W9-BNM-693

Deeper Than The Grave

Books by Tina Whittle

The Tai Randolph Mysteries
The Dangerous Edge of Things
Darker Than Any Shadow
Blood, Ash, and Bone
Deeper Than the Grave

Deeper Than the Grave

A Tai Randolph Mystery

Tina Whittle

Poisoned Pen Press

Copyright © 2014 by Tina Whittle

First Edition 2014

10 9 8 7 6 5 4 3 2 1

Library of Congress Catalog Card Number: 2014938569

ISBN: 9781464202629   Hardcover
        9781464201643   Trade Paperback

All rights reserved. No part of this publication may be repro-
duced, stored in, or introduced into a retrieval system, or
transmitted in any form, or by any means (electronic, mechanical, photocopying, recording, or otherwise) without the prior
written permission of both the copyright owner and the pub-
lisher of this book.

Poisoned Pen Press
6962 E. First Ave., Ste. 103
Scottsdale, AZ 85251
www.poisonedpenpress.com
info@poisonedpenpress.com

Printed in the United States of America

For Toni Deal,
who has always been there for me,
and for Trey and Tai, who will always be my BFF. Love ya!

Acknowledgements

This book, and I, owe an enormous debt of gratitude to lots of people. And even though I am a word-ish woman, I know that words can never truly demonstrate how much I appreciate them. The best I can do is put it in black and white, here on the page—I am blessed to know some fine, talented, generous people:

My critique group—Jon Bryant, Amber Grey, Ann Hogsett, and Kate Stockman. My Mojito Literary Society Sisters, especially Susan Newman, Katrina Murphy, and Laura Valeri. My fellow Sisters in Crime, including the members of my home chapter, the Low Country Sisters in Crime. My patient friends—Toni Deal, Sharon Hudson, Theresa Moore, Danielle Walden, and Robin White. Kira Parker, my PR/promo maven. And—of course—my excellent and forbearing family: my parents, Dinah and Archie; my parents-in-law, Yvonne and Gene; my sibling and siblings-in-law, Tim and Lisa, and Patty and Rich; plus my wonderful niece and nephews—Connor, Sydney, Drew, and Hayden.

Much gratitude to the fine folks at Poisoned Pen Press—especially Barbara Peters, Annette Rogers, Rob Rosenwald, and Suzan Baroni—a writer's dream team that serves writers and writing in exemplary fashion. I am also grateful to my fellow PPPers—the Posse—for their smarts and generosity and unwavering support.

And—as always and forever—much love to my husband, James, and daughter, Kaley Grace. Whenever I count my blessings, you two are at the top of the list.

Chapter One

Trey's mouth was at my ear, his chest solid against my back. "Slowly."

"Got it."

"Firm and gentle pressure."

I sighed. "I have done this before, you know."

"And yet you're still snatching." He adjusted my grip on the revolver so that the butt of the gun rested solidly in my left palm. "Take a breath. Half exhale. Then squeeze. One smooth motion."

His voice was muted through the fancy electronic hearing protection muffs, but that hardly mattered—he was saying the exact same thing he always said. I wiggled my nose to adjust the safety goggles, sighted along the barrel. The revolver's sights bobbed red against the target, a human-sized silhouette with concentric rings highlighting its heart. I took one deep breath in, trickled it halfway out. Then I dropped the barrel a smidgen and squeezed. The .38 kicked in my hand as a fresh bullet hole appeared at the target's groin.

Trey examined the result. "You're supposed to aim for center mass."

"I'm supposed to stop the threat. Which I certainly did."

His blue eyes flashed annoyance behind his safety glasses. "Do you want to learn proper technique or not?"

I sighed again. Then I took my stance and emptied the rest of the rounds into the target. The holes clustered in the figure's chest region, right at the heart. Or where the heart would have been had I not pulped it.

I gestured with my chin. "There. How's that?"

Trey eyed me reproachfully. He was a stickler. I could recite his mantras from memory—watch your muzzle cover, watch your periphery, watch your background.

"Why didn't you do that with your first shot?" he said.

"Jeez, boyfriend. Unwind a bit, it's just practice."

"It's not practice, it's training. There's a difference."

"So you keep saying. Over and over again." I double-checked the cylinder to make sure the gun was empty before laying it on the shelf in front of me. "Let me try yours."

Trey retrieved his H&K nine-millimeter, popped the empty magazine. He thumbed bullets into the mag, then clipped it into place with the heel of his hand and handed it to me, careful to keep the muzzle downrange.

"Feet hip-width apart, slight lean forward, right arm straight, not locked."

I racked the slide. "Yeah, yeah, yeah. Got it."

Trey's P7M8 was very much like him—sleek, powerful, efficient—and I savored the control and punch of it, even if the pleasure came with an edge now. It had been only four months since I'd held that same gun in my hand, the sights centered not on a paper target but on a human being. I remembered that same gun in Trey's hands, later that same rain-slashed night. Three shots, precise and ruthless.

I squeezed the grip to cock it, then fired three times fast, twice at center mass, then once at the forehead. To my dismay, only the first two hit home.

Trey stared at me. "What are you doing?"

"Mozambique triple tap."

"You don't need—"

"I've needed a lot of things I didn't think I would."

Trey didn't argue. He simply held out his hand. "Give me that."

I handed the nine back to him. He stepped up, then hit the switch with a closed fist and the target rattled its way toward him. He fired two shots, then a third a half-second later. As the target flapped to a stop in front of us, I saw two serrated holes in the center of the heart, and one final shot right below the nose. If the two-dimensional paper had been flesh and blood, the last bullet would have ripped a trajectory through the medulla oblongata, dropping the body like a meaty marionette with its strings cut.

"There," he said. "Triple tap, properly known as a failure drill. Useful in circumstances when direct hits to center mass do not stop the target, most likely due to a tactical vest." A cock of the head. "Is that what you want to learn?"

I fingered the ragged paper. "Yes."

"Okay. Then work on your stance, your form, your breathing, your aim, your draw, and the ability to target center mass. Because without those basic skills, you'll never master this one." He checked his watch. "We've got fifteen minutes. Back to triggering."

Chapter Two

Trey drove me back to the gun shop. During our time inside the range, the sun had set, and I huddled into my jacket as I stepped out of the warmth of his Ferrari and into the night. The evening wasn't terribly cold by most standards—low fifties, zero wind—but I was a creature coddled in the briny marsh of the Georgia Lowcountry, where winters were mild and smelled of clean pine and the ocean. February in Atlanta, however, was twenty-eight odd days of seasonal mood swings. All during the summer and fall, the cold lay low in the upland mountains, deep within the granite, until sometime around Christmas when it came slinking down into the city. Now it sprang like a wild animal from unexpected places, bolting up stairwells, rushing at a canter across parking lots.

Trey had moved into his winter wardrobe months ago—the Prada trench coat and the Armani wool suits, the finely textured cashmere scarves and leather driving gloves, everything black as bituminous coal. He stood very close behind me as I wrestled with the door to the gun shop.

I felt the deadbolt give. "Wait here a second. I want to surprise you."

"I don't like surprises."

"Go with it, this one time."

He made a noise of acquiescence, so I ducked inside, punching in the security code that would disable the multiple alarm systems, then taking him by the hand and pulling him in after me. The smell of sawdust and fresh paint and industrial adhesive rolled over the threshold in a wave, clean and chemical mixing in a singular wallop. Trey stepped gingerly, his patent-leather Brionis making soft echoes on the linoleum.

I punched the light switch, and the overhead fluorescents sputtered to life. "Ta da."

He opened his eyes, and his expression shifted to pleased astonishment as he took in the front room. My counter, formerly paint-splattered, now stripped and refinished in a rich golden maple. The newly scrubbed and re-waxed floor. Fresh yellow paint on the walls.

Of course the rest of it was a mess. Dozens of my Uncle Dexter's framed photographs remained propped against the walls, waiting to be rehung. I'd managed to find space in the storage room's gun safe for all the firearms, but the ammo was still on the floor, the edged weapons crammed into a single display case. The cash register sat in the empty planter boxes, the dead marigolds in the trash, and I'd stuffed all the reenactment uniforms into a friendly blue and gray tangle, a Confederate-Union mishmash that would have offended my uncle no end had he been there to see it. There was a rumor of order to the place, however, and Trey noticed.

"You've been working," he said.

"I have. I found every single gun missing from the inventory. I wish I could say the same for the other stuff." I shook my head. "God rest Uncle Dexter's soul, he loved this shop, but I don't know how he stayed in business."

Trey surveyed the box next to the cash register, a jumble of looseleaf papers that I was attempting to turn into an official Acquisition and Disposition book for the ATF. "Will you have this ready by Friday?"

"I will."

"Are you sure?"

"I'm sure." I smiled at him. "And don't worry. I destroyed all the paperwork surrounding our little 'sex for handguns' arrangement."

He ignored the joke and reached inside. "I could—"

I intercepted his hand. "Leave it be. I want to do it myself."

"But—"

"For real, Trey."

He reluctantly left the scattered A&D materials alone, but it pained him physically, I could tell. And he was right to be concerned—all joking aside, if I didn't pass the audit, I lost my Federal Firearms License, and without an FFL, I couldn't sell guns and ammo and black powder. And there would go seventy-five percent of my income.

He surveyed the rest of the shop. "You took down the new security camera."

"Did not."

"Then where is it?"

"You tell me."

A pause, then his eyes tracked the room. He scanned the empty shelving units, the cabinets, the walls, finally stopping on the deer head mounted behind the counter. He stepped closer and scrutinized the mangy relic.

I joined him underneath it. "Damn. That was fast, even for you."

"Where did you get…that?"

"The attic." I knocked on the muzzle of the cockeyed creature, its left antler broken at the tip, its nose dented and dinged. "It's fake, felt and plastic on the outside, hollow as a balloon inside. Perfect for a single-lens covert camera."

Trey peered into the deer's glassy eyes. "You hooked it into the wireless grid?"

"Yep."

"What about the—"

"Primary and secondary power supplies, yes." I put my hands on my hips. "You think I don't listen to you, but I do. Every word."

He pulled out his phone and tapped in a code. Two seconds later, his screen filled with an image of the shop, the two of us looking up at the deer head. Even in two-dimensional black and white, Trey was a six-one, black-haired, haute couture hot dish. My charms were more down-to-earth—dirty blond curls rioting under a baseball cap, faded jeans, scuffed work boots. We seemed utterly mismatched on the tiny screen, like two people on a disastrous blind date. Regardless, there he was, at my side. As usual. I took his arm in mine, watched my video twin do the same, and then the image switched to the back lot, where my Camaro was parked next to the dumpster.

Trey pulled up the third feed, the parking lot out front, with the entrance, burglar-barred windows, and his Ferrari in plain view. There was no fourth image, however. This was Trey's current worry point.

"Have you talked to your neighbor about setting up a camera in the alley?" he said.

"Brenda? I tried, twice, but she won't go for it. And since the alley is technically her property, not mine—"

"But that makes no sense."

"Sure, it does. Dexter sold access rights to the previous owner, when Aunt Dotty got sick and he needed the money. Now Brenda's using that to make me miserable so I'll leave and she can have this end of the square all to herself." I folded my arms. "She complained about your Ferrari, you know. Said it damaged her ears."

Trey made a scoffing noise. "The threshold for short-term hearing damage is one hundred and twenty decibels. The F430 produces ninety-six point nine decibels at full throttle, which—"

"My point is she has an agenda."

But Trey wasn't listening anymore. He abandoned me under the deer head to check out the new door to the storage room. It was an innocuous-looking hunk of wood—beige, bland as baby food—but he ran his hand across it with an almost sensual reverence.

"It came," he said.

"It did." I stepped beside him. "I was expecting something less ordinary."

"It's designed to look ordinary, but underneath the veneer is a hardwood core with fiberglass sheathing. It has a UL rating of four, which is military grade. Guaranteed to defeat ballistic assaults up to .44 magnum caliber, resistant to .50 cal."

He punched some numbers on the keypad, and the deadbolt clicked opened with a well-engineered snick. I saw the twitch at the corner of his mouth that was almost a smile.

He stepped inside, and I followed. What used to be Dexter's secondary storage room was now a state-of-the-art safe room. Well, not as state-of-the-art as Trey wanted—he'd envisioned something along the lines of the Pentagon—but an adequate compromise. The walls were already concrete, the ceiling inaccessible from the front room. All it needed was a bulletproof door, which I now had, thanks to him.

He walked under the casement window, a three-paned hand-cranked antique installed when Dexter built the place back in the sixties. The window was one foot tall and three feet wide and provided the only outdoor light in the room. Trey glared at it.

I stood beside him. "I know you don't like the window, but it's staying for the time being."

"But—"

"It's ten feet off the ground and too narrow for a person to get through. Plus you've got glass-break sensors on it."

"Nonetheless—"

"One thing at a time, boyfriend. I'll fix it when I get the camera situation figured out and the audit completed."

"Still—"

"Hush." I slipped my arms around his waist, resting my palms flat against his lower back. He smelled like gunpowder and the ghost of his Armani aftershave. "Use your mouth for something besides talking."

His eyes narrowed. "You're trying to distract me from the point, which is—"

I stood on tiptoe and kissed him quiet. On the training mat, at the range, he was pure masculine force—direct, active, aggressive. In all matters romantic, however, he preferred to follow my lead. I moved my hands upward, across the plane of his back, the familiar geography of rhomboids and deltoids.

"It's been two weeks since I've had my way with you, boyfriend."

"Six days. Don't exaggerate."

"We can fix that, you know. Upstairs. Where there's now—surprise surprise—an honest-to-goodness real bed. With 600-thread-count, Egyptian cotton Frette sheets."

He leveled a look at me. "You took my sheets."

"The spare ones, yes. Also your shampoo and a pair of pajamas. And some towels. Do you mind?"

He shook his head. I could almost see the picture forming in his mind. No longer was my upstairs living space a wretched hovel. Tiny, yes, as cramped as a ship's cabin. But thanks to a trip to Goodwill and a teensy raid of his bathroom closet, well stocked with everything he'd need to feel at home, at least for a few hours.

I looped my arms around his neck. "Stay here tonight."

"I can't, I've—"

"So stay right now."

"That doesn't…Oh."

I flicked a glance at his watch. "It's seven-fifty-five. Your bedtime is nine o'clock. The drive will take forty-eight minutes tops, which leaves seventeen free minutes."

His eyes slid to the right, the better to access his perfectly sharp left frontal lobes, the seat of logic and time management and schedules. The right side of his brain had some hiccups still, an artifact of the car accident three years earlier, but the rest of him agreed with me, that two people could do a lot with a new mattress and seventeen minutes.

I moved closer, hip to hip. "Sixteen minutes and counting."

He exhaled softly, his posture loosening, and I knew the battle was mine. His left brain made a formidable opponent at times—rigid, calculating, inclined to lock down the systems at the slightest emotional chaos—while his right brain tended to lurch into paralyzed befuddlement. My strategy was simple—bypass the neuronal circuits and go straight for the body, which had its own agenda.

I reached to loosen his tie. And he froze.

"Tai?"

"Yes?"

"Did you hear footsteps?"

Chapter Three

"What?"

He cocked his head. "Footsteps. In the alley. There shouldn't be anyone back there this time of night."

I listened, but all I heard was the buzz of overheads. Our breathing, suddenly quickened. "I don't hear anything."

He pulled out of my arms. "I'll go take a look."

"Trey—"

He slipped his gun from the holster. "Stay here."

I recognized the tone. It always happened so fast, the shift from boyfriend to bodyguard. I felt the chill, involuntary, a flash of memory. Not all stalkers stopped with stalking. Some shot at you from across great distances, the crosshairs trained on the back of the skull, or the T-zone between your eyes, or the bull's-eye where your heart and lungs pumped....

I grabbed his elbow. "Don't go out there."

"Tai—"

"I'm serious. Call 911."

"I have to check."

"Trey!"

He slipped backward into the hall, then slammed the door behind himself so fast I didn't have time to stop him. I snatched at the handle, but without the code, the door wasn't budging. I kicked it once for good measure, but Trey was already out the back door and into the night.

Cursing loudly, I shoved aside two garbage bags filled with packing peanuts and climbed on top of the display table, then stood on tiptoe and peered through the window into the lot below. The yellow haze of security lights bathed the deserted pavement, washing my red Camaro a sickly orange. The dumpster squatted directly below me, surrounded by shadows as darkly impenetrable as the mouth of the alley, which I could barely see from that vantage point.

No sign of Trey.

I cranked open the window and pressed my face to the opening. "Goddamn it, Trey, get back here right now and let me out of this room!"

No answer. My lips felt numb, my hands too. I rubbed them together, but the sensation spread.

"Trey!"

Still no answer. I climbed down, but the coldness remained. I willed my heart to stop galloping, my body to stop shaking, my vision to stop collapsing, but my body wouldn't respond. I dropped cross-legged to the floor, my back against the wall, and drew my knees to my chin.

I did hear footsteps then, outside, leather on pavement. Trey. Finally, I heard the back door open and close. A series of beeps, and then the inner door opened and he came inside, his gun back in its holster.

"Whoever was there never left the alley," he said, "so the camera didn't…Tai?"

I looked up at him and tried to speak, but no words came. The shivering intensified, and my chest hurt as if I'd taken a punch.

He knelt in front of me. "What happened? Are you hurt?"

"No, I…"

I tried to stand, but a new wave of dizziness crashed and broke. All I could see was Trey, his face centered against a collapsing gray blur.

"Give me your hands," he said.

I did as he said, automatically, and he squeezed my fingers, his touch firm and steady.

"Good. Now breathe."

I tried, but the air wouldn't go in all the way. My eyes flew open. "Omigod, I can't...I don't..."

"Breathe on my count. In for two, out for two."

I drew in a shaky breath as he counted. *One, two, one, two.* Gradually the shaking subsided. My throat opened, my chest too. The anger rose then—at him, yes, for dashing off into the night, but mostly at myself. Suddenly I wanted to be anywhere else than on this dirty floor.

I fought down tears, but they flowed anyway. "Damn it, I don't know why this is happening! I'm not some panicky spaz girl!"

"Tai—"

"This isn't making any sense, I'm not...I don't..."

And yet there I was, on the floor, in the dark—embarrassed, angry, suddenly exhausted—with my boyfriend assessing my vital signs. I stretched my legs in front of me, fighting an itchy restlessness. Gradually the cramping pain in my chest subsided, and my vision cleared, and when I inhaled, the air went all the way in.

Trey rocked back on his heels and watched me, fingers at my pulse point. Part of me wanted to yell at him some more, but another part held onto the sensation of his hand against my skin like a drowning person clutching a life preserver. It was physical, grounding, real.

Trey assessed my progress. "How are you feeling?"

I glared at him. "Don't you ever shut me up in this room again, you hear me?"

He glared right back. "I heard footsteps. In the alley. Where no one should have been."

"For which there are a dozen possible explanations."

"Yes, including the fact that someone could have been in the alley."

"Checking is one thing. Pulling your weapon and stomping out there is something else entirely!"

"Are you saying I overreacted?"

"Hypervigilance is the official term."

His head snapped back a quarter inch, but he showed no other reaction. I knew he recognized the word, though. It referred to an enhanced state of sensory sensitivity accompanied by exaggerated threat-detecting behaviors, and his psych profile was littered with it.

He kept his expression neutral. "We're discussing your reaction—"

"And now we're discussing yours. It happened to you after the accident, this same thing."

"Not the same."

"I saw the symptom list."

"Then you also saw the diagnosis. Post-concussive syndrome. It was resolved within six months."

"I know. But I also know that anniversaries can trigger relapses. And Sunday is three years to the day you went head to head with that concrete embankment."

He dropped his eyes to the floor, but he stayed calm. I was getting back to calm too.

"Trey?"

"I heard you. But the anniversary of the accident isn't a trigger for me. It never has been."

"Something is, though." I kept my voice steady. "I may be the one on the floor, but I'm not the only one cracking up."

He looked puzzled. "What do you mean?"

"I mean the nightmares."

"What nightmares?"

"The ones you've been having almost every single night."

He looked astounded. "I have?"

"Tossing, turning, mumbling nonsense. I tried to wake you up once, but you got a little…" I pantomimed a right hook. "Punchy."

All the color drained from his face. "Did I—"

"Of course not. I got back on my side of the bed fast, and you went back to sleep."

He exhaled slowly, shakily. "I am so sorry. I would never… Why haven't you told me?"

"Because I thought you knew. Why wouldn't you know?"

"Because this kind of nightmare is very different from normal dream states. There's no recall, just a feeling of…I don't know. Mental exhaustion." He dropped his eyes again. "You're right, however. Combined with the rest of the symptoms, they're a clear PTSD indicator."

"The rest of what symptoms?"

He kept his eyes down. "The headaches. Backaches. Tiredness. I know you've noticed."

I had. The migraines that floored him for hours at the time. Muscle spasms in his lower back. A lack of interest and energy bordering on depression. Things he'd explained as a hard afternoon at the gym, an extra-long day at work, the shorter days and longer nights of winter. Suddenly I realized what a great job the two of us had been doing at playing denial.

I tried to meet his eyes. "Trey? If it's not the anniversary, what is it?"

He didn't answer. I pulled his face up so that I could look at him straight on. I saw a muscle in his jaw tic. I got another flash of memory—the rain, the lightning, the desperation—and felt light-headed again.

"It's what happened in Savannah, isn't it? For all your training and Special Ops smarts, it got to you too."

He exhaled heavily, then sat next to me, his back against the wall, our thighs touching. We made a pair of peculiar bookends, Trey and I, as he propped his arm on his bent knee. He leaned his head back against the wall, stared at the ceiling.

"It doesn't make any sense. I've been in multiple threat scenarios; that's what I trained for. And yet…Savannah was different."

"How?"

"I don't know how to explain."

"Can you try?"

"No."

"But—"

"Talking about how I don't know how to talk about it is not going to help."

He had a point. I leaned my head on his shoulder. He flinched again, and then forced himself to relax.

"Is this who we are now?" I said. "The PTSD poster couple? I slump in a panicked stupor while you pull your weapon at the least provocation?"

He shot me a sharp look. "I heard footsteps."

I didn't feel like arguing anymore. I stood, a little wobbly, but on my own two feet. I held out my hand. He took it, eyeing me from top to bottom as he let me pull him to standing.

"Come back with me to Buckhead," he said.

"I can't. I've got—"

"Please."

Damn it. He had to go and use the p-word. "Fine. If it makes you happy."

"It does. Go get your bag." He held the door open for me. "I want to check the cameras one more times, video and audio, see if they caught something. And you really do need to talk to your neighbor about that dead zone in the alley. There's absolutely no reason—"

I let him gripe. It was forty-five minutes back to the steel and glass safety zone of his Buckhead apartment. One short elevator ride to the thirty-fifth floor, then the triple-lock system would engage, the deadbolts and the Schlage platinum keyswitch and the security alarms too, all the primary and secondary and tertiary systems. No more quickening panic. No more opportunity for everything to slide and crash.

No more surprises, of any kind.

Chapter Four

The next morning, the sky had the low ponderous weight of a mudslide. Yet there I was standing under that sky with an umbrella and a bag of pastries, the sideways rain and thick humidity playing havoc with my hair. The headquarters of Atlanta's FBI Field Office loomed before me. Somewhere on the top floor of that graphite-glassed cube was the temporary office of Dan Garrity, Trey's former partner and slightly estranged best friend, who had recently been promoted to the Atlanta Metro Major Offenders Task Force. Though still technically an Atlanta PD detective, Garrity's main gig for the next two years would be here, with AMMO—assuming he didn't go to prison, flee the state, or get shot down in his driveway like his three predecessors.

I tucked the phone between my ear and shoulder. When Garrity answered, I waved. "Look out your window, Secret Agent Man."

A few seconds' silence. "Is that you under the umbrella?"

"Yep."

"There's a tornado watch on, you know. Not the best idea, standing out there like a lightning rod." A pause. "So what's in the bag?"

"Doughssants. Like croissants, only doughnutty. With brandied peaches on top."

"That's a real thing?"

"Smells real. Wanna take a coffee break and find out?"

◇◇◇

Garrity met me in the lobby under the official FBI seal, with its corona of navy and gold flourishes and the stalwart motto: *Fidelity, Bravery, Integrity*. I sat on the bench with my knees together, raindrops beating against the window, stronger now. Not a single dark-suited agent spared me a second glance, which meant, I knew, that every single one was examining me with the thoroughness of an X-ray.

Garrity brought two coffees in paper cups. "Compliments of Uncle Sam."

He unbuttoned his navy jacket and sat next to me. He looked very special agent-y, even if his hair refused to conform to suit-and-tie standards, flaming about his head in rust-colored cow-licks. Despite his quasi-federal status, he still wore the Atlanta PD shield on his belt and the department-issue S&W on his hip.

"Still a cop," I said.

He grinned. "A cop with my own urban tactical team and a Sikorsky Black Hawk helicopter at my disposal. Beats that old Crown Vic any day." He accepted the bag, tested its heft approvingly. "So…what have you done now?"

"Nothing."

"Come on, you only bring me food when you want something. What's up?"

He had a fox face, with a sharp nose and sharper eyes. I still found it hard to picture him and Trey working together—Trey with his detached, mathematical precision and Garrity with his kinetic street smarts. They'd met on the Atlanta PD's infamous Red Dog Squad, and Garrity still maintained a fierce protective-ness, but sometimes I saw loss in his eyes, the heart-gouging kind.

I took a sip of coffee. "So there is this one thing on my mind."

Garrity pulled a doughssant out of the bag, waved his hand in a "get on with it" gesture.

"Sunday is the anniversary of Trey's accident."

"Right."

"Does that ever…I mean…" I tried to keep my tone easy, nonchalant. "Does that ever look like PTSD?"

He put down the pastry, suddenly serious. "What's going on?"

I told him about the previous night—the refurbishing of the gun shop, the footsteps in the alley, the drawn gun. I told him about Trey too—the nightmares and headaches, the battening down of the psychological hatches. Garrity listened without interrupting. He had an interrogator's knack for silence—he could twist it like a screw when he wanted—but he could also be gentle with it.

"How long has this been going on?"

"Months." A hard burst of rain lashed the window—stronger now, laced with hail—and I jumped.

Garrity noticed. "You're feeling it too. Leftovers from Savannah?"

I started to deny it, then nodded. Whenever it rained, I remembered the driving wind, the terror of helplessness, the soaking obliterating storm. And then Trey, as rending and total as a lightning strike himself. There had been no charges filed against him for the shooting; it hadn't been lethal, after all. Obviously in self-defense, the officials had said, as if they couldn't quite believe the Trey they'd seen in the aftermath—battered, soft-spoken, deferential—could have been capable of killing anyone.

But I knew better. And so did Garrity. I'd seen Trey come close to homicide, but he'd seen Trey actually do it—one night years ago, a robbery gone bad, Trey putting a single bullet right through the bad guy's heart. Garrity and I weren't fooled by Trey's dropped eyes and quiet voice. Not by a longshot.

"I don't know what happened to me last night," I said. "All I know is Trey shut me in that room, and I lost it. Lots of ungood things. He was the one stuffed in the hold of a boat down in Savannah, not me, so I don't know why…it makes no sense."

"Have you talked to Eric about this?"

I closed my eyes and rubbed the bridge of my nose. My brother. The occupational psychologist with a sub-specialty in PTSD.

"Not yet."

"Why not?"

"Because my brother is an alarm bell you can't unring. He'll sink his hooks into whatever freaking complex he thinks I have this week. Besides, things are otherwise good. Trey's got this new project—resilient security systems—and he's re-doing my storage room into a state-of-the art safe room."

Garrity snorted. "That's what always he does right before the anniversary, throws himself into some project. Then on February ninth, he hides in his apartment and avoids all contact with his fellow humanity. Won't answer his phone, won't respond to e-mail or texts, won't answer the door. He denies this is what he's doing, but he does it anyway. Like the rest of his life. He knows it's all one big mirage, but as long as it keeps him functioning, he doesn't poke too hard at it."

I knew what Garrity meant. Trey's mirage was of fabulous construction—the Ferrari, the wardrobe, the black-and-white condo, all of it pulled from the Italian style issue of a *GQ* magazine. Trey knew the life he inhabited was psychological scaffolding. But when pressed about it, he would say only that it worked, the implication being that until it stopped working, he'd be keeping the whole package, thank you very much. And I did not argue.

"So how do I know whether this is the normal weirdness or some new weirdness?"

"The short answer is, you don't. Recovery can look like relapse and vice versa."

"So what—"

"Talk to your brother. And if you see a PTSD episode coming, do the thing."

"What thing?"

He looked incredulous. "You know. The thing. I've seen you do it a hundred times."

"I swear I have no idea—"

He placed one hand on my bicep and squeezed—just once, quickly and firmly. I suddenly remembered all the times I'd done that very same thing whenever Trey threatened to go off the rails. I remembered how he would tense, and then relax under my touch.

Now I was incredulous. "That's a thing?"

"Uh huh." Garrity returned his hand to his lap. "You know why it works?"

I shook my head.

"Back in his SWAT days, he led up entry teams, usually as the number one guy, front of the stack. That's a hard place to be—God knows what fresh hell on the other side of some door, your team in line behind you. You can't hear a damn thing with the riot helmet on, you got body shields and flashbangs and rifles clattering around, it's dark maybe. You can't make a move until every single man on your team is in place, but you can't ask, can't look, can't break formation."

Garrity talked with the concentrated enthusiasm of a football coach, his hands moving as if he were describing a play-by-play. His eyes gleamed with that peculiar cop shine, like a flash of light along a blade.

"Trey needed a signal to know everybody was in place. So when the last man in line got into position, he squeezed the shoulder of the guy in front of him. The guy in front of him did the same, and they passed the signal up. So when Trey felt that hand on his shoulder, he knew his men had his back. Literally. That's what he's remembering, every time you touch his arm. And his brain kicks down the same message now that it did then—got your back, man."

I didn't know what to say. All around us, the office hummed with purposeful activity. Everything in its place, everything with a purpose. It was suddenly overwhelming, and I had to restrain myself from bolting from that bright contained lobby.

Garrity tilted his head. "You okay?"

"Yeah, yeah. Just…it's a lot sometimes."

"I know. But we'll get him through this. We're his team now. And if you ever need to talk, about anything, holler. I know what dealing with him is like—better than anybody." He flashed a wry grin. "Well, except maybe Gabriella, but she doesn't count because she's French."

That pulled a half-laugh from me. Trey's ex. Gorgeous, intelligent, sophisticated, and very much still a part of his life. Like

Garrity, she knew Trey From Before. But I couldn't imagine sitting across from her discussing the only thing we had in common, that we both knew what a complicated delight it was to be the woman in his bed.

Garrity got serious again. "Tai? There's another explanation, of course. For last night."

"Which is?"

"He really did hear somebody in the alley."

I shook my head. "There was no one there. He checked."

"Doesn't mean there wasn't someone there, someone smart enough to bolt when Trey came barreling out the back door with a gun drawn."

"Could have been doesn't equal was."

"True enough. But regardless, you've got trouble brewing, my friend."

"I think I can handle—oh crap, seriously?" I pulled my phone from my pocket and swiped it to stop the shrill beeping. "You've got to be kidding."

"What is it?"

"The shop's alarm system. Again. Which means that any second now—"

My phone rang, this time with the authoritative and slightly demanding ringtone I'd grown familiar with.

"—Trey will be calling." I shoved the rest of the breakfast bag at Garrity as I put the phone to my ear. "I know, boyfriend, I know. I'm heading up there right now."

"Don't do that."

"Why not?"

"Because I don't have exact coordinates for the touchdown yet."

I shouldered my bag and stood. "That sentence makes no sense whatsoever."

"The tornado, Tai. I don't—"

"The *what?*"

Garrity grabbed my elbow and showed me his phone, a radar map pulled up on the screen. Sure enough, it flashed with the dreaded words—Tornado Warning—and churned with a red clot of nasty weather spinning and fuming right over downtown Kennesaw.

Right over my shop.

"Aw hell," I said, and bolted for the parking lot, not even bothering to open the umbrella.

Chapter Five

Driving in the storm's wake felt like following a stampede. Branches littered the road. Whole tree limbs lay in the ditches like road kill.

I crossed my fingers. "Please please please, let the shop still have a roof."

Trey's voice was muffled through the speaker phone. "It has a roof. I can see it."

I switchbacked the Camaro around a hump of debris, flipping the volume up to hear him better. He had the shop's live CCTV on his work computer at Phoenix, plus the alarm schematic up on his phone. The former showed no damage, but the latter was insistent there had been a breach at the storage room window. It had taken every bit of convincing I had to keep Trey at his desk and not racing the Ferrari up to Kennesaw.

"Walls too?"

"Yes. All of them."

"So it wasn't a tornado?"

"Not that I can see."

"So what set off the alarm?"

"I don't know. It could be another false alarm. You've had three of them over the past month, ever since I upgraded the system. You can check the recording when you get there and see what happened, but I've got no information here. Are you sure—"

"I'm sure. You stay put. The Kennesaw PD is on the scene. I'll call you back when I know something."

◇◇◇

When I got to the shop, I saw young Officer Butch out front, the squeaky-clean, buttermilk-complexioned guy who showed up at every alarm, false or otherwise. I suspected he had a crush on me, what with all the blushing and hat-in-hand chivalry, but he wasn't crushing this morning. He was all business, rain-slickered and serious-faced, deep in discussion with a woman in a pink raincoat standing underneath a pink umbrella. I opened my own umbrella and muttered an under-the-breath curse.

Brenda Lovejoy-Burlington heard me coming and swiveled to face me, her ash-blond flip unfrizzled and smooth even in the rain. She stood yardstick straight, hips cantilevered in a beauty queen stance. A recent import to the area from parts Up North, Brenda was the third wife of a local businessman. She was also president of the Kennesaw Revitalization Commission and had recently—oh, joy of joys—set up shop in the vacant office right next to Dexter's building.

I joined them in front of the shop. It didn't looked tornado-battered. The burglar bars on the front windows were intact, the gravel parking area unfazed. The bleak morning light empha-sized every twinge of tacky, from the paint-flaking sign to the faded brick, but I saw no damage. The rest of the square seemed untouched too—one rectangular acre of inexpertly maintained hedges and dilapidated benches bordered by buildings like mine on all four sides, all of it waterlogged but exactly as it had been the night before.

Officer Butch nodded his head in greeting. "Hey, Tai."

"Hey, yourself. What's up?"

Brenda smoothed her hair from her forehead. "Somebody tried to break in to your *shop* again, that's what's up. Probably trying to steal your car, which is another reason it shouldn't be parked out back."

I crossed my arms over my chest. "It's where I've parked for a year."

"Yes, but now the lot is shared property—"

"The lot is, but the parking space is not. It belongs with the apartment, which is a separate address from the gun shop."

"It doesn't matter, it's all together as far as the criminal element is concerned." Brenda glared at me, looking for all the world like a frostbit petunia. "Your *shop* attracts them."

She said "shop" as if it were code for "whorehouse" or "opium den." Never mind that I'd cleaned up the storefront considerably, taking down Uncle Dexter's more eccentric posters and handbills, putting marigolds into the window boxes. I glanced at Brenda's storefront, ablaze now with summery posters and sunshiney images of cleanliness and prosperity. A giant banner unfurled above it all—*Kennesaw: Moving Forward!*—and the craving for a cigarette hit me fierce and bright and zig-zag powerful, like a bolt of lightning.

I pulled a sucker from my pocket. "Maybe if you'd let me put up a camera in the alley, the criminal element would have a harder time tromping around *our* area."

She rolled her eyes. "Another camera won't solve anything. Cleaning up this square, making it family-friendly, pedestrian-friendly—"

"Yeah, yeah. Whatever, Brenda." I nodded Officer Butch's way. "I'll meet you out back. Where it's quieter."

And then I started walking. Brenda kept talking, something about enhanced livability criteria. But I knew the real score. The Kennesaw Revitalization Commission wanted to revitalize me right out of the square. I unwrapped the sucker and shoved it in my mouth, then cracked it between my molars. It was going to be a long day.

◇◇◇

It really was quieter behind the shop. No Brenda, no traffic, only the pattering of rainwater on the brick pavers and Officer Butch on his radio, his voice a mumble of ten codes interspersed with the scratchy rasp of static.

"So what happened?" I said.

He stood in the mouth of the alley. "Hard to say. The back window alarm triggered, we know that. No evidence of a break-in, though. Nothing broken, front and back doors are still locked."

"Another false alarm?"

He shrugged. "You've had several of those."

"Yeah. My boyfriend upgraded the system. Everything's real touchy now."

Officer Butch rubbed his chin thoughtfully. "Seems like it. But here's the thing—the alarm still needs a trigger. And I suspect I found it."

I followed his eyes to the mat in front of my door. It took me a second, but then I saw what he was talking about—the mat had several pieces of gravel on it, some of them pea-sized, but some almost as big as golf balls.

I knelt and examined them. "This isn't from the storm."

He shook his head. "Nope."

"Somebody tossed these at my window."

"Yep."

"From the alley, where the security cameras couldn't catch them."

"Yep."

"And then made no attempt to break in." I stood. "Does that make any sense to you?"

"Nope. Unless this was a test of your security system. In that case, you need to be real careful. As much as I hate to admit it, Ms. Lovejoy may be right. Some unknown perp may be casing your place."

I felt a cold wash of realization…and guilt. Trey had been right. There had been somebody in the alley the night before. It hadn't been hypervigilant paranoia that had him chucking me in the safe room.

"I'll tell Trey. He'll make the proper adjustments." I pulled out my keys. "You want to come in while I double-check the cameras?"

He tucked his radio back under the slicker. "Not right now. I just got word the tornado touched down near the park, and we're all on emergency response for the duration. I'll come back when I can finish the report."

The park meant Kennesaw Mountain Battlefield National Park, the three thousand acres of rolling range around Kennesaw Mountain. It was a place of winding trails and forest and tumbling stone, a place where Mother Nature could really pitch a hissy fit.

"Is anybody hurt?" I said.

"Some tourists got throwed around, but no serious injuries were reported. So if you don't mind—"

"No, no. I'm good. Take care of the real trouble. I'll call you if I find something."

He headed back into the alley, hesitated, then turned to face me, his eyes serious. "Tai? You might want to watch out for Ms. Lovejoy." He craned his neck left and right to see if anyone was listening. "She's been down at the station a lot. Asking about city codes and violations and penalties."

"You don't say?"

"She and her husband bought that building real cheap. I think they have plans to sell it not-so-cheap once they make this square more…beautified."

"That doesn't surprise me one bit."

"I'm just saying. This is the fourth callout you've had this past month, including that firearm-discharge violation on Robert E. Lee's birthday."

"That wasn't me, that was Raymond Junior, and it was black powder and shooting caps, not bullets, as I explained to Brenda when she came stomping over here. Every other call-out was a false alarm from the new security system."

"That's even worse, and you know it. They don't like nuisances down at the station." He put his hands on his hips, all official-like. "Keep things as calm as you can, okay?"

I surveyed my shop's back door, the scattered gravel, the alley that was apparently Perp Central.

"I'll do my best," I said.

◇◇◇

Inside, the darkened shop felt as ominous as a Hitchcock movie. I flipped the switch, and the fluorescent overheads flared and hummed, revealing the boxes and display cases in all their ramshackle glory. I felt a possessive warmth rise at the sight. This place was *mine*. I'd cleaned the dead flies from windowsills. Squeegeed the windows. Planted marigolds, even if they always died.

Mine.

I tossed the keys on the counter, the toe of my boot scuffing the photograph propped there—Uncle Dexter and Aunt Dotty on opening day, their arms about each other's waists. In the photo, Dotty's pixie-cut hair was dark and thick, and Dexter already had the barrel chest and luxuriant mustache of his latter days. I'd taken down his enormous Confederate Battle Flag with a lump of guilt in my throat, folding it with military precision and tucking it away in Dotty's cedar chest, like laying it in the coffin of a fallen soldier.

I wondered what he'd think of his shop now, of me. I wished I could ask him. I knew what he'd say, though. *Stop wasting time and get to work, girl.*

I shook off the bittersweet and rolled up my sleeves.

Chapter Six

I'd barely finished sweeping up when I heard the unmistakable growl of twin cam engines and the crunch of tires on gravel. I put down the whisk broom and dustpan. Sometimes dealing with Trey was as complicated and messy as the gun shop, but like the shop, he was all mine. So I wiped my hands on my jeans and went into the main room, where I found him brushing rain from his jacket, his briefcase beside the door.

I shook my head at him. "I told you not to come."

"I came anyway."

"So I see. I thought you had a busy day."

"I'm taking a long lunch." He went behind the counter and rolled a chair in front of the computer. "Have you reviewed the footage yet?"

"There's no reason to. The perp—to use Officer Butch's favorite word—took advantage of the blind spot in the alley. So until Brenda sees fit to let me put a camera up, it's gonna be open season on my back door. A fact she seems to be enjoying."

Trey wrinkled his forehead as he pulled up the video screen, tapping in the key code that got him access to the archived footage. I joined him behind the counter, watching as he ran the video backwards and forwards, frame by frame, looking for some clue in the grainy footage. The camera we did have couldn't capture the alley, but it did show the back lot clearly.

He pointed. "There."

I followed his finger. Sure enough, I could see gravel strike the casement window, and sure enough, it came from the direction of the alley.

I cursed and fished in my pocket for another sucker. "Doesn't Brenda realize that blind spot could backfire on her one day?"

"One would think."

"One certainly would." I shoved the candy in my mouth and hopped up on the counter next to him. "Unless she doesn't care. I mean, there's nothing to steal from her space except City of Kennesaw propaganda, whereas I've got a shop full of expensive weapons."

"A hazard of the profession, yes."

I swung my feet. "This means you weren't hearing things last night. There really were footsteps."

Trey kept his gaze riveted on the screen, but I saw a slight twitch at the corner of his mouth. He sat back abruptly, index finger tapping the arm of the desk chair.

"It could have been a would-be burglar testing the system," he said.

"Officer Butch suggested the same thing. He also suggested you might want to dial down the sensitivity just a hair. The false alarms are getting me grief down at the station."

Trey started to reply just as my phone rang. I checked the readout. "Hang on, this is one of my clients. I keep telling them I'm closed this week, but they keep calling." I put it to my ear. "Sorry, Richard, still closed."

"Hey, I heard on the scanner they sent a police unit your way—everything okay?"

Richard was one of my uncle's oldest clients. They'd been members of the same reenactment unit—the 41st Georgia Infantry, Company B—and had both shared a commitment to authenticity that Richard continued. His voice was richly timbered, like Kentucky bourbon, but it held an edge this morning.

"A minor mishap," I said. "Nothing storm related."

"Wish I could say the same. Tornado hit the Amberdecker family cemetery."

I yanked the sucker out of my mouth. "Is everyone okay?"

"All my work crew's checked in, but I can't find Rose anywhere."

Rose Amberdecker, his employer, matriarch of the Amberdecker clan. From what Richard had told me of her, she was pushing sixty, stubborn, cantankerous. And now she was missing.

"Have you called 911?"

"Hell no! Rose'd kill me if I did that. She's right particular about who gets on her property, and the government especially ain't welcome."

"But aren't you worried that she's...you know?"

"Of course I am. But as far as I know, the tornado only touched down in the cemetery, and she's not there. She's somewhere on these three hundred acres, and I need to tell her before she finds out herself."

"Tell her what?"

"That the twister took her great-great-grandfather into the wild blue yonder."

I let the words sink in. "You mean—"

"Braxton Amberdecker's tomb is a bunch of rocks now. Broken and empty as Easter morning."

I tried to put the snatches of the story together from my memory, something about discovering remains on the Amberdecker property that bordered the park, an interment in the family cemetery with full Confederate honors. I remembered Dexter coordinating the effort and his description of the tomb, a massive granite and marble mausoleum designed to look as if it had been constructed in 1865.

Richard kept talking. "They didn't find the poor son of a bitch until almost two years ago, now he's all scattered to kingdom come. All the burial goods went with him too. Word gets out about that, I'll be running relic hunters out all morning. Law says I can't shoot 'em, but I swear—"

"Don't shoot anybody. What do you need me to do?"

The edge in my tone—or perhaps the word "shoot"—caught Trey's attention. He looked up from the video monitor, pen poised on his notebook. *Tornado*, I mouthed. Then I waved my hands around to illustrate. Trey put the pen down and rose from the chair.

"I've got the crew looking for Rose, but I need you to help look too, find what you can before the crows and riffraff do. You still got your uncle's metal detectors?"

"They're here somewhere."

"Good. Grab 'em and get up here."

"I'm not sure how much help I'll be. I haven't worked a search grid since I was twenty, and that one was underwater."

"If you can follow a map and keep your eyes on the ground, you're good. Because that's what we need this morning—as many eyes as possible. Rose is out there. So's her great-great-grandfather. I'd prefer to have him back in place before she gets back, or my ass is grass."

"I'll be right there."

"And I'll be grateful. Meet me at the cemetery next to the chapel. You know where the Amberdecker plantation is, don't you?"

"Vaguely."

"It's just past the Visitor Center, left on Old Mountain Road. I'll leave somebody at the main gate to let you in. Ask him for directions to the chapel." His voice was gruff, but there was emotion running underneath the rough tenor. "And thanks. Your uncle would be proud."

He hung up, and I stared at the phone. Trey cocked his head, one eyebrow raised.

"What happened?"

"Tornado hit a cemetery. Now a little old lady and a Confederate soldier are missing." I smiled at Trey in a pretty-please way. "You did say you were taking a long lunch, right?"

Chapter Seven

As it turned out, Trey's boss granted him plenty of time for lunch. Or to be more specific, for the Amberdeckers. She'd immediately e-mailed him a file, which he was perusing on his phone as I drove us out of downtown Kennesaw.

"Marisa wants you to schmooze?" I said.

"That was not her exact word, but in essence, yes. She's been courting Rose Amberdecker for several months, she said, but the family has resisted hiring any outside security services."

I clicked the windshield wipers into high. We were behind the storm's trailing edge, weaving though a road littered with debris. I slowed down to pass a tree limb blocking the right hand side, a gnarled mass that looked like the foreleg of some prehistoric raptor. The forest would have been beautiful with a clear blue sky behind it. Pines and oaks, ancient hardwoods, granite outcroppings running with rain. But the sky remained low and yellow, the oily hue of weak sunlight and thick humid air.

Trey checked his seatbelt—again—then pulled up the weather map on his phone—again. I couldn't tell which had him more nervous, the storm or my driving, but he'd grudgingly admitted the Ferrari wasn't the best vehicle for traveling into the wilds and joined me in the Camaro. The Z-28 was hardly ideal, but it rode higher off the ground and, most importantly, had trunk space for three metal detectors.

I downshifted through a particularly slick patch. "What makes Marisa think today is the day to make contact? On the morning Rose Amberdecker's cemetery gets ripped up by a tornado?"

"She wants me to be a presence. Her words."

"Which means she wants you to show up and be helpful and then when she runs into the Amberdeckers ever-so-accidentally a week from now, she can say, ah yes, you remember Trey, my number one man, he who was so helpful during your recent unpleasantness, and then the Amberdeckers will throw money at her."

Trey considered. "That sounds correct."

A stray branch whipped across the road in a whirling dervish, and Trey tightened his grip on the seat. We had a ways to go, up through the winding roads of the Kennesaw Mountain National Battlefield Park. During the Battle of Kennesaw Mountain, the mountain had stood like a great wall between the Union army and their eventual war prize—Atlanta. I'd last visited the area back in June, the height of summer, when the park held its commemoration of the battle's sesquicentennial. Birds singing, grass greening, a sky so blue and bright it looked like it might crack open any second and candy fall out. People had told me the land was haunted, that I would sense darkness there, but I hadn't. I'd felt only the colorful violence of summer. Now the violence was more chaotic, destructive. Mother Nature's mean side showing.

"So tell me about these Amberdeckers," I said.

"I thought you knew them personally?"

"No, I know Richard, their caretaker, the one who called this morning."

"I've met him, haven't I?"

"Yeah. Burly guy, beard. He's in the shop at least once a week. But I know very little about the Amberdeckers."

Trey swiped the screen. "Rose Amberdecker, formerly Rose Amberdecker Farwell, formerly married to John Farwell of Farwell Bank and Trust, Farwell Financial, Farwell Insurance and—"

"Got it. Filthy rich white people."

"—mother of Evie and Chelsea Amberdecker, thirty and twenty-five respectively, both living and working downtown.

The family is currently embroiled in a legal battle to separate the Amberdecker assets from her matrimonial ones, hence her return to her maiden name. And her daughters' legal adoption of it."

"The kids took *her* name?"

"After their mother's divorce, yes. Which effectively extinguished any linkage to John Farwell. Or so they are arguing."

"Who's coming for the family money?"

"The state. Before Farwell died, he was convicted of seven counts of fraud and ordered to pay eighteen million in restitution. He died in prison. Heart attack. Rose is arguing that the payback responsibilities died with him."

I was a little confused. "Then why is Marisa so interested? There doesn't seem to be a lot of spare change floating around this family."

"No, but thanks to the discovery of their ancestor's remains two years ago—the same remains you've been asked to find this morning—and the Amberdecker exhibit at the Atlanta History Center—opening this weekend—their social capital has, in Marisa's estimation, increased exponentially. Especially now that Evie, the older daughter, serves as assistant to the state archaeologist."

"So they're the darling of the preservationist set."

"Yes. But most importantly, Chelsea, the younger daughter, is engaged to Jeremy Pratchett."

Trey pronounced the name with a decided emphasis. And it was familiar, in an oh-I-heard-that-on-the-news kind of way.

"And he is?"

"Vice president of marketing for Intercontinental Exchange, headquartered here in Atlanta."

And then I remembered. It had been big news among those in Trey's circle, not so important to people like me, the rinky-dink owner of a rinky-dink gun shop.

"You mean the company that bought the New York Stock Exchange."

Trey nodded. I whistled.

"I see why Marisa's interested. That's some tall cotton."

Trey frowned. The metaphor puzzled him for a second, but he eventually got the gist. "Yes. Marisa sees this as an opportunity to make some valuable connections, and Rose Amberdecker is the…I need a word, two syllables, starts with L."

"Linchpin."

"Yes. Exactly."

A wind shear bumped the car like an enormous invisible battering ram, and Trey whipped his attention out the window again. He stared belligerently at the passing wilderness, as if he were preparing for the trees themselves to leap out at us. He still had the road map open in his lap, but I didn't have the heart to tell him it wouldn't help. We were about to be off the grid, on Amberdecker land.

"Doesn't the Boss Lady remember what happened last time she pimped you out? Or the time before that?"

"What are you suggesting?"

"I'm suggesting bad things happen when Marisa gives you this kind of assignment. Fires, shootings, corpses."

"Those things weren't *my* fault."

"They weren't *mine* either."

Trey clutched the dashboard. "Deer!"

I slammed on the brakes as the buck tossed its head and bounded into the road, nimbly dodging a branch toppled in the left hand lane. I looked over at Trey, who stared straight ahead, one hand braced against the dashboard, the other wrapped around the door handle. The deer stamped its foot, snorted once, and disappeared with a leap. Trey didn't let go of the door, though.

"Welcome to the jungle," I said, and shifted the Camaro back into first with a growl of gears.

Chapter Eight

We passed through the first gate, a swinging fence post guarded by one of Richard's crew, only to be confounded by the second, an intricate wrought-iron barrier with no entrance that we could find. Eventually Trey realized we were supposed to follow it, not enter it.

"It's the boundary that protects the main house," he said. Indeed, I could glimpse the Amberdeckers' white Greek Revival mansion through the black lines of the gate, behind rows of pine trees. Richard had told me it was an exact replica of the original, except that the current version had an elevator, and the slave quarters had been replaced by a sprawling greenhouse.

Trey pointed to the left. "Try that way."

I followed his instructions. He kept his notepad open as I drove, his pencil in constant motion as he sketched and erased, the blank page unfolding into charted landscape. Eventually we found the path, a single-car dirt lane that curved and looped through the woods, finally ending at a clearing. White headstones and ghost-pale statuary dotted the terrain, bordered abruptly by deep woods.

I parked next to the chapel, a compact structure of quarried river rock twined with ivy, a flagstone path leading to its wooden door. As we got out of the car, I saw the path the twister had taken. The chapel looked unharmed, but a massive magnolia lay sprawled on top of gravestones, roots exposed. That wasn't the only damage. The corkscrew storm had gouged a channel through the woods, ripping shrubs into salad and saplings into toothpicks. Raindrops plop-plopped in sloppy mud puddles, thick as soup, and the air felt too heavy to breathe.

I buttoned my rain jacket and headed for the edge of the cemetery, leaving my car beside the chapel. Trey walked beside me, his umbrella over our heads.

"Damn," I said.

Private Braxton Percival Amberdecker's tomb was a ruin. The Corinthian columns that had once guarded the Confederate soldier's final resting place lay cracked and split, the white marble dirt-pocked and filthy with scraps of vegetation. Stone blocks scattered like breadcrumbs across the rough grass, and the figure of a grieving angel had been toppled, one pale arm still curled around its head.

I pulled the rain hood over my head. "This used to be twelve feet tall. Stone Mountain granite over brick. Cement fortified."

Trey didn't reply. He was a little overwhelmed. His dry-clean-only trousers and leather lace-ups weren't suited for slogging through mud and rain, neither of which he liked very much. Nor did he care for being in the woods with nature spilling its guts all around him. He was mustering through, though, probably because I'd seen his eyes light up at the words "search grid."

He nodded toward the tree line. "That's Richard over there, yes?"

It was indeed. Dressed in workingman's jeans and a flannel shirt, Richard looked sweaty and hot despite the freezing temperatures, his thick sorrel curls hidden under a Ford truck hat. He had small eyes that held a cowboy squint, with high cheekbones and a sun-darkened complexion. The beard, however, was straight out of a Mathew Brady daguerreotype, even if his stocky frame wasn't.

He pulled his gloves off. "You got here fast. Considering."

"It didn't get bad until we got past Barrett." I nodded Trey's way. "You remember Trey, right?"

"Of course."

He extended his hand, and the two men shook. Another man silently joined us. He wore overalls, and his lined forehead and mulish gaze gave him a look of profound contrariness. He ignored Trey and me, kept his eyes on the woods.

"What got hit besides the tomb?" I said.

Richard shoved his hat back. "The chapel lost some roof tiles, but that's fixable. That magnolia was over a hundred years old, though. Rose is gonna split her seams."

"You haven't found her yet?"

"No. Best I can tell she took off for a walk this morning, probably down to the edge of the property."

"Do you think she's all right?"

"I'm sure she is. But I want to have those bones safe and sound before she gets back."

I looked around at the acres of pine and hardwoods, kudzu and meadow. "They could be anywhere."

"So we'd best start figuring out where they ain't." Richard pulled out a terrain map, which he'd marked with an approximation of the tornado's path. "There's a tally of the burial goods on the other side. I pulled it from your uncle's notes. Every button, every buckle accounted for."

"Got it."

Richard looked at me seriously as he handed me the map. "I need to warn you about the bones."

"Don't worry, I've seen bones before."

"Not like these. These are red, mottled like they've been dipped in blood. Evie—you know, Rose's daughter, the archeologist—she says it's from being buried on Amberdecker land for a hundred and fifty years. We got a peculiar kind of clay down by the ravine. Striated, Evie calls it."

The old man made a noise and pulled his hat down low. "Or red from being cursed. Best leave him in the clay, I say."

Richard didn't look up from the map. "Nobody asked you, Joe Ben."

But Joe Ben was on a roll. His dentures didn't fit properly, giving him an odd lisp. I could smell the chewing tobacco on him, and saw the corner of a Red Man pouch peeking out from his overall bib. His eyes were pewter-gray and nail-sharp.

"The mountain wants those bones, and we'd best not interfere lest we pay the price too. It's eye for an eye out here."

Richard's voice grew taut. "This ain't the End of Days. Our job is to find those bones, repair the tomb—"

"The mountain don't want no tomb. You mark my words—"

"Do your job, Joe Ben, or I'll find somebody who will. Now go get a radio and start hunting. And if you see Rose first, keep your mouth shut. I need to be the one to tell her about this."

Joe Ben spat a thin stream of tobacco juice to the side, then headed for the chapel. He moved without hurry, as slowly as he could get away with without provoking Richard further.

Richard watched him, then turned to me, shaking his head. "Old men and their stories."

"Stories sometimes have truth for a backbone, you know that."

"I got real backbones to worry about." He jutted his chin toward his pickup truck. "You ready to get started?"

Richard set Trey and me up with handheld radios. The plan was a simple quadrant search—clear one square, then move on to the next. Like a crime scene zone search, Trey had explained, although tornadoes didn't play by the same rules as human perpetrators. Humans tended to drop things in concentric circles. Tornadoes, however, had a peculiar logic all their own.

Trey stopped at the edge of the woods. "Richard said he needed a point person, so I'm staying here and coordinating."

I pocketed the radio. "Where'd he go?"

"One of his men called and said he'd found something."

"The bones?"

"He thought it was a piece of the coffin, but he needed Richard to make sure." Trey hooked his own radio to his belt. "Call off when you've cleared an area, and I'll keep track on the main grid."

I hoisted the metal detector and the accessory bag. "Got it."

"Good. Channel nine. Keep to your quadrant." He tilted his head, examined me thoroughly. "And be careful."

◇◇◇

The woods were dark this morning, and deep. I paced off the coordinates Trey had given me, which took me from the edge of the cemetery to a small ravine. Here, the anemic light grew thin and gray as dishwater. I was glad I'd worn heavy work boots. The red clay mud sucked at the soles like something from a horror movie.

I pulled the headphones from my pocket and plugged them into the detector. I also had a small trowel and handheld probe, but didn't expect I'd be needing them. Tornadoes flung things around, but they didn't bury them too deeply. The detector penetrated to three feet, definitely enough for this particular mission.

The detector wouldn't find bones. That would require a sharp eye, especially since I knew Private Amberdecker's might not be the only remains around, thanks to the nearby battlefield. The Battle of Kennesaw Mountain had claimed over four thousand Confederate and Union casualties, including hundreds of men missing in action, like the Private. And although the Piedmont soil of the Kennesaw area wasn't especially conducive to preserving body parts, the Amberdecker lands created an exception. With loamy soil and red clay deposits veining the earth, this particular landscape coddled bones like a cradle. It was private land, off-limits to looters. That didn't stop the relic-obsessed, however, a fact Richard knew all too well.

I settled the headphones on my ears, listened to the whine of the machine. No, bones would not register, but one of those buttons or buckles would. And if I found one of those things, with any luck, the bones would be nearby.

I straightened up, swung the detector left and right, then set off into the woods.

The tornado's initial impact was precise and obvious. After that, the damage grew more sporadic. There was a petulance to the destruction, like a temper tantrum, but I knew it was only physics at work. Here the trees stood, but the tumbled branches in the pine needles were proof that a lacerating wind had ripped through. I kept my eyes on the ground, swinging the detector back and forth in a neat arc.

Thirty minutes later, all I had found were pull tabs and broken tool parts. None of the private's burial goods, and not a sign of Rose. I was beginning to think Richard's faith was misplaced, that any second now I'd be stumbling on the unfortunate corpse of a little old lady, pearls clutched to her crushed chest…

The metal detector threw off a high-pitched whine, the signature of something big. I looked down. A muck-covered length of metal lay at my feet. I nudged it with my toe. A pry bar, probably from some unfortunate resident's toolshed. I marked an X on my map and kept searching.

I didn't have to search long. The detector whined again, this time in a short sharp burst. I knelt at the foot of a massive oak and parted the top layer of leaves with my fingers. They were cold and slimy and smelled of ripe decay, but they covered something solid underneath. I peered into the mulchy mess. Then I cursed and snatched my fingers back fast.

The brown-stained skull grinned up at me, dead leaves in its teeth, a chunk of its cranium caved in at the back. I didn't even try to brush the mud off. I reached for my radio.

"Trey? You there?"

It sputtered and crackled. "Ten two, Seaver here."

He was in SWAT mode, all last name and ten codes. I pressed the talk button. "I found the skull. Bring the rest of the metal detectors, and we'll grid this area with an intensive."

"Copy that. Text me the coordinates."

"Will do." I dropped my voice. "I love it when you talk cop, have I ever told you that?"

A tiny pause. "Copy and out, Tai."

I tucked the radio back into my pocket and started to move some more leaves out of the way. But before I could, I heard a stomach-dropping noise to my left—the unmistakable "ka-chunk" of a pump action shotgun. And then a woman's voice, cold and authoritative.

"Hold it right there, you goddamned thief!"

Chapter Nine

I put my hands in the air so fast I almost fell over.

The woman came striding toward me—tall, purposeful, her shearling coat pulled tight around a sturdy figure. She stopped fifteen feet from me, the shotgun swung into firing position, the butt tight against her shoulder. I saw it was a twelve-gauge, and whether it was loaded with cartridges or slugs, it could cut me in half before I could take a step.

"Stand up!" she said. "Real slow."

I did as I was told. An ice-gray braid fell over her shoulder, and her eyes flashed pale blue. Despite her tanned skin, I could see spots of color riding high on her cheekbones, and her mouth was a flat line in a square, tightly set jaw.

I kept my hands high. "I'm not a thief. And I'm not armed either. So if you could just put down the shotgun—"

"I'll put it down when I'm good and ready. Who are you?"

I took a deep breath to steady my voice. "Tai Randolph. Richard asked me to help with the search."

"What search? Where's Richard?"

"He's with my boyfriend—"

"Your boyfriend is tromping around too? This is private property, girl, and what you're doing is trespassing. Didn't you see the POSTED signs?"

She was angry, but calm. I relaxed a little. Itchy trigger fingers made for deadly trouble, but there was nothing itchy about this woman.

I lowered my hands a smidgen. "First of all, my boyfriend is a highly trained security operative, so to say that he's 'tromping around' is highly inaccurate. Second, Richard called me and asked me to come. So if you don't like that, your problem is with Richard, not me."

She kept the shotgun leveled at my head. "You always talk back to someone holding you at gunpoint?"

"Unfortunately, yes. It's a character flaw. But I only do it when I'm not really worried about getting shot. And I'm not."

"Why not?"

"Because I'm not doing anything worth shooting me over. And you don't strike me as a woman who wastes ammunition, Mrs. Amberdecker."

She scowled, then lowered the gun. "Put your hands down, you look ridiculous. Where's Richard?"

"Back at the chapel. There was a tornado—"

"Don't you think I know that? Damn thing came through like a freight train. Did it hit the chapel?"

"The roof lost a few tiles, but Richard said he can fix it."

She huffed in relief. She came forward, the wet leaves crunching underneath her boots. Her expression was still hard, but curious. Matter-of-fact instead of angry. She hadn't released the gun, though, so I kept my hands where she could see them.

"Then what did Richard call you for?" she said.

"The chapel may be fine, but your great-great-grandfather's tomb isn't."

She froze. "How bad?"

"Bad enough that Richard's got me out here looking for bones. One of which I've just found, by the way."

"What? Where?"

I pointed with the toe of my shoe. She followed with her eyes, but didn't turn her head or gasp or even act startled. She just stared at the skull the same way she'd stared at me.

"I think they found the coffin too," I said. "We'll know when we get back to the chapel. Richard wanted to get the remains located as soon as possible. He knew you'd want that too, so he called me."

She shook the rain from her eyes, squinted at me. "You're Dexter's girl, aren't you?"

"Yes. His niece."

"I remember. Your uncle helped us bury Braxton the first time we found him." She nodded toward the skull. "Where's the rest of him?"

"I don't know."

She knelt and examined the skull, her shotgun butt-first on the ground beside her. She looked up at the sound of voices behind me, then footsteps. Trey and Richard coming up the path. She hoisted the gun and went to meet them.

Richard hurried over at a jog. "Rose! Where have you been? I was two seconds from calling the police!"

"Goddamn coyote got one of the new kids—I heard it bleating and screaming all the way from the kitchen. So I tracked the varmint down and blew it to kingdom come. Then the damn twister came through and I had to lay low in the culvert over by the south field. And now I come back to this mess."

Trey came forward—cautiously, deliberately—a borrowed rain slicker dripping water on his shoes. He directed a top-to-bottom assessment Rose's way, then mine. Only when he was satisfied that the situation wasn't about to erupt in gunplay did he speak.

"You said you found the skull?"

I nodded toward the tree. "Underneath the leaves. I haven't had a chance to look around anywhere else, but…"

"But?"

I knelt at the base of the tree. "A skull wouldn't set off the metal detector, not by itself. There's something else down there."

Richard came over and stood at my shoulder. "Probably one of the buttons."

"This was too big for a button."

I moved my fingers through the detritus around the skull, suppressing a quirk of disgust. It was just leaf mold, I told myself, rainwater and mulch. And the bones were just ossified calcium, one hundred and fifty years old. But there was something about this skull, something…not right.

Trey crouched beside me, pushing back the black plastic hood of his rain gear to take a closer look. He pointed at a tangle of roots. "Is that what set off the detector?"

I followed his index finger, dug my own fingers into the leafy muck until they brushed something hard. I wiped the leaves and dirt away, then bent closer. And then I got a chill. It was a piece of metal, rusted and mud-choked. And it had no business being where it was.

I stood up, wiping my hands on my jeans. "Looks like you need to call the police after all."

Rose frowned. "Why?"

"Because that's not your great-great-grandfather's skull."

"How do you know?"

I pointed. "Because there's no way Braxton Amberdecker was buried with a NASCAR belt buckle."

Chapter Ten

The interior of the chapel would have been a welcome spot in the summer—a cool place of stone and shadow—but this winter's day, with rain slashing against the window, it was dreary and depressing. It seemed designed to be intentionally dark, with only three windows, all of them stained-glass pieces at the front of the church. There was no electricity; we had to make do with the guttering light of paraffin candles.

Trey and I were the only occupants at the moment. Richard's crew had been sent home for the day, leaving Richard behind to assist the sheriff's deputies, who were treating the area like a crime scene, not an archaeological artifact recovery. Not that there was much difference in my book—both prioritized procedure, preservation, and hasty meticulousness—but I was sure there would be quibbles.

Trey paced in front of the windows, his footsteps echoing, leather against slate. He'd converted one end of the front bench into a makeshift office, covering it in papers bearing his meticulous notes in the margins, his research into resilient security systems. He'd tried to explain. He'd talked of tolerance fluctuations via design parameters, redundancy and diversity, reactive versus proactive control. Now he was trying to have a conversation with his boss, but the connection was spotty, and he kept repeating himself.

His voice held a twinge of frustration. "No, I did not find the body, Tai did."

"It wasn't a body," I said, "it was a skull."

Trey ignored my protests. He moved back and forth in front of the stained glass. The windows faced east, and during most mornings, the first light of day would have illuminated the reds and golds and blues, firing them into life. But this morning left them as dull and washed out as the rain itself.

The centerpiece was a cross—not a crucifix, that was too gory and idolatrous for sensible Baptist tastes. White lilies and red roses entwined in profusion around the border, a rising sun piercing the horizon behind it. The other panels told a familiar New Testament story, the Parable of the Prodigal Son, writ large in two scenes—the first, the prideful richly dressed son setting out on his own, leaving his wounded father and stoic dutiful brother behind. The second, the same son's weeping return to his father's welcoming embrace. The dutiful son was missing in the second image. Probably off grumbling and pouting, I decided, as older know-it-all siblings were wont to do. Only the father, welcoming the boy with open arms, forgiving him, preparing the feast. I couldn't help but wonder what that kind of love felt like, that kind of acceptance…

I shook my head clear. This wasn't my personal saga. This was another family's story, and I could not trespass.

The colors of all three were clear and clean, in stark contrast to the drippy cramped chapel, with its creaky benches and moist cloistered air. I ran a finger along the glass—it was smooth, covered by only a light layer of dust. And then I understood. The windows were new, unlike the rest of the chapel. Not original, a reproduction. I peered at the writing underneath, an inscription in Latin that was a separate window in its own right, making four overall. I didn't know Latin, but I did catch a familiar *Domini* in the phrasing. I got a pen and scribbled the sentence down on the back of my hand.

Trey remained engrossed in his phone conversation. "They *did* call in an archaeological team, but until the authorities release the scene…No, I don't know. I won't know until we've completed our interviews. We're waiting on the detective." He checked his watch. "At least four hours, that's my best guess. Because it's a crime scene now, and…Marisa? Are you still there?"

I sympathized with his frustration. Already behind schedule, he was trapped in the Kennesaw boondocks until he was officially interviewed—yet again—about a suspicious incident involving me—yet again.

Trey shook his head. "Because it's clearly not a historical interment. Because the skull was…" He lowered the phone. "Tai, what was the word?"

"Grotty."

"Not your word, their word."

"Putrescent."

"Putrescent," Trey repeated. "Which means it's now a suspicious death investigation. Because we're witnesses. No, not like that. Nonetheless."

He listened while Marisa continued her diatribe. She was a woman like a Valkyrie, with platinum hair and an imposing figure that reminded me of the prow of a ship, and she had Agendas. But Trey was patient, I had to give him that. Outside I heard the grind and pop of tires on gravel. A new car arriving. I crossed my fingers that it was our highly awaited detective.

Trey resumed pacing. "I saw Mrs. Amberdecker, but haven't spoken with her. Tai talked to her. Briefly. She was held at gunpoint, equally briefly. No, Mrs. Amberdecker had the gun on Tai. A twelve-gauge shotgun…No, I can't say I've ever contemplated such."

He slid a glance my way, and I was surprised to see a sparkle in his eyes. I smiled and held up a middle finger. *For the Boss Lady*, I mouthed.

He looked away quickly. "What was that? Oh. Certainly. I'll finish up tonight. Of course. Goodbye."

He returned his phone to his jacket pocket. With a roof over his head, he was in a better mood. In fact, he was in a damn fine mood considering.

"Marisa giving you trouble?" I said.

He shook his head. "No. She is a bit…baffled, however. She says you're cursed. Her word. She says I should get a voodoo charm to protect myself."

"She's so sweet." I sat on the bench and patted the hard wood. "Sit."

"I'd rather—"

"Sit."

He sat. The rain-spackled Armani was a little worse for wear, but Trey himself was cool and collected. Not a single hint of hypervigilant paranoia, powder-keg frustration, or control freak shutdown. His expression was placid, no sign of the worrywart wrinkle between his eyes.

I frowned. "Are you okay?"

"Yes. Why do you ask?"

"Because we're trapped in the hinterlands, waiting on cops to quiz us. Because there have been shotguns and tornadoes and grumpy old men, and there's no good cell phone coverage and Marisa is annoyed and—oh, yeah—there's this *skull*. And you have yet to deliver a single grumpy I-told-you-so speech about any of it."

"Why would I? You were asked to help, and you said yes. The complications arising from that decision were entirely unforeseeable."

"So that's what annoys you? When I get into trouble that I should have seen coming?

"It's not about predictability, per se. It's…" He glanced over my shoulder to the front door. "Never mind. The detective is here."

Chapter Eleven

Trey stood, buttoning his jacket as he did. I stood too, and the slab of a front door creaked open and a woman bustled inside. She tussled with her umbrella at the threshold, muttering under her breath for a full thirty seconds before giving up and abandoning it on the flagstone path outside. She stamped the water from her feet, then pulled back her rain hood. A cloud of dark brown ringlets fell to her shoulders, kinking and frizzing around her hairline. She smiled—lots of white teeth, like a toothpaste ad—but I couldn't stop staring at her rain boots. Bright purple. With flagrant daisies.

"Tai Randolph?" she said.

I looked up quickly. "That's me."

"Detective Anita Perez, Cobb County Police."

Her voice wasn't Southern. There was a lilt there I couldn't place, a singsong rhythm she was trying to cover with a crisp official tone. Her skin was the color of honey, her dark eyes thick-lashed without a lick of mascara. She was plain, but it was a carefully orchestrated plain, designed to conceal as much as any makeup.

She unbuttoned her rain racket. "Heard you found a skull?"

"That I did."

"Care to tell me the story?"

And so I did. She listened without interrupting, her field-issue recorder clicking away while I talked. She took notes too, little jottings in a notebook, almost afterthoughts. Trey waited in the background—poised, alert, a black-and-white silhouette against the muted splendor of the stained glass.

"And that was the only body part you found?" she said.

"Yes. I stopped looking when Mrs. Amberdecker showed up locked and loaded."

"How about any of the other artifacts?"

"None that belonged to the private. Here's the list." I pulled out Uncle Dexter's tally sheet and handed it to her. "There were some personal items, buttons, and a CSA belt buckle, but my Uncle Dexter provided the flags, a Confederate Stars and Bars and a state flag of Georgia. Those were replicas, but the personal artifacts were real."

She examined the list. "Nobody found any of this?"

I looked at Trey—he'd been in charge of the master tally—but he shook his head. Perez's eyes tracked the items. She looked at lists the same way Trey did, as if feeding data directly into her brain, and her lips moved slightly as she added up figures in her head.

"This stuff is antique, right?" She ran her tongue behind her front teeth, calculating. "How much money are we talking here?"

"I'd have to do a little research to let you know the range. Depends on the condition, provenance, all that."

"Were they worth enough to rob a grave?"

I saw what she was getting at. If there had been nothing in the coffin but dusty old bones, there would be nothing to find in the field but the same, and the metal detector would have been useless.

"I suppose so. But that would have been unlikely."

"Why is that?"

"Because they buried him in a mausoleum, an aboveground tomb, and until that tornado ripped it open, the thing was sealed shut." I looked at Trey. "Didn't you tell me that one of Richard's men found the coffin?"

Trey nodded. "That was the report, yes. I didn't get a chance to confirm, however."

Perez didn't say anything. She was keeping some information in her back pocket, I could tell. That was how the game worked. I'd been on the suspect side of the table enough times to recognize that particular play.

"Any idea who our non-historical bones belong to?" I said.

She wiped water from her nose. "That's exactly what I was going to ask you."

"I'm not the one who can help you, Detective. I'm assuming you've asked Richard and Rose this question."

She shook her head. "I like to talk to whoever discovered the body first."

"Not a body. Just a skull." I pointed at the tally sheet. "And a non-CSA belt buckle. But where there's a belt, there's usually pants, and where there's pants, there's usually a wallet. Did you find one?"

She stared at me for two seconds, then smiled. "My job is to wait for the ME to finish his report. Until then, nobody touches a thing. Not even if that skull had a damn driver's license between its teeth. Because…" She looked at my chest, frowned. "Is that a Confederate flag on your shirt?"

I looked down. "Oh. Yeah. I forgot." I pointed to the words underneath. "That's my shop. Dexter's Guns and More. Currently the 'more' part means Civil War gear, both authentic and replica, including—"

"Key rings? Like this one?"

She pulled out her cell phone and showed me a photo of a grimy hunk of metal. Despite the bad lighting, I could make out the familiar crossed bars of the Confederate Battle Flag, etched in the blacksmithed iron. I felt my heart skip faster.

Perez peered at me, her eyes narrowed. "You recognize it?"

"I do."

I reached into my jacket pocket and pulled out a similar one, only instead of being clogged with gore, mine was polished by constant handling, dinged on the edges. I handed it to her.

She held it side by side with her photograph. "Do you still sell these?"

"They've never been for sale. My uncle made it for me, as a gift."

She examined it closer. "Do you mind if I borrow it?"

"Actually—"

"I'll keep it safe. I need to do a comparison, that's all."

"With the one you found on the body, right?"

Her expression gave nothing away. "I can't discuss specifics. But I'll give it right back as soon as I've got some photos. I promise."

Suddenly, the door to the church flew open. It was an entrance so abrupt it startled even Trey, who immediately went into a defensive stance, slipping one hand under his jacket. I put a hand on his shoulder as a woman stomped down the aisle, her eyes blazing under a khaki slouch hat, her boots echoing against the stone floor. Unlike the uniformed police officers hurrying behind her, she wore sturdy jeans tucked into a pair of high mud boots, a dirt-stained corduroy jacket, and thick oilskin gloves.

She ripped off her hat. "Who the hell authorized this?"

Perez rounded on her. "Excuse me?"

The woman flung a hand toward the door. "Do your people know anything about in situ preservation? Shovel-testing? Subsurface reconstruction? The archaeological record of this land is an artifact in its own right, and until I get my team together, you are under direction of the Department of Natural Resources to cease and desist the disturbance of this previously filed archaeological dig site."

Perez listened to this spiel with patience. So did Trey. His hand no longer hovered near the hem of his jacket, but he stayed in neutral stance, eyes keen, utterly fascinated.

Perez looked straight at the woman. "You're Rose's daughter. Evie Amberdecker."

Evie's eyes flashed. "*Doctor* Evie Amberdecker."

"Did your mother call you?"

She folded her arms. "No. The state archaeologist did."

Perez nodded. "Right. I've already talked to him too. I promised he'd hear from me again as soon as the ME finished his report as per Georgia Code Section 45-16-24 which states that any law enforcement agency notified of the discovery or disturbance, destruction, defacing, mutilation, removal, or exposure of interred human remains shall immediately report such notification to the coroner or medical examiner of the county where the human remains are located, who shall determine whether investigation of the death is required."

Evie looked askance. "Don't quote the law at me, I know it backwards and forwards."

"Then you know that since the ME has said that yes, indeed, an investigation is required, that's *my* scene out there, not yours, not your family's. Mine." She still had the dazzling toothpaste-ad smile on her face. "Now stick that in your dig site and shovel-test it."

"You can't—"

"I can. I did. And if you or any of your people interfere, I will clap you in handcuffs and haul you to jail and charge you with violation of said Georgia code plus interfering with an ongoing investigation. So put away the trowel, Dr. Amberdecker, and go get some coffee. You're gonna be sitting this one out."

Evie flushed crimson, and I could have sworn I hear a sound like a kettle whistling. She glared at me, glared at Trey, then turned on her heel and stomped out.

Perez pulled out a radio. "Hey Jim, it's Anita. If Little Miss Thang tries to cross the tape, throw her in a squad car, won't you? You're a peach." Then she turned back to Trey and me. "Don't go anywhere. I'll have this key ring back in a second."

She squeaked out of the church, her galoshes flopping with each step. Trey watched her go. I watched him just as carefully, but he no longer seemed likely to shoot up the vestibule, so I relaxed. "Your thoughts?"

"I think this situation just became even more complicated."

"I think the same. Luckily, that's not my problem. My problem is that Uncle Dexter is apparently connected to that grotty skull." I stood. "Perez said there was coffee. I'm going to get some. Wash it down with a nicotine patch and some more suckers. You want to stay here, or come with?"

He reached for his umbrella.

Chapter Twelve

The coffee came courtesy of Richard, who had a giant metal urn set up in the back of his truck. It tasted like someone had stewed a rusty nail in creek water, but I didn't care. The warm cup felt good in my hands, and the caffeine went straight into my bloodstream.

Trey chose to stay at the edge of the police tape-enclosed area. He'd given over his sketches and grids to the police officers and watched as they used them to make notes, navigate the area. He stood stoically, arms folded, keen on their every move but unable to participate. I felt a pang for him.

Richard refilled my cup. "Your boyfriend did a good job."

"Yeah. His heart beats for this stuff."

I could see flashlights every now and then beyond the timberline, bobbing and weaving like giant fireflies. Detective Perez was finishing up her interviews. Dr. Evie Amberdecker remained apart from the cluster of people, talking on her cell phone. So far no one was telling her what she wanted to hear—that she could kick Perez and company off her land.

"Evie assisted with the first dig?"

"Yep. Almost two years ago." Richard leaned closer. "Between you and me and the gatepost, Evie wants this whole place dug up and put on display. Rose, however, wants everything left exactly as it was two hundred years ago. But Evie's got that exhibit to think of."

"The one at the History Center? It's opening this weekend, isn't it?"

Richard nodded. "In the new wing. Which Evie is hoping will soon become the Amberdecker Wing. All she has to do is convince the board to make the exhibit a permanent display."

I remembered the History Center. Rico and I had spent an afternoon there the weekend of Uncle Dexter's funeral, during that blazingly bewildered time after I'd learned about his will, and my inheritance. Dexter had volunteered at the Center as a docent, dressing in his 1865-era working clothes, beating out metal on the blacksmith's forge. The new wing had been in process then, a mass of hammers and drills as noisy as the dark smith barn.

"It was under construction the last time I was there."

"You should see it now. Evie's pulled together some serious donations, but the hardest part was convincing her mother to give up the family goods. Like I said, Rose wanted things to stay the same, and that included all the stuff in the house and all the relics buried out here. She wanted them in the dirt."

Something in his voice caught my attention. "You disagree?"

He sipped his coffee, looked thoughtful. "Rose is a sensible woman, and I agree with her on most things, but leaving that stuff in the ground ain't right. Every soldier, no matter what side he fought on, deserves respect and honor. The dirt don't honor nobody."

"So you support the exhibit?"

He shrugged. "Better than the dirt. But personal effects belong with the families, not in a museum. The swords and buckles need to go home the same way those boys needed to go home. Proper like."

So he didn't support either approach one hundred percent. This was an interesting tug of war—Richard and Rose and Evie, all pulling hard on their own agendas. Across the field, Trey put his phone to his ear. Marisa again, I was betting, wanting an update on either his Amberdecker assignment or his progress with the resilient security systems report. I guessed the latter when he started back toward the chapel.

I wrapped my hands tighter around the coffee. "One of my favorite parts of my job is reuniting people with things that belonged to one of their kinfolk. It doesn't matter if it's valuable or not. Just being able to hold some real thing, no matter how small, matters."

"It does. That's why I hate looters. Looters don't see nothing but price tags."

"I suppose I look like a looter to Evie."

"Everybody looks like a looter to Evie. And Rose."

I laughed, but Richard's eyes were far away, and I knew what he was thinking about Dexter, and the last time they'd been on this soil together. As we gazed over the three hundred acres of Amberdecker land, I wondered how many stories remained under that dirt. How many women and men and children, with no stone to mark their graves? There had been slaves here, indentured servants too, and before them, the Cherokee and the Creek and the Muscogee, all the way back to the Stone Age. They had died and returned to the earth. But now they rested unmarked, uncherished, unknown.

Richard wiped his forehead. "As if looters weren't bad enough, now a tornado comes and tears up the place. Rose is gonna rip me a new one."

"For what? Calling me in to help?"

He laughed. "For letting a tornado in."

"You can't help a tornado."

"No. And you can't help Rose, either. She's a force of nature herself."

He said it with pride in his voice, the peculiar Southern appreciation for the rebellious and stubborn, but something else too. Something deeper. I was having a hard time sharing his appreciation. Having been in Rose's crosshairs, I was inclined to classify her as a cantankerous nut job with a possessive streak. But I didn't say such to Richard.

He jabbed his chin toward the chapel. "On the upside, there might be some restoration funds coming in now, especially for the roof and the gravestones. And the publicity would be good for Evie's exhibit. I may not agree with everything Evie's doing, but I gotta say, I was glad she got those windows taken care of."

"You mean the stained glass ones?"

He nodded. "Evie got a restoration team down here to fix them up, and they look mighty nice now. She's right, that chapel is going to wreckage out here, and I don't know much that can save it, short of taking it apart stone by stone and rebuilding it someplace stable." He shoved his hat back. "But Rose won't listen. She says she'd rather it crumble on Amberdecker land than stand forever on someone else's."

I shook my head at him, suddenly confused. "Wait, those are the real windows?"

"Why wouldn't they be?"

I remembered the smooth sheened glass, free from bumps and occlusions. "I don't know, they seemed so…perfect."

"They're restored. Evie got the team together herself."

"But—"

"Tai. Don't be messing with the windows, you hear?"

He had an edge in his voice, and I realized I'd blundered into a minefield of some kind.

"I hear," I said.

"Good." He clapped me on the shoulder. "You'll figure it out later, all by yourself. I'm sure of it."

Together, we looked out over the field, beautiful even in ruin. When the fog settled this way, wet from the mountain, the movements of the men shrouded in it, I could believe that the past rose from the ground like a slumbering beast, tangible and real. Like the ghosts might actually start talking.

"Dexter told me you were the one who found the bones the first time," I said.

"Me and one of my workers, out near the park border. One of the oaks fell, and I found Braxton's skull tangled in the roots. I remember walking in the house that morning, bright summer day, everybody having lunch. Evie got on the phone in two seconds flat, started the whole process with the state."

"And the rest of them?"

"Rose wasn't too happy about none of it, of course. She doesn't like the government messing around private affairs, and I don't blame her. But there's rules, you know, when you find bones. And she calmed down when Evie promised to return him to family soil as soon as possible. No labs, no exhibition. Bury him where he belongs, here, on his homeland."

I remembered the photos of the reburial. Dexter and Richard in full dress grays, the cannon smoke rolling through these fields, brilliant with fall color. It had taken the family several months to work through the red tape surrounding the recovery of human remains, and to build the tomb. Much time and money, now all for naught.

"What did the other daughter think about the situation?"

"Chelsea?" Richard snorted. "She didn't have an opinion one way or the other. Just between you and me, that girl won't look at nothing what ain't wearing tight jeans and driving a fast car."

"I thought she was engaged to what's-his-name? The guy whose family runs the New York Stock Exchange now."

Richard thumbed a cigarette out of his pack. He offered me one, but I shook my head, and he stuck it between his lips, cupped his hands and lit it. I rubbed the nicotine patch harder, thought of England, France, Turkey, anything but the sweetly acrid hit of the smoke.

Richard held the cigarette at his side. "Chelsea snagged her a fine young man, that's for sure. Back in the day, though…She had a taste for wild game, that one."

I filed that idea away. The older responsible daughter with a vested interest in the bones, the younger wild child who was bringing home some bacon in a completely different way. All of it riches for the Amberdecker coffers. All of it a nicely wrought life preserver made of wads and wads of money.

"You have any idea who the skull belongs to?" I said.

Richard shook his head. "Nope. But I'm betting that lady detective does."

"She took my key ring. The one Dexter made me."

"She took mine too."

"How many did he make?"

"Don't know. But whoever that was in the woods, I bet he had one too, the poor bastard." Richard took a long drag on his cigarette and blew a thin stream of smoke toward the trees. "Sometimes I think Joe Ben's right, that this place is haunted. It used to be peaceful and quiet, and then the day Braxton's bones saw the sun again…"

"You say that like a man who believes in ghosts."

"I believe the other side ain't nothing to be getting definite opinions about." His radio crackled, and he pulled it from his belt. "Yeah?"

The voice at the other end was raspy with static. "Detective Perez says everybody can go now. They've got the scene secured. She says it would be very helpful if nobody left town, though, especially not that girl from the gun shop."

I sighed. Of course. Different corpse, same story.

Chapter Thirteen

The clouds fell away behind the departing storm, leaving a chilly wind and diamond-on-velvet sky to see us home. Trey hurried to the car without looking up, then belted himself in and submerged himself in paperwork. He was finishing up another call to Marisa when I climbed behind the wheel.

I managed to back out without ramming any of the dozen official cars parked willy-nilly at the gate, including an ambulance just arriving. "I hate to tell them, but it's way too late for an ambulance."

Trey pulled a penlight from his pocket. "It's procedure."

"Sometimes procedure makes no sense. Like when you stick a grotty skull in an ambulance." Once we cleared the gate, I flipped on the high beams. "So what do you think happened?"

"About what?"

"About the skull. There was a crater in it, like somebody took a baseball bat it."

Trey remained immersed in his papers, his penlight a slim focused beam as he read in the darkness. "I don't have enough evidence to theorize."

"Then guess."

"I'm not good at guessing." He turned his attention to me. "Why are you asking?"

"Because it's looking like that skull's connected to Uncle Dexter in some way."

Trey switched his penlight on me. His cranial lie detector didn't work very well in a dark Camaro, but it functioned well enough. He'd damaged several cognitive functions in the car accident, including the mechanism that let most people ignore verbal deceit. The "white lie shield," my brother called it, explaining that after the accident, Trey didn't have one anymore. Lies hit him square between the eyes now. What this meant for me was that I had a devil of a time hiding anything from him. Every not-quite-factual word I spoke glowed like a road flare.

"Tai," he said, "your part in this is over. This is a suspicious death investigation now, possibly a homicide."

"I know. That's why I'm not getting involved."

He reached up, flipping on the interior lights to better scrutinize my micro-emotive expressions, and I could tell by the tone of his voice that he was cranking his neurons into high gear. "If you're not getting involved, then why do you have notes written on your hand?"

"That's not murder-related. That's from the inscription below the stained glass. Latin. *Et tu Domini* something."

"*Et ut inhabitem in domo Domini in longitudinem dierum.*"

The words flowed from his tongue with practiced ease, lovely as a sonnet. They were a direct contrast to his expression which had all the softness of granite.

"How could you possibly remember that?" I said.

"I learned it in third grade. It's the Twenty-third Psalm, Twenty-second in the Latin Vulgate: 'And I will dwell in the house of the Lord forever.'"

Sometimes I forgot that he'd gone to Catholic school. There was nothing of the religion in his present life, no Mass, no confession. He seemed to have escaped from the nuns without a single mystical bone in his body.

"So correct me if I'm wrong, Mr. Former Altar Boy, but that quote doesn't belong with the Prodigal Son story, right? That story ended with something about the brother who was dead being alive again, fatted calves, the whole forgiveness thing."

"Correct."

"Then why is a quote from the Psalms under there instead?"

"That I don't know."

"Aha! See? Something weird. And it has nothing to do with the skull. This is my historical curiosity being stirred, nothing more."

Trey shot me that look, the one that showed he didn't believe a word coming out of my mouth. I ignored the look.

"And while we're on the subject of those windows, did they look like the real thing to you?"

"What do you mean?"

"Real antiques. Richard said they were, but they seemed awfully new to me."

"I have no expertise in that area."

"Neither do I. But still…" I finished up the last of Richard's awful coffee. "Windows, key rings, skulls. You gotta wonder how it's all connected."

"Tai—"

"But like I said, I'm leaving this particular mess to the cops."

His gaze tracked across my face, lingering around my mouth. He shook his head and narrowed his eyes. "No, you're not."

Once we returned to the gun shop, I walked Trey to his Ferrari. "And it's not as if—"

"Tai. You explained. I heard you."

"Yes, but you think I'm about to do something stupid."

"I think you're becoming…I don't have the word."

"Overly curious?"

"Overly something." Trey opened the car door, slipped his briefcase behind the seat. "As for the rest of it, I've ordered a new video monitor for the safe room. It should be here tomorrow. But unless Brenda agrees to shared access on her property, the alley will always be a vulnerability."

"I'll do my best with her, but she's not being cooperative."

He turned to face me. The wind had died down, leaving a tenacious, heavy cold in its wake. I moved closer to him, but he kept his arms crossed. In the amber glow of the street lamp, his eyes were almost turquoise, his face a study of shadow and light.

"You did good out there today," I said, "heading up the search team. You really miss it, don't you?"

"What, searches?"

"The whole cop thing."

"That's not my job anymore."

"Maybe. But you still miss it."

He didn't reply. I burrowed under his coat, wrapping my arms around his waist, pressing myself into the circle of his warmth. He uncrossed his arms to let me in, but that was his only response. If I wanted a goodnight kiss, I'd have to take it. As usual.

I looked him in the eye. "Trey Seaver, what do I have to do to get you to make a move on me?"

He blinked in confusion. "I'm sorry, what?"

"You know. A move. A pass. Something—anything—that will end with us having sex."

He cocked his head. "Are you asking me to seduce you?"

"Yep. That's it. Got it in one."

"Oh. Okay. I can do that." He leaned back against the car, pondering. "I'll need your help, of course. Because you're somewhat difficult to seduce."

I resisted the urge to thump him between the eyes. "You've got to be kidding. You've never even tried, you jackass."

His eyes flashed. "I've never had the chance. You're very…I need a word, multisyllabic, starts with A."

"Assertive?"

He shook his head.

"Aggressive?"

"Fast. You're very fast."

I glared at him. "Fast doesn't start with A."

"Nonetheless." He looked down at his shoes, a slight flush running warm along his cheekbones. "Fast isn't a bad thing, of course. I like fast. But I'm…"

"Slow?"

"Not slow." He raised his head. "Just less fast."

I caught his scent then—subtle, as always, carried on body heat and proximity, the mixture of that evergreen aftershave and the musk of skin. My fingers itched as I remembered the muscles camouflaged under the sleek Armani suit, the sure touch of his hands, the intense pleasure he could deliver...

I move my mouth closer to his. "I could take you now if I wanted."

"I know."

"Right up against this Ferrari. You wouldn't put up any resistance whatsoever."

"None at all. But that would hardly count as a seduction on my part, now would it?"

I almost caved. The pull of him was gravitational, like planets circling into suns, ever closer, as reckless and heedless as physics. It was science, chemicals and laws and rules, and all I had to do was kiss him, and he'd kiss me back, and the chain reaction would begin...

I forced myself to take one step backwards. "There. That's me being less fast."

He watched me. Considered long and hard. Then he got in the car, leaving me standing alone in the freezing solitary night. He started to close the door, but I stopped it with my hand.

"What the hell, Trey?"

He looked up at me. "What?"

"That's it?"

He nodded. "For now."

"Are you serious?"

"Of course I'm serious."

He said it calmly, softly. But his eyes gleamed, even in the low light. Yes, he was serious—he was always serious. But this was a new kind of serious.

I leaned forward into the car. "Trey. Boyfriend of mine. I don't know what you think seduction is, but this isn't it."

I saw the quirk at the corner of his mouth, and a fresh desire flooded me like sap in the springtime, especially when the quirk deepened into one of his rare crooked smiles. He kept his eyes on me as he started the Ferrari, all four hundred horses under its hood leaping and snorting in a growly eight-liter rumble somewhere close to ninety decibels.

"Of course it is," he said.

Chapter Fourteen

The next morning dawned sunny and clear and bitter cold. I kept the engine running and the heater blasting as I parked in front of my brother's house. His lawn wore the dead of winter well, the leafless dogwoods and winter-spare azaleas complementing the lines of his Arts and Crafts bungalow. I knew better than to honk in his part of Virginia Highlands, but of course I didn't have to—Eric was already coming out to meet me, suitcase rolling beside him like a well-behaved dog.

Maybe it was the bright clear light, but he looked thinner, more gray hairs among the dark blond tousles he so carefully cultivated. He'd turn forty this year, I remembered with a start. I had thirty in my headlights and no gray yet, but my brother's hair was a portent of things to come. He popped his luggage in the trunk, then slid into the passenger side, balancing a travel mug as he arranged his messenger bag between his knees.

"I could have gotten a car," he said, fastening his seatbelt. "The coffee's for you, by the way. Blue Mountain. Sugared and creamed."

I took the mug from him. "Let me guess. Organically sourced from a single cow in Switzerland."

"Oh, you are full of funny this morning, aren't you?"

I laughed as I pulled the Camaro into his driveway for a quick turnaround. Despite the sunshine, his street was empty. Usually there were joggers, retired couples walking fancy dogs clipped like topiary, but temps in the thirties had the neighborhood shuttered and silent.

Eric dropped his glasses to his nose and frowned. "Why aren't you taking Virginia?"

"Virginia's blocked at Monroe. They're filming some movie at Piedmont Park this morning."

"So take Highland to Ponce and then—"

"I know how to get to the airport."

"But—"

"Trust me."

Eric shook his head doubtfully. He looked exactly like our father when he did it—eyebrows lowered, jaw set, the barest waggle of chin. He didn't argue, though, just checked his phone for any messages he'd missed between the doorstep and my front seat.

"So how's it been?" he said. "I haven't seen you for weeks."

"I've been hunkered down in the shop, trying to get it ready for the ATF audit."

"How's that coming?"

"Good."

I watched as he typed out a quick text with his thumbs. Apparently the known world would dry up and sift away if he stopped answering his messages for five minutes. I took the next left, crossing my fingers that the Connector wasn't suffering from extended rush hour gridlock.

I tried to sound nonchalant. "I've got a question."

He didn't look up from the phone. "Shoot."

"Did Uncle Dexter give you a key ring like this one?"

I reached around the steering column and fingered the black iron curlicue of my Dexter-made key ring. Eric examined it, nodding.

"He did. For Christmas, I think, a couple years ago?"

"Your initials on it?"

"Uh huh. The engraving was a bit wonky, but then, he'd only been blacksmithing for a little while, right after he lost Dotty. Then his hip got too bad to stand at the forge all day."

I was a little surprised at how much my brother knew, and a little guilty. I'd visited Dexter every time I'd come up to the city, but I'd visited because he was an irascible old coot, good for a story. I'd loved him, sure enough. But I hadn't paid attention. Apparently Eric had.

My brother ran his fingers along the key ring. "He made those pointy things too."

"Tent stakes?"

He snapped his fingers. "Those. For his reenactment unit, when they went camping. And the things you hang pots with."

"S-hooks."

"Right. Simple things, he called them. Good for a beginner."

"Do you know who else he made key rings for?"

Eric shook his head. "You could ask the rest of his reenactment unit, or the folks at the History Center. They could probably answer most of your questions." He eyed me then, keenly. "Because you have lots of questions this morning. Why is that?"

I shrugged. Eric gave me the therapist look, which sometimes made stuff fall out of my mouth that I had no intention of telling him. I managed to resist this time, however, setting my jaw, tightening my grip on the steering wheel.

Eric thumbed a number into his phone. "Fine. I'll call Trey."

I reached over and pushed his fingers away from the screen. "Don't you dare."

"Then tell me what's going on."

So I explained. Thing were going well until I got to the word 'skull.'"

Eric's eyes widened behind his wire-rims. "You found a body?"

"No, I found a skull. Kinda grotty, but— "

"Tai! Why didn't you call me last night?"

"This is why! Because you overreact!"

He yanked his glasses off his face and polished them furiously on his sleeve. "It isn't overreaction, it's concern. You have an unfortunate tendency to throw yourself into dangerous situations. Situations involving skulls, for example."

"Jeez, Eric, I asked you one question, about a key ring."

"That's always how it starts. Innocently. But at some point you cross a line, and you cross it deliberately, and then you start doing sneaky things like offering to drive me to the airport just so you can quiz me about a piece of evidence in a murder investigation!"

"Nobody said anything about murder." I eased off the gas and settled reluctantly into the middle lane. "And that's actually not the reason I wanted to talk to you."

That caught him off guard. "Then what is?"

So I told him that story too, which took a lot longer. I started with the night in the gun shop, when Trey had thrown me in the safe room, then backed up to the nightmares, the insomnia, his lack of interest and energy in pretty much anything until he'd been handed a search grid.

Eric listened. He'd heard it all before, when he'd helped Trey recover after the accident. He listened with a new perspective now, for Trey was no longer one of his clients—he was the guy dating me—and that complicated the situation. Which explained the seriousness in his voice when he started talking.

"Tai, you know that Trey's particular brand of instability is not only dangerous for him, it can be dangerous for anyone in his immediate vicinity, including you."

"I know. But the truth is, he probably did hear somebody, probably the same somebody that set off the alarms yesterday. Maybe the other false alarms too. I'm not sure that was provocation enough to pull his weapon, though."

"It's what he's trained to do. It's his fallback."

The memory of Savannah flashed again. Deep parts of Trey had come to the surface. And while some of them had been downright mouthwatering, I'd seen the darker aspects too. I sometimes forgot that Trey was capable of killing in various total and professional ways—with his hands, with a knife, with a sniper rifle. I'd been forced to confront that part of myself too, the part that could kill, would have killed, and had wanted to, very badly.

My brother kept his voice level. "How aware is Trey of his behavior?"

"The PTSD part? Quite. There's other stuff going on I'm not sure he sees, though."

"Like?"

"Like how utterly starved he is for something exciting to do. His entire professional life is now charts and graphs, and he adores them—yes, he does—and he's great at them—yes, he is—but there's something missing, and he thinks he can fill that empty spot with paperwork."

I pulled up to the Delta terminal, but Eric didn't get out immediately. Instead he opened his messenger bag, pulled out a pen and scribbled something on a notepad. He tore the paper off and handed it to me. It was a book title: *Post-Traumatic Stress Disorder: A Cognitive Behavioral Approach.*

"Trey has a copy. It's an excellent primer, lots of practical advice. I'm sure he'll let you borrow it."

I folded the paper and stuck it in my pocket. "Thank you."

"Because we're coming up on the ninth, you know. And anniversaries can trigger—"

"I know. We've talked about it."

"Good." Eric shouldered his messenger bag and climbed out, pulling his suitcase from the backseat. "I'll be back Sunday night. We can talk more then."

"Okay."

He hesitated, then leaned back in the car. "I don't know why a skeleton had one of Dexter's key rings. I don't think that's something you ought to be trying to figure out. I *do* know it would mean a lot to Dexter that you're still making a go of the shop. Dotty too. And it would mean even more to them—and to me, and to all of us who love you, including Trey—if you can manage to stay alive while you're doing it."

I felt my throat constrict. "I'll do my dead level best."

He shut the door. I threw him a wave, pulled back into the stream of traffic. He waved back, but didn't move from his spot in front of the terminal. I watched him as he became a shrinking speck in my rearview mirror. Eventually I couldn't see him anymore. But I knew he was there.

Chapter Fifteen

From Peachtree Street, the Atlanta History Center looks deceptively urban and bland. Behind its beige exterior, however, lie thirty-three acres of greenness, including several vegetable gardens, a 1928 Classical-style mansion, and a Civil War-era farmhouse that somehow survived Sherman's torch. Unfortunately, the outdoor exhibits were deserted this morning, including the blacksmith shop.

"We don't have another blacksmith program scheduled until Saturday," the docent at the front desk said. She was a slight woman, with jet black hair and red nails and a librarian's hushed voice.

"Perhaps you can help me. My Uncle Dexter used to volunteer here."

I pulled out the photograph I'd found of Dexter, delivering his presentation amidst the smoke and hot bellowed air, metal glowing in his tongs like a miniature sun, his face red and cheerful in the firelight.

Her eyes lit up. "I remember him! Big guy, walked with a cane?"

"That's him." I showed her my key ring. "Do you remember him making these?"

The docent examined the key ring. "Sorry, no. I can always ask Dr. Amberdecker about it. She's busy right now, of course, but—"

"Evie Amberdecker? I don't suppose there's any chance I could see her?"

The docent pursed her lips. "Oh no, that wouldn't be possible. Would you like to leave a note?"

"That will do, I guess."

She sent some paper and a pen my way. I jotted down my contact info with a quick summary of the situation. I handed it back to the docent, who folded it neatly and placed it in a memo box. And then she handed me a map and schedule.

"Enjoy your visit!" she said, beaming.

I walked to the middle of the main atrium, where hallways branched into the separate exhibit areas. Had I been in the mood, I could have explored Atlanta's role in the Masters Tournament, the Centennial Olympic Games, the Southern Folk Art Revival. But of course I was drawn to the hallway concealed behind thick crimson curtains and a CLOSED sign. The Amberdecker exhibit—"Homecoming: The Life and Death of a Confederate Soldier."

I looked back at the help desk. The nice lady docent chatted up a new visitor, while her assistant worked the phone. I looked back at the exhibit. No guard, no locked door, nothing between me and the shadowed interior but a red velvet rope. Another quick check down the adjacent hallways, and I stepped over the rope and slipped behind the curtain, letting the drapery close behind me with a heavy exhalation, like the doors of a church.

I eased around a partition, grateful for the recessed overheard lights that warmed and softened and, I hoped, concealed. The space was silent except for my sneakers on the golden hardwood and the thunder of distant cannonade, sound effects from hidden speakers. The exhibit was arranged in a walk-through fashion, each display leading further into the labyrinth. It was probably enormous in that hall, yet it felt close, intimate.

And it started with a life-size replica of the gentleman himself. Private Braxton Percival Amberdecker. Rose Amberdecker's great-great-grandfather.

His likeness wore the uniform of the Confederate infantry-man—a gray shell-jacket and a pair of gray cloth trousers and a sky-blue kepi with a dark blue band. A replica of his .45-caliber Whitworth rifle, a rare and legendary firearm of the finest workmanship, rested in his arms. The bayonet attached to it was genuine, found with his remains—I could barely make out his name engraved on the blade. The figure's eerily realistic features bore an expression of stoic, blue-eyed acceptance. I could see Rose in those eyes, and in the square chin, but the heartbreaking softness of his freckled cheeks above the mustache was his alone.

I'd looked him up in the second volume of Dexter's dusty *Roster of Confederate Soldiers*. The private had served in the 41st Georgia, Company B, seeing action at Vicksburg before returning to Georgia late in the summer of 1863. A fractured arm earned him a thirty-day furlough back on the Amberdecker plantation, after which he returned to his regiment. The summer of 1864, he went missing during the Battle of Kennesaw Mountain, presumed dead. And that was the end of his story until yet another hot summer day two years past, very much like the day he'd disappeared.

A voice startled me. "Excuse me, but this exhibit isn't open to the public yet."

I turned. Dr. Evie Amberdecker stood there, no longer in field gear. She wore a smart maroon suit with pantyhose and sensible heels, her brown hair subdued in a bun. In the half-light, the resemblance to her ancestor's effigy was stunning, right down to the assertive jaw and the freckles spattering the bridge of her nose.

I stuck out my hand. "Hi again, I'm Tai Randolph. From yesterday?"

Recognition bloomed on her features. She took my hand. Her grip was soft but strong, calloused below the thumb, a scholarly hand that also did hard labor. "Evie, please. Despite my performance yesterday, I don't usually pull the 'Dr. Amberdecker' routine." She winced. "I do apologize. I think I yelled."

"It was a tough morning. No apology necessary."

"Richard told me afterward that you were Dexter's niece. He said you came out to help, and I didn't appreciate that at the time. But I do now, and so does Mama. Really."

"You have a sister too, right? Chelsea? Was she there yesterday?"

Evie's nose wrinkled slightly. "No, she was tied up with yet another dress-fitting."

"That's right. Richard said she's getting married soon."

Evie's mouth twitched, but she covered it with a tight smile. "In two weeks. Her bridal luncheon is tomorrow, at the High. As if I didn't have enough to do with the opening happening the *same* weekend, and now Braxton's remains in the wind. Literally."

There was tension between the sisters, that was clear. A simple big-sis-little-sis squabble? Or something deeper, more entrenched? I tried to gauge Evie's expression, but she'd made her face as bland as the mannequin's.

"So they haven't found the bones yet?" I said.

"Not yet. Which makes this whole homecoming theme rather poignant." She inhaled briskly. "I'm going back this afternoon, once I can get the reporters out of my hair and these clothes back in the closet."

"I thought it was still a closed crime scene?"

"Not anymore. The cops did an aerial surveillance, gathered what evidence they could, then called it a day. Which makes it my scene again."

"So they've identified the skull?"

"If they have, they're not telling me about it. I couldn't care less, though. Probably some looter tripped and cracked his head open, which serves him right. I'm tempted to let Mama start shooting them. Or simply shoot them myself. It's been a while since I took the Winchester out, but pulling a trigger is like riding a bike."

She had her mother's remorseless practicality, that was certain, and probably her overprotective streak too. I thought hard about my next move and decided that straight-up honesty was my best bet.

"I'm sorry to sneak behind the rope like that, but I've got my own family mystery to unravel." I showed her the key ring. "My Uncle Dexter made this. He worked as a docent here a few years ago, in the blacksmith shop. Do you remember him?"

She smiled, in genuine delight this time. "Of course I remember!"

"Do you remember if he made these for anyone else?"

She shook her head. "I'm sorry, I don't."

I slipped it back in my pocket. "I saw his demonstration only once before he died. But I think he's connected to your family, and that skull, in some way I haven't figured out yet, so I'm hoping…I don't know what I'm hoping. But I look at this exhibit, at the work you've done, and I think you understand why I have to find some answers."

The straight-up approach worked. Evie checked her watch. "I have an hour before the news crew arrives. Would you like to join me on my final walk-through, Ms. Randolph?"

"Call me Tai," I said. "And absolutely."

Chapter Sixteen

I moved quietly through the exhibit, Evie at my side. She stopped me at the first display, where a pretend fireplace burned with orange licks of faux flame. A dark-haired female mannequin dressed in black mourning sat in a rocking chair, a notebook in her lap. Another female figure—also in black, her blond hair in an elaborate plait—gazed at the mantel, one slender plastic hand resting there, the other on top of her pregnant belly. Between them stood a matronly figure in a dark slate housedress, hands on hips, gray hair in a netted bun, eyes like blue bullets.

Evie gestured with an upturned palm. "Meet the Amber-decker women. That's my great-great-great-great-aunt Violet, Braxton's younger sister, in the rocker. We used her sketches, including her self-portraits, to create the models you'll see today."

I examined the three figures. "They're incredibly lifelike."

"Part of that is technology—the hyperrealism of silicone skin—but the rest is Violet's talent. She had a way of capturing not only each person's distinct features, but also each unique personality. Unfortunately, all we have of her are her sketches. Her diaries and journals were lost in a kitchen fire just after the Battle of Kennesaw Mountain."

I stepped closer. Violet seemed poised on the verge of springing from the rocker, her blue eyes bright in her pale pixie face. Childlike, but not innocent, an unsettling combination.

"She look a little manic," I said.

Evie's expression remained smooth. "Violet eventually went mad and was committed to a mental institution, where she died at the age of twenty. Suicide from an overdose of laudanum."

Her words hung heavy in the air. "That's awful," I said.

"It was. I have a special fondness for Violet, who was the black sheep of my family in many ways. But more about that later. Let me introduce my great-great-great-grandmother now."

We moved to the left of the tableau, stopping before the pregnant blonde. This figure seemed prissily bored, the slight curl in her tiny rosebud mouth rippling with genteel contempt.

Evie folded her arms. "And this is Evangeline Davenport Amberdecker, Braxton's wife."

"She looks annoyed."

"She was. The daughter of wealthy Northerners, Evangeline was betrothed to Braxton in a marriage that was more business arrangement than love match and which was bitterly unhappy on both sides."

I pointed at the swollen belly. "They managed to get along for a little while."

Evie laughed. "Well, that was their duty, of course. She was carrying their first and only child when he went missing in action at the Battle of Kennesaw Mountain. Her parents had moved her back to Maryland by then, however, so that child—my great-great-grandfather—was born in Chesapeake Bay. He didn't return to Georgia until 1895, when he reclaimed the land that is now the Amberdecker plantation and rebuilt it."

I stepped to the edge of the display, looked the stern central figure in the eye. "And this is?"

"Augusta Rose Amberdecker, my great-great-great-great-grandmother and the matriarch of the clan. You'll notice she's not in mourning. That's because she refused to acknowledge Braxton's death. This put her at odds with her other two children, and with her daughter-in-law, who seemed quite eager to be a widow and put her unfortunate marriage, and Georgia, behind her."

"Augusta Rose. Is she your mother's namesake?"

Evie nodded. "And not just the name got passed down. Mama also inherited her stubborn streak."

"Richard told me your mother wasn't too happy about parting with the family heirlooms for this exhibit."

"My mother would keep everything in the closet if she had her way. Sometimes I think she expects the Yankees to make another run at us." She started walking. "There's only one section of our land that has ever been excavated, and that was back when the greenhouse was built over the ruins of the old slave quarters."

I stopped abruptly when I reached the next tableau. This shadowy corner explored a darker aspect of plantation life—the labors of the enslaved—and as such contained the artifacts of an everyday, ordinary evil. The ten-pound bucket of nails that was a slave's required daily output at the forge. The slave ship manifests listing human beings as cargo. Every mundane thing, from the soup ladles to the pottery, felt touched by a sadness so pervasive it would never rub off.

Evie's voice was calm, however. "These artifacts tell the Amberdecker story as much as the rest. They speak of their participation in an inhuman institution. But they also demonstrate that by all surviving accounts, my ancestors were not brutal people. They provided religious services and health care for the enslaved workers, and Violet often taught the children how to read and draw—"

"But not write," I said. "Because that was illegal."

Evie's eyes widened in mild surprise—she hadn't expected me to know that—but she recovered smoothly. "Correct. Violet flouted the law, however. She was reprimanded multiple times for bringing free persons of color onto the plantation under the guise of religious instruction, when in reality, they were probably underground educators. It's one of the reasons I have such a fondness for her."

Evie started walking again, and I followed, relieved to put that display behind me. I was on a fact-finding mission, I reminded myself, not a soapbox. But I couldn't help the dull seethe of anger. Or the guilt. Both were part of my Southern baggage, inextricable.

We stopped next at a three-dimensional replica of the Kennesaw Mountain battlefield and surrounding land, including the Amberdecker property. I recognized the area I'd trekked the day before, now rendered in miniature, bordered by the ridge of Kennesaw Mountain. I poked one of the push buttons lining the perimeter, and the terrain lit up where Braxton's bones had been found. Another button illuminated the chapel and the cemetery, pristine and intact, unlike their real-life counterparts.

I resisted the urge to touch the tiny gravestones. "I've heard rumors this land is haunted."

"You've been listening to Joe Ben, haven't you?"

"He does talk." I pressed another button and watched the front line of the Confederate defense light up across the mountain, where sharpshooters had hidden in the red clay earthworks, as gray and silent as ghosts themselves. "I used to be a tour guide in Savannah. The supernatural was my specialty. And the War Between the States."

Evie kept her eyes on the display. "This is a story of a haunting, yes, but not how Joe Ben thinks. Violet had a premonition that her brother would never return from battle. She had a dream, she said, her brother dying in the forest, undiscovered. That was a pervasive fear then, even more than dying, so much so that some soldiers pinned their names to their backs, or etched them into their daggers and bayonets, as Braxton did. Indeed, his personalized bayonet was instrumental in identifying the remains as his."

"You didn't run DNA?"

She shook her head. "My mother wouldn't allow it. And really, it wasn't necessary. We had anecdotal evidence that established his identity—a fracture of the left ulna, documented in his medical papers—plus the bayonet."

"Richard said the evidence indicated he was trying to get home from the battlefield."

"All we know is that he was buried prone, arms splayed, the

Minié ball that killed him still in his skull." Evie rubbed the bridge of her nose. "A single shot, right between the eyes."

I winced. Minié balls were notorious for the damage they inflicted—tearing, lacerating, splintering. Over sixty thousand amputations were performed in the Civil War, most of them due to this deceptively small piece of lead.

"The in situ presentation demonstrated that he wasn't given a proper Christian burial—that's usually face up, supine. It suggested that he died where he fell and was covered with dirt, his body eventually becoming entangled in the roots of a tree growing nearly. That's how he was found, you know. When the tree fell."

"Richard told me. He said the bones were red."

"They were, as you can see from the photographs in the program. They were buried in stratified red clay, which created a staining pattern quite unlike anything I've ever seen. Beautiful, actually." Evie stepped forward, pulling open a set of drapes. "Braxton left us his bones, Violet her art, Augusta Rose's stubbornness left us these."

She pressed a button, and a previously dark alcove flooded with light like morning sunshine. The stained-glass windows flared to life. Unlike the ones in the chapel, these weren't blandly perfect. They thrummed with vitality, broken and authentic, as if the hundreds of eyes that had gazed through them over the centuries had burnished them brighter, as if the figures were poised to step out of the leaded panes, lungs pumping, blood surging.

I spun around to face her. "I knew the ones in the chapel weren't real!"

"I used the renovation as an excuse to switch them out with replicas. As the whole world will know on Saturday, including my mother. And then there will be hell to pay. But I decided it would be easier to ask forgiveness than permission."

"You fooled Richard."

She shot me a pointed look. "I did not. Richard knows, but he doesn't want to admit it because then he'd have to tell my mother, and he doesn't want to do that. And neither do I."

I remembered Rose's eyes above the twelve-gauge. I wasn't about to mention it either.

Evie gazed at the triptych, her skin burnished by the reflected glow. "The Amberdeckers commissioned the windows the day they received word that Braxton was missing in action at the Battle of Kennesaw Mountain. They are extremely valuable, even without the historical provenance, an exquisite example of Henry Sharp's pre-1870 work. Today, it would cost approximately $143,000 to reproduce them. The images should look familiar to you—that's Braxton as the wayward prodigal, his brother Nate as the older son, and their dearly departed father as the patriarch."

"Nate?"

"Braxton's older brother. Look around the corner."

I did. And there he stood, a strapping, black-haired specimen of Confederate manhood in full officer's dress, his cadet gray jacket sleeves accented with the gold Austrian braid indicating his rank. Nate had the same angled jawline as his brother, but there was no tenderness in his lean cheeks and narrow eyes.

"Nate was the oldest of the Amberdecker siblings," Evie explained, "and a proud son of the South. He'd barely graduated from the Citadel when the call to arms went out, and he voluntarily joined the Army of Northern Virginia as an officer. He was home on leave when the Battle of Kennesaw Mountain began and his brother went missing, effectively leaving him as head of the household during the Siege."

The windows were mesmerizing, as tantalizingly mysterious as the story behind them. "But if this is the prodigal story, why is the inscription panel from the Psalms?"

Evie smiled. "Therein hangs the tale. The inscription panel was a memorial gift from the Davenports, Braxton's Northern in-laws. It was supposed to be Luke 15:32—'For this thy brother was dead, and is alive again; and was lost, and is found'—but instead the Davenports sent the last line of the Twenty-third Psalm. 'And I shall dwell in the house of the Lord forever.'"

"They decided Braxton was dead."

"They decided it was in their best interest to sever their ties with the Southern aristocracy, especially the Amberdeckers, who were left in, shall we say, reduced circumstances as the war progressed. Evangeline's status as a Confederate wife-in-waiting kept her from moving into respectable widowhood."

"And further marriageability."

Evie inclined her head. "Yes. Which is why they brought Evangeline back to Chesapeake Bay and got her engaged as soon as possible, this time happily, to a Unionist. Augusta Rose resisted, of course—it was in her best interest to have a wealthy daughter-in-law and an heir in her pocket—but in the end, the Davenports won that skirmish."

I was dazzled by the brilliant rubies and golds, the textured opalescence of the skin tones. The yearning in the father's face, the despair in the son's, the stern flat judgment in the brother's.

I pointed. "Why isn't Nate in the second panel?"

"He used to be. Look closer."

I saw it then, barely perceptible, a person-shaped collage of sky the tiniest bit lighter than the surrounding glass, thicker and duller too, without the same quality and workmanship.

I traced the outline in the air with my finger. "There."

"Yes. The day after it was installed, Violet smashed a rock through the window, cutting herself so badly that she had to be hospitalized. It was this incident that forced her family to commit her to the asylum. Augusta had it repaired, but funds were too limited for a full restoration." Evie shook her head. "Poor Augusta Rose. It helps me understand why she denied Braxton's death for so long, why she tried to keep Evangeline in Georgia. Her daughter-in-law carried the only grandchild Rose would ever have."

"Nate never had a family?"

"He never married. After the war, he did his duty to his mother and father and what was left of the plantation, but his heart remained on the battlefield and the Glorious Cause. He died bitter and alone in the house I grew up in. So yes, I would say 'haunted' is a fine word to use for our land. And our history."

I stared at the window, a story woven in leaded lines and shimmery glass. Betrayal, insanity, misplaced blind faith. The template for every Southern tragedy ever written. I suddenly didn't blame Rose one bit for wanting to keep this tale buried.

Evie checked her watch and winced. "I'm sorry, but I have to get ready for the reporters now." She handed me a program for the exhibit, scribbled her number on the back. "That's my cell. If you hear anything about the other bones, please let me know." She paused, as if preparing to tread delicately. "Richard said the man who came with you yesterday works at Phoenix?"

Suddenly I figured out why I'd rated a personal one-on-one tour. Score one for Marisa.

"His name is Trey Seaver," I said, pulling out one of my own cards and scribbling his contact information on the back. "And he's a premises security genius. You'll see."

Evie smiled at me. Transaction completed.

"Thank you," she said, gesturing firmly toward the exit. "This door will take you out."

Chapter Seventeen

I returned to Kennesaw to find my shop engulfed in a noisy stew of grinding engines and shouting construction workers. A bulldozer worked the square, scraping dirt and brush into a pile, the whole block bordered with yellow tape. I saw Brenda in front of her office putting out a sign—CAUTION! REVITALIZATION IN PROGRESS! She threw me a smug wave. I slammed the door and pulled the blinds, making sure the CLOSED sign was showing.

Then I dumped my tote bag on the counter and got down to business.

After talking with Evie, I'd gone straight to the gift shop and bought everything that had the word "Amberdecker" on it, including the book with Violet's sketches. Her drawings of Braxton captured the softness of his youth, while the ones of the older Nate caught the practical, relentless gaze of a man trying to keep a crumbling world intact. Evangeline's wan beauty was rendered in blurry lines and smudged shadowing. Violet's self-portraits were equally expert, but they felt unfinished, as if she'd cut the process short. Unwilling to look at herself whole.

I paged through the program. I'd seen most of it during my tour with Evie, but the most fascinating part was the photography spread from the Amberdecker dig site, including shots of the bones still tangled in the tree roots. They were mud-smeared and covered with debris, but clearly mottled red, just like Richard had warned me. From the earth to the tomb to the earth again.

Three knocks at the door jolted me back to reality. I frowned as I stood. Trey didn't knock anymore. Neither did my customers. I came around the counter and peeked through the window. Detective Perez stood on my doorstep.

I opened the door. "Good morning."

Perez trooped inside. "Morning yourself."

She had file folders under her arm and a harried expression on her face. No daisy-adorned galoshes this time, only sensible heels and slacks. She'd tamed the hair with a headband, but still wore no makeup.

I closed the door on the surging noise of the square. "Can I get you some coffee?"

"No thanks. I have to make this quick." She reached into a folder and sent a photograph along the counter. "Do you recognize this person?"

The photo showed a twenty-ish man, straw-colored hair in spikes above a lean tanned face. A goatee flourished along high cheekbones and down to a pointed chin, and pale lashes rimmed quartz-chip eyes. He wasn't smiling—the image had the odd posed look and washed-out lighting of a mug shot or a driver's license photo.

I sent the photo back. "I don't know him."

"Are you sure? Because he used to work here, in this shop."

"I've only been here eleven months. Maybe if you could tell me more about him, I could help."

She pulled another piece of paper from the folder. "His name is Lucius Dufrene. He worked for your uncle until he skipped town a year and a half ago, right around the time of Braxton Amberdecker's reburial. Lucius was a thief. Two hits for pickpocketing in Albany, plea-bargained to time served. This is a copy of the police report filed by your uncle after Lucius disappeared."

I followed her pointing finger. It was a terse write-up, Dexter's statement that he was missing two swords, a shotgun, three revolvers, and a whole bunch of ammunition, all of which was recovered at Dufrene's apartment during the subsequent investigation. The report concluded with an active warrant for his arrest.

"Great. So what's this Lucius person done now?"

"He got himself killed."

"Can't say I'm surprised. He strikes me as a wrong-place-wrong-time kind of guy."

"Funny you should mention that." Her eyes were suddenly sharp, with a whetted, polished gleam like the arrowheads I used to find. "Because it's likely that the skull you stumbled across yesterday belongs to him."

I closed my eyes. Lord have mercy, I did not need this again. It was bad enough that I'd found yet another corpse—even though that shouldn't have counted against me seeing as how I'd been asked to actively look for said corpse. Or some other said corpse. Suddenly there were too many corpses to keep track of.

"What happened to him?"

"Somebody caved in his skull with that pry bar you found in the woods. And then somebody also—maybe the same some-body—went to his apartment afterward, stirred the place up but good. Looking for something. Which is why I'm here talking to you, since as best we can tell…" Perez consulted her notes. "Your Uncle Dexter was one of the last people to see Lucius alive."

"No, whoever killed Lucius was the last person to see Lucius alive. The person who went looking through his apartment later. That person. Not my uncle."

Perez gave me that look, the one that was designed to make me feel like she was on my side. But I'd learned that cops didn't have a side. Their job was to suture the societal fabric that ripped open whenever one human being violated another. All of us—criminals, witnesses, even victims—were dangling loose threads in their efficient hands.

"Ms. Randolph—"

"It's Tai. Short for Teresa Ann. Long story."

She flashed a smile. "Tai. We found a key ring matching yours on the body. We have reason to believe it belonged to your uncle since we found his initials on it." She pulled a set of keys with plastic ID tags zip-tied to them. "These are copies the lab made for me. I'd like to try them out in your shop, if you don't mind."

"Be my guest." I gestured toward the ash-blond door now protecting my storage room. "That's the only new lock. The rest were here when I inherited the place, so the keys should fit."

But they didn't fit. Perez slipped the keys one by one into every lock in the place, but none of them worked. As she double-checked, I noticed one looked very different from the others—shorter, more jagged.

"That's not a door key."

Perez shook her head. "Nope. Not a display-case key either."

"Padlock maybe?"

"You have one?"

"No. Everything around here is combination lock."

She returned the keys to their plastic bag. "Your uncle change the locks regularly?"

"My uncle was cheap. If he changed the locks, he had a reason. Which I'm guessing might be because his keys got stolen." I tapped Lucius' photo. "By this guy."

She put her hands on her hips. "That guy you conveniently remember very little about."

"Like I told you, I wasn't here then." I put my hands on my hips too. "How *do* you know he worked here? I haven't seen Lucius' name on any of Uncle Dexter's payroll statements."

"Your uncle's report said that he helped out around the store, and I'm guessing it wasn't out of the goodness of his heart." She cocked her head. "Did your uncle wear his costume when he was at work?"

"It's not a costume, it's a uniform. And no, he didn't."

"Any idea why Lucius would have been wearing a Confederate uniform when he died? Was he a reenactor like your uncle?"

"A *replica* uniform, I'm sure, and I don't know. But he was also—correct me if I'm wrong—wearing a NASCAR belt buckle, and Dexter wouldn't have tolerated that on the field. He wasn't a farby by any means—"

"A what?"

"A farby. A seriously hard-core reenactor."

Perez frowned. "Spell that."

I did. "Farbys constantly nitpick. They're called that because they're always saying 'Far be it from me to criticize" before they tell you everything you're doing wrong." I held up both hands. "Don't get me wrong, I love farbys. They're the guys who buy my hand-stitched 1865-style long underwear. But they can be a pain in the ass."

"Your uncle wasn't a farby?"

I snorted. "Dexter wore Fruit of the Loom under his uniform. But he did believe in presenting as authentic an impression as possible. He would never have allowed Lucius on the field or in this shop dressed sloppy and half-assed."

Detective Perez didn't lose the pleasant curiosity in her face. "So there were conflicts between them?"

Damn it. There I went again.

I took a deep breath. "Except for Lucius apparently stealing him blind? None that I know of."

"Did your uncle have any other employees who might remember more?"

"I can check the records for you, tell you if I find anything."

"That would be very helpful. Thank you." She headed for the door. "And if you do find something, call me. I'll be happy to return and pick it up."

She said "happy" with an odd inflection. Of course she'd be happy. She'd be utterly thrilled to come poking around my shop, downright delighted to knit what she found into a story that would hold water, with a solution she could sell to her supervisors and file under "case solved."

She opened the door to leave, the door bells a cheery jingle in her wake. "Oh, one more thing—I found this on your front door."

She handed me a piece of paper. The message was folded so that the watermarked KRC showed. The Kennesaw Revitalization Commission. I opened it, skimmed it, felt my ears grow hot.

Without even waiting for Perez to get in her car, I stomped next door. Brenda looked up as I entered, but remained seated behind a two-acre conference table. The walls glistened a saccharine moss green, and spa music flitted from corner to corner, zither and pan flute and harp.

I slapped the paper down in front of her. "What the hell?"

"I see you found your revitalization plan."

"Paved parking. New sidewalks. I can't afford any of that right now!"

She folded her hands demurely. "You're taking this personally."

"Damn straight."

"I don't think we can have a productive discussion until—"

"Admit it. You're trying to run me out of business. That's why you won't let me put a camera on your property, because you *want* me to be robbed and pillaged and burgled!"

Her eyes sparkled, and her pink mouth curved. "Why, yes. I do. You attract the wrong element—you are the wrong element—and whatever happens to you serves you right." She pushed herself to standing, elbows braced on the table. "I am trying as hard as I can to get rid of you. So why won't you just go?"

I waited for a few seconds. "Are you done?"

"No. I'm just getting started. You have no idea the kind of enemy I can be. Leave. Find somewhere else to peddle your retro wares. The rest of us are marching forward without you and your kind. It's the New South. Wake up and smell the progress."

I realized I'd clenched my hands into fists, so I took a moment to open them, shake them out. Take a deep breath or two. So we were moving into open warfare. Good. It suited my skill set better than skulking and backstabbing.

I smiled at her. "You'd better watch it, Brenda Lovejoy-Burlington. My kind doesn't like being told what to do, so I suggest you cut this shit out—"

"Or what?"

She said it sweetly, with sugar on top. I smiled wider, without a bit of sweetness in it.

"Or things will get ugly."

"Is that a threat?"

"Yep. Clear threat. Directed at you. From me. Stay out of my business. Or else."

I headed for the door, leaving behind the pretentious slab of a table, the pastel-scented air, the unscuffed floor. Brenda scurried after me, her voice pitched high against the bulldozer's drone.

"The next time you park out back, I'll have you towed! You, your friends, even that damn Ferrari!"

I threw a middle finger over my shoulder and didn't look back.

Chapter Eighteen

"And then that bitch Brenda had the nerve to…hang on." I thumped the computer screen. "Rico? Are you there?"

Rico's voice came through the speakers, but his on-screen image didn't move. "I'm here."

"You're frozen."

"That happens with Skype. Just wait."

I sat cross-legged on the floor of the shop, my laptop in front of me, and dribbled another finger of bourbon into my glass. I was an island in a sea of Dum Dum wrappers and dusty paper boxes, a ham and cheese sandwich balanced on one knee. Rico kept his baseball cap pulled low over his forehead, shadowing his café au lait features, but I didn't need to see his eyes to realize he was a walking hangover. His neon-splattered black hoodie was the brightest thing about him, and it was as wrinkled as a shar-pei.

His screen image unfroze, and he blurred into motion again. He was sitting on the edge of his unmade bed, Fourth Ward Park showing through the window behind him. Martin Luther King, Jr. had walked those streets, preached at New Ebenezer, and usually the area was a colorful tapestry of locals and tourists. It was empty now, for even though the sky was a brilliant blue, the temps hovered in the upper thirties.

I'd been griping. He'd been patiently listening, or seemed to be anyway.

"This isn't the same as face-to-face," I said.

"So drag your ass down to the East Side for a change."

"I will, I swear, once this damn audit is done. And this mess with the skull."

Rico considered. He'd been my best friend since high school, and we'd developed a strong tolerance for each other's idiosyncrasies. We counted on each other for both brutal honesty and unconditional support, and as he'd listened to my story, he'd managed to serve up helpings of both. His final word on the matter was clear, however.

"Skull mess ain't your mess."

"The cops seem to think it's my mess."

"That makes it a mess to run away from as fast as possible. You do not want to be hanging around when The Man decides it's time to put the handcuffs on somebody."

I started to argue as I heard the Ferrari pull up. "Speaking of The Man, mine just arrived."

"Trey will agree with me. Leave it be, baby girl." A pause. "Miss you."

"Miss you too."

Rico logged off just as Trey came through my front door. He assessed the situation—noting the Jack Daniels bottle and candy wrappers—then paused in the threshold.

"I thought we were going to dinner," he said.

"We were. But that was before Detective Perez informed me that Uncle Dexter is a person of interest in the case of the grotty skull. Before I went next door and yelled at Brenda, who swears she's going to put me out of business. Before I decided to go through all eleven of these boxes I dragged out of the storage room."

He stayed in the doorway, briefcase in hand, my new monitor under his arm. "What's in the boxes?"

I swept my arms out. "You are looking at the fossil record for Dexter's Guns and More. You name it, Dexter saved it. Old A&D books. Newspaper clippings. Photographs. Grocery lists."

Trey put his things down and came over. "Why is everything…"

"Dumped on the floor?"

"Correct."

"Because Detective Perez asked for all of Dexter's records involving Lucius Dufrene."

"Who?"

"The guy whose skull I found in the field. Apparently, he used to work for Dexter."

"So you're…"

"Doing what I'm told, boyfriend." I reached for the bourbon again, then changed my mind. Maybe I'd had enough bourbon. "Me following orders. Brave new world."

I waited for Trey to ask another question, make another declaration, voice a complaint. Instead, he took off his jacket and draped it neatly on the back of the chair behind the counter. The holster went next, the dark leather shoulder rig with his H&K and the extra mags, right into my private gun safe. Then he stood and faced me, loosening his tie.

"Would you like some help?" he said.

I patted the linoleum. "Pull up a square of floor."

Trey started by rolling up his sleeves and sitting next to me, thigh to thigh. Paperwork mesmerized him, absorbing him in a zone of almost sensual concentration. I remembered what it was like to be the center of that sustained, unwavering focus, and I almost reached for him. Almost. But then I remembered our agreement.

"This had better be part of your strategy," I muttered.

He looked up. "What?"

"Never mind. Continue." I propped my chin in my hand. "I'll watch."

He eventually created two large stacks—the professional and the personal—breaking those down into smaller piles. Some of Dexter's things fit both categories; these Trey handed to me to make heads or tails of, and I did the best I could. There was an arcane logic to the materials in the box, but it wasn't logic like Trey was accustomed to.

He shook his head in bewilderment. "Why didn't your uncle collate his payroll? Or keep electronic records? Or—"

"I think I just found out why." I handed him a blue-ruled notebook with rings at the top. "Look at this."

He opened it and frowned. "What is it?"

"Keep reading and you'll see."

Trey ran a finger down the columns of names, dates, and transactions, all of it rendered in Dexter's tight, cramped scrawl. "It's an off-the-books payroll."

"Look at page nineteen."

He flipped through the pages until he found the list. The month before the Amberdecker burial, my uncle had paid Lucius seventy-five dollars to unload a delivery truck, install new shelving in the storage room, and clean the ductwork. I squinted at the last phrase—which involved a word that looked suspiciously like "bats"—and shook my head. Didn't want to know.

"Dexter kept everything under the table," I said. "Nothing official."

"But it demonstrates that Lucius did work here, in some capacity."

"So make a Lucius pile and stick it in there."

Trey did. We finished up the remaining materials in the cardboard box and moved to the most daunting task—the photographs. Two paper boxes overflowing with black-and-white shots, candids, studio portraits with Kmart scenery in the background. Uncle Dexter never got rid of a photograph, it seemed, and never spent a penny on albums.

I took a deep breath. "Have mercy, this is going to take forever. There must be fifty years of photos here."

Trey didn't reply. When I looked his way, I saw him staring at a five-by-seven, his expression puzzled. He cocked his head. "Tai? Is this you?"

He handed me the photograph, and I felt a blush of embarrassment rising. "Aw, hell."

In the photo, I was sixteen, wearing a white froth of a dress. I was also deep in a curtsy. It's a hard thing to pull off, a proper curtsy. It takes grace, poise, and well-muscled thighs. I'd had none of those things except the thighs. Thanks to all the water-skiing Rico and I had done that summer, I had the quads of a Russian gymnast.

"Is it your prom?" Trey said.

"No. It's the winter cotillion, this pseudo-debutante thing at my parents' country club."

Trey listened politely, waiting for me to share the story. It was a painful one, however, one I'd always glossed over. But I remembered all the deep things he'd shared with me, and knew I had to try.

"Dad and I had been very close when I was little, but right after I turned thirteen, he started drinking. A lot. Mom said it was because he'd gotten the promotion to department chair, that he was stressed, but…" I hesitated, feeling my voice shake. "Some drunks get loud and mean. My dad got quiet and cold. This ridiculous dress was a last-ditch effort to get his attention. It didn't work. Two months later I got banned from the club for driving a golf cart into the lake, and I never had to mess with that crap again."

Trey's voice was soft. "I'm sorry."

"Yeah. It sucked." I stared at the person I'd been, the forced smile like a mask. "Your dad abandoned you when you were two, mine when I was thirteen. Different methods, but equally effective."

Trey examined the photograph more closely. "Are you wearing boots?"

"Yep. Black snakeskin. Nobody noticed them until the curtsy." I managed a half-smile. "Rico bought them for me. They're the thing that got me thorough."

Trey nodded. Far more than most people, he understood how physical things could be talismans.

We sat that way for a full minute—knees touching, silent. And then he stretched, unknitting the knots in his lats and traps and deltoids, working the tight tendons supple again. He took his time with it. I let him. I knew digging through the dusty avalanche of photographs was going to be sloggy work, tedious and hard on the lower back. But if my uncle's life was about to become an open book for the Cobb County Police Department, I had to know what they'd find there.

Trey pulled the box toward him. "Do you want to sort these? Or would you rather watch me some more?"

I swatted him on the knee. "Don't be getting all cocky. You haven't even come close to seducing me yet."

Chapter Nineteen

The next hour went by quickly. I finished my sandwich. Trey ate two of his protein bars. The sky darkened, and a harder cold fell, like a sandbag tumbling to the ground. I was getting antsy going through the photographs one by one, but Trey was settling into a rhythm. Pull, sort, pile, pull again.

"By the way," I said, "Marisa's little plan worked. Evie will be calling Phoenix to discuss security services. Apparently they've decided that Rose plus shotgun does not equal a secure environment."

But Trey wasn't listening. "Tai? Look at this."

I peered over his shoulder. He held a daguerreotype in his lap, or a photograph made to look like one, with stark black-and-white exposures and formally posed subjects. There was Dexter in front, with his walrus-like mustache and big belly, Richard at his side. And there, in the back corner, Lucius. He wore a Confederate kepi, but the eyes were the same—rakish, devilish, intelligent. And his uniform bore the insignia of the 41st Infantry.

I pointed. "That's him. Right there. Lucius Dufrene."

"He was a member of Dexter's unit?"

"Sure looks like it."

"Is that from the Amberdecker burial?"

I flipped the photo over. "No, it's dated six months before that." I pulled the box into my lap and rifled through the images, stopping when I found what I was looking for. "But this one is."

In this photograph, Dexter himself manned the cannon as he fired the salute, the smoke rolling through the red and gold trees. Evie was in the image too, as was a plush blonde I assumed to be her sister, Chelsea, the two of them beside three women in stiff black Victorian dresses, reenactors portraying mourners. Far to the left, separate from the main grouping, Rose Amberdecker stood as straight and still as one of the marble statuary. None of the Amberdeckers had gone for period clothes, but all of the men in Dexter's unit had donned the dress grays, rifles held at parade rest.

I handed the photo to Trey. "I don't see Lucius in this photo. According to Detective Perez, he disappeared around this time. And that was the last anyone saw of him until I found his skull."

"A tentative identification?"

"Yes."

Trey and I both knew that fingerprints didn't exist on a corpse eighteen months rotting, that the cops would be looking for family and dental records. Should the dental prove a bust, they'd move to DNA. But the reality was— thanks to the cold-case nature of his death and the subsequent stirring of the pot by the tornado—Lucius' death was a case best solved by asking a million questions of the people connected to him. Hence Perez's visit to my shop.

I leaned back on my elbows. "I can't believe the stuff I know now."

"Meaning?"

"Meaning I'm not thinking of Lucius as a tragic and perhaps oddball circumstance, I'm thinking of him as a case. My case."

Trey put down the photograph. "Tai—"

"I know, I know. Not a licensed security professional."

"And—"

"I can't drag you into things and expect your license to cover me. Trust me, these things have all been explained very clearly by various official people." I paused. "But technically, I *was* asked to help locate the bones."

"You were asked to locate the bones of Braxton Amberdecker. The bones you found belong to an entirely different person."

I sat up quickly. "You're right. Lucius' bones are of no concern to me."

Trey's eyes grew wary. "True. Which means we should—"

"Follow Braxton's bones instead."

He frowned. "That wasn't what I was going to say."

"I know. But they haven't been found yet." I stared into the box full of photographs, layers upon layers of memories, buried one upon the other. "Trey?"

"Yes?"

"This is purely speculative, I know, but…what if Braxton's bones weren't in the coffin?"

"What do you mean?"

"I mean none of Richard's crew found them. Evie's crack archaeological team didn't find them. The cops didn't find them. What if at some point between their original discovery and that coffin going in the ground, they were stolen? What if nobody's found the bones because there are no bones to be found?"

"Why would someone steal bones?"

"I don't know about bones, but collectors are hot for relics." I started searching the piles around me, almost knocking over my bourbon. "There's a list of the burial items around here somewhere—"

"Don't you think the police would have considered this too?"

"Of course they would have. But they would have tucked that close to the vest and let Evie's team keep searching, knowing full well they were on a wild goose chase." And then it hit me. I reached out and grabbed Trey's knee. "Omigod!"

"What?"

I clamped tighter on his knee. "What if it was Lucius in that coffin instead of Braxton?"

Trey didn't react at first, but eventually he got the picture. "You mean—"

"I mean, what if somebody took the contents—bones, burial goods, the whole shebang—then killed Lucius with that pry bar and then stuffed it and his body in the empty coffin? Which then got cemented up in that tomb out in the cemetery. Which then got scattered across the Amberdecker woods by a tornado?"

"But—"

"You saw the coffin, didn't you? Yesterday morning?"

Trey shook his head. "No. Richard said one of his crew had found it, and he was planning to investigate, but then you found the skull and we rendezvoused with you instead. And then Rose held you at gunpoint."

Now he was getting intrigued. I could see him snapping to attention again, his index finger tapping, his brain sparking and whirring.

"If that coffin had Lucius in it instead of old bones, it would have looked as grotty as that skull."

"It would have, yes."

"And nobody would have noticed the extra weight during the re-burial." I pointed at the photograph. "They had it on a caisson. Just roll it up to the vault and slide it right in—one, two, three, shove."

Trey reached for his yellow pad and sketched out a bubble map, then jotted a quick timeline in the margin. I tapped my foot while he evaluated and analyzed. Finally he put down his pen and exhaled. "It's a plausible theory."

"I knew it! Which means that if we find the bones, the killer—"

"No, no, no." Trey shook his head adamantly. "We aren't finding bones, or killers. That's—"

"Hold on a second."

"—and plausible does not mean probable. There's a matter of mechanics, and a means/motive/opportunity breakdown, and…who are you calling?"

I tucked my phone between my shoulder and ear. "Richard."

"But—"

"I need to know if he actually saw that coffin and if so, what shape it was in, and…crap. Voice mail." And then I remembered. "Damn it, he's taken his unit on an encampment. They left an hour ago."

"Tai—"

"I'll have to catch him later."

I ran my hands though my hair. The floor was a jumbled mess on my side, a series of neat stacks on Trey's. I dragged the photograph box into my lap and started pawing through it.

Trey peered over my shoulder. "What are you looking for?"

"Any other pictures of...aha!"

I snatched another photograph out of the box, this one of a young brunette side by side with Lucius, his hand on her waist. He was wearing a Confederate jacket, but he'd paired it with jeans and his giant NASCAR belt buckle. At first glance, the girl seemed to be in Civil War dress. She wore a red corset and matching crinoline, but copper buckles accented the stays and the skirt ended in a ragged hem far above the knee. Her purple-streaked hair was cut short and razored in the back, with long jagged bangs, and a Victorian blunderbuss pistol was tucked into a holster at her hip.

"From a reenactment?" Trey said.

"Not a reenactment. Steampunk. This Victorian mad scientist thing. See?" I tapped my fingernail on the pendant she wore, what looked like a cast-iron infinity symbol with a copper gear mounted in the bottom loop. "Definitely not reenactment jewelry, or dress. But look behind them. That's Dexter's counter in the background."

"Do you recognize the girl?"

"No. But that's definitely Lucius. He's not steampunking, though, not with jeans and that belt buckle and a tee-shirt with a picture of a..." I held the photo closer to my face. "I swear that looks like a pig in a leather vest."

"Wait. I know that pig." Trey took the photo from me. "That's a shirt from Hog Wild."

"Which is..."

"A bar in Buckhead, near the Triangle. I used to get call-outs there."

"Bad place?"

Trey considered. "Problematic is a better description. Most of the calls were for drunk and disorderly, but occasionally we handled more serious violations. Drugs, shootings, stabbings." He tapped Lucius' image in the photograph. "That's the shirt the servers wore."

So Lucius had been dressed for work, not play. I leaned closer, placed a gentle hand on Trey's knee. "You do realize I'm going to go roughnecking at Hog Wild tonight?"

His expression was one of stoic resignation. "I suppose I do."

"Would you like to join me?"

He kept his face averted, but I saw the spark kindle in his eyes. "I suppose I should."

Chapter Twenty

Hog Wild occupied one of the seamier seams that knit Buckhead together. Several miles removed from the high-end boutiques and see-and-be-seen dinner spots, it ferreted itself behind an industrial grind club near the intersection of West Paces and Peachtree. One look and I understood Trey's assessment of "problematic." Nothing like a bunch of hormone-amped youths of privilege mingling with the genuinely dangerous to create a powder keg.

Trey paused outside the door, dirty neon and jukebox guitar washing over him. I could smell the gray haze of cigarettes, hear the ceramic clack of pool balls in a fast break.

I inhaled deeply. "You can get drunk just breathing this air."

Trey glared at me. "You say that as if it's a good thing."

"It's home-sweet-home to me. The bathrooms are probably an all-access pass to hell, but I bet the beer is cheap. And I bet there's a dartboard."

"I'm sure there is. There always is."

"Are you coming or not?"

He squared his shoulders. "I'm coming. But stay close. And don't get near the dartboard."

Inside, the sticky floor sucked at the bottom of my boots. I pushed in next to the bar, Trey as close as my shadow. There was only one empty seat, so I took it. Trey put his back to mine and surveyed the room. I didn't have to look to know we were getting more than our fair share of attention.

"I told you not to wear the jacket," I said.

"I can't wear the holster without the jacket, and I wasn't coming without the holster."

"You look like a former Red Dog."

"I am a former Red Dog."

"Which is exactly why you shouldn't look like one."

I leaned backwards slightly and my shoulder blades connected with the muscles of his back—the latissimus dorsi and the rhomboids, warm and solid—and for the first time in my life, I understood what it meant for someone to *literally* have my back. I remembered what Garrity had told me, about the SWAT team and the hand on the shoulder, and knew that Trey took it literally too.

At the pool table, a bald guy with a beard down to his belly-button eyed me as he leaned over his shot. Two other men moved to stand beside him, all of them wearing jeans and leather vests, their forearms intricate snaking webs of tattoos. They talked quietly, but kept their eyes in our direction, and I felt every one of Trey's muscles tense.

"Tai—"

"I know. I see them."

His voice was calm. "We need to leave. Now."

"Nope."

"Tai—"

"Trust me. I've been in the middle of enough bar fights to know when one's about to break out, and it's not, so hang tight, boyfriend."

"Bar fights?"

I showed him the pale slashing ripple across my palm. "See this? Bar fight."

"You said you cut it on a broken bottle."

"I did. During this bar fight."

"Tai—"

"Just be quiet, okay? We're cool."

Trey made a noise of annoyance. I kept the bikers in my peripheral vision. They were menacing-looking, all right, but there was something…calculated about it. A slinky blonde in a tight black dress moved into their midst and whispered something into the ear of the brawniest, who smiled in our direction.

The bartender came over. He was a late-twenties guy in jeans and a black Hog Wild tee like we'd seen in the photograph, pecan brown hair just beginning to recede, his small suspicious eyes the same hue. "What can I get you?"

"Jack on ice."

"And your friend?"

"The same."

Trey shook his head. "I don't want—"

"Give me your credit card. The black fancy one."

Trey made the noise again, but he complied. The bartender brought the drinks and stuck them in front of me. I slid the card his way. He stared at it, then at me. "What exactly are you looking for here?"

"Information."

"Then why did you bring a cop?"

"I didn't."

He jabbed his chin at Trey. "He's a cop."

"He was, but he got fired for bad behavior."

Now Trey was double annoyed. "I did not, I—"

I elbowed him, and he stopped talking. He was suspicious and confused, a gasoline-and-matches combination, but he was too concerned about the growing menace at the pool table to make an argument. To a novice, the room continued much as before—the jukebox played Toby Keith, the smoke curled like dragons' tails above the pool tables. The only tipoff was the conversational noise, dropped low now so that every ear could tune into what I saw saying.

"We're here unofficial-like, and we don't want any attention either. We're looking for information, that's all." I showed him the photograph. "You know either of these people?"

The bartender shook his head. "Nope."

"Even the guy wearing the same shirt you're wearing now?"

"Before my time."

"How do you know that if you don't know him?"

"Because I said so."

I looked to Trey for some reinforcement, but he wasn't paying the least bit of attention to the bartender. He had moved shoulder to shoulder with me, his back against the bar, hands loose, ready to launch some Krav Maga in any particular direction.

I kept my voice calm. "If there's really nothing you can do to help me, then fine. I'll take my questions to the cops. Maybe they'll help me. Or maybe they'll show up here. Who knows?"

I heard the peculiar silence then, like the soft lifting ripple of the hairs before a lightning strike. And then a woman's voice cut through the gathering tension.

"It's all right, Eddie. I'll talk to them."

She came in from the back. It took me a second to recognize her—the girl from the photograph, a few years older. Gone were the lace explosions of her skirt and corset. In their place were low-slung jeans and a tight black tee, cut short enough to reveal hipbones. The hair was longer and deep purple all over now, but the eyeliner was still thick, foundation too, covering skin rough from her not-too-distant adolescence.

I slid the photograph across the bar. "Did you know Lucius Dufrene?"

"You know I did. You got the damn photograph."

"Were you two dating?"

"Dating?" She rolled her eyes. "Who are you, my mom?"

I took a steadying breath. "I just need an answer."

"Then you should start asking better questions."

She delivered the line with a little sideways jerk of the head. Lord help me, I recognized that too. Had I really been that cocky? Probably. I tried to find some compassion for the girl standing in front of me, the girl I'd been then—angry, spiteful, mad at anyone who presented themselves as a target—and failed utterly.

I made my expression as neutral as possible. "Like what?"

"What do you mean, like what?"

"I mean what kind of questions should I be asking? You tell me." I put my elbows on the bar. "I'll just sit here and drink... Oh, I don't know. Whatever you have. We'll put it on Mr. Seaver's credit card."

I heard what sounded like a growl from Trey. I crossed my fingers that it was only a steadying exhale and smiled. "Well?"

She sidled a look at the bartender. He shrugged. "Whatever you want to do, Cat."

Cat plucked the credit card from my fingers. "What'll it be? Ma'am?"

I bit back the response rising behind my teeth. "Whatever you'd like to bring me. Kid."

◇◇◇

She brought me a shot of something that tasted like she'd set a dead pine tree on fire, put it out with cough syrup, then stirred the ashes into kerosene. It was the vilest, nastiest stuff I'd ever forced down my throat, and I'd slammed back some rotgut moonshine in my time.

She grinned. "Smooth enough for ya?"

Eddie the bartender chuckled. They hadn't had this much fun in a long while. Trey, however, looked like he wanted to call 911. Not for the cops. For an ambulance.

"Are you sure you know what you're doing?" he said.

I took another sip, coughed, and thumped my chest with my fist. "Yeah, yeah. Fine. I'll probably go blind tomorrow, but I'm good for now."

Cat watched. She didn't offer me any water. She didn't offer me any answers either.

"How did you and Lucius meet?" I asked.

"At the gun shop where he worked. The owner took that picture of us."

I tried to keep the surprise out of my face. "Dexter?"

"Yeah. He made the necklace I'm wearing. He was a black-smith, cool for an old guy. I liked him. He wasn't crazy like the rest of those Old South redneck nut jobs."

"Why did you take up with Lucius then? He was into that Old South stuff too."

She eyed me steadily. "Lucius thought that whole thing was a crock of shit. He was good at pretending, though. He could be anything he needed to be."

"Like?"

She shook her head and poured. "One question per shot."

I threw back the remainder of the clear liquid, coughed some more, then leaned across the bar. "Okay, here's a question. Did Lucius steal a dead soldier's bones right out of his coffin, or was that you, because I don't know right now, but considering somebody most likely cracked Lucius' skull open then stuffed him in that same coffin, I'm leaning toward you, and if you can't help me figure out why it *wasn't* you, then I'm taking this photo to the cops on my way home and letting them have a shot, so can you maybe start being a little more thorough in your answers, yes or no?"

She blinked at me, her face suddenly pale beneath the makeup. Eddie the bartender placed a gentle hand on her shoulder.

"Cat?" he said. "Time to get serious."

She looked up at him, shaken. "Fine."

The bartender turned to me. "Cat will take you to my office. You can talk in private there."

Trey shook his head, his eyes still on the roughnecks with the pool cues. The bartender saw where Trey was looking and dropped his voice.

"Hey, don't worry about those guys. They're not real bikers. They're just extras from the movie. I promised I'd keep that on the down low, so…"

He pressed a finger to his lips. Trey exhaled in a huff. I recognized the sound, equal parts wariness and frustration. If things went dicey, he'd never let me forget it. But I had a feeling. And I needed that back room and some alone time with Cat to sort it out.

I touched my fingertips to the inside of his wrist. "Trey?"

"Fifteen minutes," he said.

Chapter Twenty-one

Eddie had a bottle of Johnny Walker Blue Label in his drawer, my father's special-occasion drink back when drinking was a special occasion, before it became his life and a two-hundred-dollar bottle of scotch wouldn't have made it through the weekend. Cat left it untouched and pulled down a bottle of Maker's Mark, however.

"Lucius was big trouble," she said, tipping a half-finger of the liquor in a highball glass. "He thought he was smarter than everyone else. And he was."

"How?"

"Not book smart. Clever smart. Smart like a rat that could chew out of any trap. He liked cons. He liked angles. He dropped out of high school, so people thought he was dumb." She laughed and popped her feet on top of Eddie's desk. "He liked that too. He could turn on that corn pone when he needed to, play good ol' boy the whole day long."

Cat struck me as the same kind of person—willing to play dumb if it suited her purposes, willing to turn on the accent if it charmed a mark. Only she was talking to us now. Were we being charmed? Should we have both hands on our wallets and an eye on the door?

Trey didn't need reminding. He had his back to the wall next to the exit, eyes on every opening, every curtain flutter, every piece of paper that shifted. He was a wolf, his nose turned up and his ears pricked and his haunches flexed.

I swirled the bourbon in my glass. "Anybody in particular get conned? Somebody who might not have liked the experience?"

"You mean enough to kill him?" She tapped Trey's yellow pad with a black-polished fingertip and grinned. "Y'all are gonna need a bigger notebook."

"How about you? Did he con you?"

"He conned everybody one way or another."

"Including you?"

She shrugged. And looked at Trey.

I slipped a glance in his direction too. He was doing his quiet evaluation of her, filtering her words and facial expressions into the inexplicable machinery of his brain. Cat tried to look nonchalant, but she was sizing him up in return. Trey had that presence—part truant officer, part priest—that made you feel like your skin was suddenly transparent and that he could see every beat of your sinful heart. It was working on her now, I could tell, but the fact that he hadn't confronted her meant that she was on the up and up. That, or she was a dangerously professional liar of sociopathic skill, and we were in more trouble than I thought.

I tried to sound reassuring. "Trey's not here to take you in. He's not a cop anymore." I swiveled in my chair. "Isn't that right, Trey? We're here for information, not to get her in trouble."

Trey shot me a look that I recognized too. If she confessed, he would absolutely call the authorities on her. He would do it before she could get her feet off the desk. I scraped my chair back, stood, then moved right in front of him.

I dropped my voice. "I need you to wait outside for ten minutes."

He folded his arms. "No."

"You can stand right outside the door."

"I—"

"She's got something to tell me and she's not going to do it with you standing there."

He glared some more. But he unfolded his arms. "Ten minutes. Exactly."

"Thank you."

He turned and left. I regretted asking that of him—I'd been counting on his cranial lie detector as my ace in the hole—but it was a good call. Cat's demeanor relaxed the second the door shut behind him.

She cleared her throat. "Lucius dragged me into some nasty shit."

"Like what?"

"Drugs. Mostly doing, but a little dealing. I didn't have anything to do with the hard stuff either way. Weed was it."

"Okay. Anything else?"

"He was a thief. Shoplifting, pickpocketing, taking stuff out of people's cars. I saw him steal a Mennonite kid's hat once, at the farmer's market. But shoplifting was his favorite. Stupid stuff—bottles of laundry detergent, candy bars."

"Detergent?"

She shrugged. "He stole all kinds of things."

"But detergent? Like you wash clothes with?"

"Lucius called it the 'five-finger final exam.' He said only a true professional could sneak a jug of that stuff out of a store. And he could. I couldn't. I got arrested. Probation, time served. That was when my dad officially ditched me. Tough love, he said. I tough loved him back and moved in with Lucius. I thought maybe my dad would come looking, but he didn't. I guess he decided good riddance. I haven't seen him since."

I felt a jab in my heart, the echo of an old bruise. "He should have come after you. That's on him, not you."

Her eyes went hard. "You said you wanted to talk about Lucius."

"I do. I'm simply trying—"

"So let's talk about Lucius. He was a thief, and a liar, and a criminal. Every single credit card he stole, every single number he scammed, he traded it for drug cred."

"Traded?"

"Yeah, online. You know. Through his connection."

"Online?"

She gave me that look again, the one reserved for hopeless old fogeys. "Everything's online. Duh."

I suppressed the old fogey urge to tell her to watch her mouth. "So Lucius had some tech savvy?"

"Hell no. He was smart, but not computer smart, so he found somebody to help him out with that part of it." She looked uncomfortable. "I never did any of that stuff. But I didn't exactly…you know. Stop him."

I swirled the bourbon, my head buzzing from one too many shots, and thought about the story so far. Cat put up a tough front, but she really wasn't a hard case. Not like Lucius. I was beginning to think I might have wanted to kill him too.

"Was there anybody who wanted Lucius dead?"

"There was Fishbone."

"Fishbone?"

"Yeah. His real name was Marcus, but everybody called him Fishbone because of the tattoo. Fishbone thought he was a straight-up street dealer—he was always talking about the face-to-face—and his product was legit, true enough, but he didn't have the balls to kill anybody for real. He made noise about taking down Lucius, but that was just talk."

I got another zing, like a nibble at the line. "He threatened Lucius specifically? Why?"

"Said Lucius owed him money. There was something bigger going down between them, but I never found out the details. Something about turf and connection, sketchy stuff." She shrugged. "By then, I was with Eddie and totally outta there."

I picked up my pen. "Fishbone still around?"

"Last I heard, he was living in his brother's shop in Stone Mountain. He runs with the Concrete Kings now."

"Is that a gang?"

She skewered me with that look. "It's a skateboard club."

I scrawled "Fishbone Stone Mountain shop" on the back of my hand just as the door creaked open an inch. Trey stuck his head in. "Your ten minutes are up."

"I'm coming."

"Now."

"I heard you!"

He closed the door, leaving a half-inch sliver, and I shook my head at Cat. "My boyfriend. He's a stickler."

"Eddie is too. I swear sometimes."

We both pretended to be annoyed. It was a small spot of camaraderie. Outside in the bar there were two men—one keeping an eye out for me, the other keeping an eye out for her, both of them grumpy and worried and overly protective. Both of them with reason to be. But both of them willing to stand by while we did our thing, said our piece, had our way.

"The cops are probably going to drop by regardless," I said. "Lucius didn't leave town—he was killed—and they take that seriously downtown."

"I figured." She shook her head. "Dead, huh? I always had this idea he would eventually get caught and I'd see him on the news, or maybe on one of those cop shows, getting hauled to jail. I didn't see this coming."

I remembered the skull in the woods, matted decaying leaves, the rictus grin. The rest of him ripped apart and tossed like broken toys. I was pretty sure Lucius hadn't seen this coming either.

Cat rubbed her forearm. "Of course, if the bastard hadn't run off, I mighta killed him myself."

"Why?"

She turned sideways and stretched out her arm. The snake tattoo coiled and uncoiled as she flexed her bicep, lengthening with the muscles and sinew like a live thing. The black serpentine lines were more than artful ink—they were the skillful covering of scar tissue.

"Fucker stabbed me with a fork, right in the middle of the Waffle House. Said I was cheating on him."

"Were you?"

She grinned. "Uh huh. With Eddie. But Lucius was cheating too."

"With who?"

"You don't know?"

I shook my head. She grinned wider, obviously savoring the answer.

"Shit. I thought everybody knew that. He was dipping his wick uptown with the Amberdecker bitch. Chelsea. So if you want to know who wanted to kill him, I suggest you look thataway."

Chapter Twenty-two

Back at the shop, Trey insisted on checking things out before he left. I was used to this. As I unlocked the door, he watched over my shoulder, so close I could see the mist of his breath right beside my cheek.

"You should get the locks changed," he said.

"Why? Because a corpse had the old keys?"

"Because you don't know who else had the keys." He pulled his phone from his pocket and accessed the security feed. "You should also tell Detective Perez what you discovered tonight."

I flipped on the lights. "Tell her what? That Lucius' ex-girlfriend said he'd been sleeping with Chelsea Amberdecker? I have only Cat's word on that, unverified by you."

"Because you made me stand in the hall."

"She wouldn't have spilled it otherwise."

Trey didn't argue—he'd seen that as clearly as I had. And he'd heard me tell Cat she had to tell the police her story, which she'd agreed to do. I put her photograph back into the Lucius stack. The rest of the photographs lay on the floor, half in my scattered piles, half in Trey's neat stacks.

"I wonder if Richard knows about Lucius and Chelsea. He described her as having a taste for 'wild game.' If he knows, maybe he can tell us that story, because I've seen neither hide nor hair of Chelsea herself."

Trey stood in the middle of the front room, verifying that each camera worked. "Has he returned your call yet?"

"No. I wonder if he even knows they've made an ID on the skull. They camp out in the middle of some private woods. No cell phones allowed."

He stood under the deer head, switching the channel on and off with his phone. Every time he logged in, a little red light flickered behind the creature's eyes. He shot me an accusative look.

I smiled. "Just my way of making sure I know when you're spying on me."

"I don't spy." He returned his phone to his pocket, and the light blinked off. "You should also tell the authorities about… what did you say his name was?"

"Fishbone."

"No, his real name."

"Marcus something, Cat didn't know the last name. But don't worry, I'll tell Detective Perez all about him."

Once I find out a little something about him myself, I thought, deep in my head where Trey couldn't see it.

He peeked over the edge of the box at the ATF paperwork, still unorganized. "Are you sure—"

"It's under control."

He harrumphed. "At least let me install the new monitor."

"I'll do it myself tomorrow morning. It's past your bedtime, and you know how you get."

He headed for the back. "I want to recheck the security door first."

I bit my lip and stopped arguing. Checking things was the Trey Seaver version of self-medication. He had to do something to bleed off the excess energy from our night of fending off pseudo-bikers and quizzing reluctant witnesses, or his brain would fry itself.

"Did you have any messages from the Amberdeckers?" I called after him.

He knelt in front of the door. "It doesn't work that quickly. Marisa makes my assignments. It's a complicated process."

"But it can be expedited. I've seen your schedule turn on a dime when some big shot requested you."

"True. But as you pointed out yesterday, the Amberdeckers have more pressing concerns right now."

"You mean like a valuable exhibit's opening weekend? A daughter's upcoming wedding to one of the most powerful sons of industry in the U.S.? A trigger-happy old lady, surrounded by treasures ripe for the stealing? Those seem exactly like Phoenix concerns."

"It's—"

"Complicated. I know."

He opened and closed the new security door twice, which seemed to give him immense satisfaction, even if he frowned at the casement window. As if he were surprised to see it still up there, all treacherous and transparent and non UL-rated.

He came back into the main room. "Tai?"

"Hmmm?"

"Why are you doing this?"

"This what?"

"This…investigating. The bar, the History Center. I know it's not because Detective Perez asked you to."

I propped myself against the counter, covered now in materials from the Amberdecker exhibit. I'd asked myself the same thing. And I knew the answer had something to do with the fact that every month—almost every month, anyway—I'd managed to drag the shop kicking and screaming into the black. But if Dexter's reputation got destroyed, then Brenda wouldn't have to lift a finger to ruin me. She could simply watch it happen from the safety of her shop.

"I'm doing it for Dexter," I said. "Because he would have done it for me. And because no matter what it looks like, he wasn't involved in Lucius' death."

Trey kept his eyes on the file boxes. "What if you learn that he *was*?"

"He wasn't."

"Are you sure?" Trey's voice was soft, non-accusatory. "You told me he was in a difficult situation after your aunt's death. Under such circumstances, people can—"

"Not Dexter."

"Nonetheless, I need you to understand—"

"That if we discover he was involved, and I don't tell the authorities, you will."

Trey hesitated, then nodded. "I'm sorry."

"It's okay. I understand. Dexter's innocent regardless." I faced Trey over the patchwork of pamphlets, the detritus of my investigation. My case. "The real question is, are you going to help me prove it?"

He straightened a folder with his finger until it lined up exactly with the counter's edge. "Of course I am. You know that."

Chapter Twenty-three

The next morning started with me flat on my back, and not in a good way. I planted my feet and shoved myself backward another inch under the counter, struggling to keep the cell phone against my ear. "Tell me the wire I'm looking for again."

"The input line."

I poked the flashlight into the dark space. "What does it look like?"

"It's black, thinner than the coaxial."

"Damn it, Trey, there's a billion black wires up here!"

"No, there's not. Stop exaggerating."

I closed my eyes and sneezed. The dead space under the counter was good for only one thing—hiding the multitude of wires from Trey's various security devices. The latest trend was totally wireless systems, but Trey was nothing if not redundant, so he'd purchased a hybrid for the shop, a system with landline, wireless and cell phone signal transmitters, all of it with a battery backup. Of course that meant three times as much to go wrong.

"Did you tell Detective Perez about your interview last night?" he said.

"I did."

"What did she say?"

"She thanked me for the leads."

"That's all?"

"Yes."

I wiped my face with the clean part of my sleeve. I didn't tell him that I'd glossed over Cat's involvement in the whole mess, focusing instead on the mysterious Fishbone. I'd looked up the Concrete Kings over breakfast. They seemed harmless enough, a bunch of white kids who posted goofy videos of themselves attempting skateboard tricks with names like Ollie 180 and Noseslide. Fishbone was a top contributor—in his clips, he flipped and looped and gyrated, his dark hair flying behind him, occasionally flashing the skeletonized tattoo that gave him his nickname, the great dome of Stone Mountain rising behind him like a lunar landscape. The park around the mountain provided the backdrop for most of his videos, and I remembered Cat mentioning something about a brother living in the town there....

At Trey's end of the line, I heard a no-nonsense female voice in the background. Marisa.

"I have to go," Trey said. "I'll finish the installation at lunch."

"I can manage, I—" I sneezed again and the flashlight beam waggled.

"I'll see you at one."

I rolled to my stomach. Dust and cobwebs clotted my hair, and when I blinked, pieces of grit fell in my eyes. I gave up and climbed out from under the counter. The main room was cleaner, but still chaotic, with display cases waiting to be refilled, photographs waiting to be rehung. And—I couldn't avoid it—the box of still-unorganized A&D materials next to an unopened package of color-coded labels Trey had brought me. I shook the dirt from my hair, Dexter's voice echoing in my head. *Time to get to work, girl.*

The voice was right. Trey was right. But I couldn't get my conversation with Cat out of my mind. Young, defiant, with lousy taste in men, finally getting it together only to have some jerk from her past come back from the dead to trouble the waters. She'd no doubt seen the morning's newspaper. Lucius was right there on the front page, along with absorbing speculations about the nature of his death.

He hadn't been alone in the *AJC*, however. The paper's society section featured the Amberdecker-Pratchett bridal luncheon, an event happening at the High Museum in—I checked the clock on the wall—three hours. Chelsea's engagement photo showcased her hothouse beauty—lush, full-lipped, peach-skinned. Only the assertive Amberdecker jawline revealed her DNA. She and Mr. Intercontinental Exchange made an elegant power couple, and considering the state of the Amberdecker family coffers, I couldn't see either Rose or Evie complaining too hard.

I remembered Cat's accusation of the night before, about Lucius and Chelsea. Had she been telling the truth? Lying out of spite? Plain wrong? I found it hard to imagine Chelsea with a shady dropout like Lucius. But then, society women sometimes had lowbrow tastes in the bedroom.

I tapped my foot. The High Museum was a public building. How hard would it be to slip inside, pull the bride-to-be into a discreet corner, and ask one simple question—were you having an affair with Lucius Dufrene?

I looked down at my clothes. There was a smudge of doughnut glaze on my jeans, and the two pistols on the tee-shirt looked like the crossed arms of the Battle Flag. My closet consisted of jeans and tees at one end, red haute couture cocktail dresses at the other. Not a single appropriate thing for subtle surveillance at a society luncheon.

I ran my hand through my hair. If I wanted to talk to Chelsea, I had less than three hours to transform into someone I wasn't. Which meant there was only one person in the greater metro area who could help me.

Chapter Twenty-four

Gabriella ran a French-manicured finger through a sherbet selection of afternoon dresses and frowned prettily. Her boutique offerings tended toward the shabby chic, but in deference to the early Easter, she'd ordered some Sunday outfits for the well-heeled infrequent churchgoer. I'd caught her between spa appointments, so she was wearing the white pants and baby tee she always wore at the massage table. Barefoot and tiny, with green cat eyes and red ringlets piled on top of her head, she had the porcelain skin of a woman much younger than her thirty-plus years, like a fresh-faced teen ripened on Provence wine and Gallic air.

"Thank you for helping me on such short notice," I said.

She waved a slender white hand at me. "*De rien*. It is what I do, yes? Now tell me again what you are needing."

"Something fancy that one might wear to a garden party luncheon at the High."

She pulled a different dress from the rack and examined it. It was the purple of hyacinths, a blushing whisper of a dress. She held it in front of me, then put it right back on the rack, shaking her head.

"What was wrong with that one?"

"Non. Not for you."

I folded my arms, tried to make myself more compact. Being around Gabriella made me feel like a particularly uncouth bull in a particularly delicate china shop. She was a former ballerina and still moved with a dancer's precise, easy grace. Trey refused to describe her as an ex-girlfriend; the details of their coming together and breaking apart were beyond his vocabulary. He was clear about one thing, however—after the accident, she and Garrity together had saved his life.

And now she was…I had no words either. But she was the engineer of Trey's wardrobe, the entire Italian couture section anyway, and my only hope for finding a high-society outfit on short notice.

She turned a practiced eye on me again. "This is the Amber-decker-Pratchett affair you are attending, yes?"

"It is. Do you know them?"

"Not personally, no. I heard about it from Jean Luc—he is the contemporary curator at the High—and it has of course been all the talk. Chelsea is…what is the phrase? A dark horse, yes?"

I perched myself on the edge of a white and gold divan. "Do tell."

Gabriella lowered her voice conspiratorially. "Several of my clients had hopes in the direction of Jeremy Pratchett. But the young man chose Chelsea. She worked there, you know, in the Intercontinental Exchange PR department." Gabriella waved her hand around like a soft tiny tornado. "Whirlwind courtship. Very fast, very disappointing to some."

"But not for Rose Amberdecker and company?"

"Oh no, the Amberdeckers are very happy, *bien sûr*, especially considering their lack of…" She rubbed the tips of her fingers together. "How did you come to know them? Through Trey?"

"Umm…no."

So I told her. As I described the previous three days—the storm, the skull, the adventure at Hog Wild—she stopped paging through dresses and turned to face me, hands on hips.

"This is one of your investigations?"

She said the word the way that Trey and Garrity and Eric and Rico did, with pronounced suspicion. I tried to look innocent.

"I want to ask Chelsea some questions, that's all."

"About what?"

So I told her. I emphasized the part where Detective Perez asked me to share what I found out with her, downplayed the whole "crashing the party" thing.

Gabriella arched an elegant eyebrow at me. "That is no good."

"It's not like I'm trying to break up the happy couple or anything, I only—"

"That is not what I mean. I mean you are not an invited guest."

"So? It's being held in a tent on the piazza, practically in the front yard for all of Midtown to see. Lots of people coming and going, very easy to slip past the ropes."

"No, you don't understand. This party is as much a display as the Picasso or the Monet, and it will be equally as well protected. Discreetly, yes. They know everyone who will be there, you see…" She shook her head. "But they do not know you."

She had a point. "So what am I supposed to do? All I have is a rumor. I don't want to sic the police on Chelsea, or Cat, or anybody, not unless I have something concrete."

"Yes, I see. It is delicate. You do not want to ruin someone's life on a rumor." She tapped her lips with her index finger, her cat eyes flashing. "Wait here. I have an idea."

Fifteen minutes later, I wore the exact outfit she did, only in black. I recognized the uniform as the one worn by the women in her nail salon. When I put it on it, I become one of the barely perceived bodies present at every society event—the wait staff, the cleaning crew, the delivery people. I became—for all intents and purposes—invisible.

Gabriella looked me over. "You need shoes, sensible ones."

"What about my sneakers?"

She shook her head. "I will find you some Dansko. That will work. Now sit."

She moved behind me and ran her fingers in my hair, across my scalp, gathering the tangled mess into a knot. She was a woman of many skills, Gabriella, both everyday and arcane—hairdressing and massage, tarot and herbs and astrology. And as Trey's ex, she knew more about my boyfriend than any other woman walking the planet. I couldn't look at her without imagining…

"So how is he?" she said, as if she'd been reading my mind.

"Trey? He's good."

"And yet you are worried, *ma chère amie*. Why is that? Is it because the ninth approaches?"

"That. Lots of stuff, actually."

"Ah."

She pinned my hair on top of my head, securing it with tiny French hairpins. She could work magic with her hands, I knew, taming both knotted muscles and snarly bedhead with her sure touch. She was sizing me up now in the mirror, her analysis as keen as Trey's.

"Are you certain all is well?"

"I'm certain."

She curled some tendrils around my ears, met my eyes in the mirror. "We will share stories one day, you and I, over Champagne. We will talk of the mystery that is Trey Seaver, and other things. But let me tell you this much. I have never wanted to be anyone's *seul véritable amour*. And Trey never wanted me to be anything I did not want to be. That is not his nature."

I froze, suddenly confused. "I don't know what you're—"

"You have been very good for him. The rest of us worry and fuss. You let him be himself, though, and that makes him happy, and that makes me happy. But listen to me…you really must tell him."

I blew out a breath. So that was the crux of her little speech. "I will. This isn't a sneak-behind-his-back kind of mission. It's just that—"

"No, not this. This, yes, of course, but I was speaking of the other thing."

"What other thing?"

She put her hands on my shoulders and regarded me in the mirror. "You and Trey, your outsides are so very different. He is Virgo, and you are Aries. But I have drawn your birth charts.

His Venus is in Leo, as is yours. He has a fire heart, as do you, and fire calls to fire."

I shook my head warily. "I'm not sure—"

"Hush hush." She smiled and tucked a stray strand of hair behind my ear. "He already knows, of course, but it's the telling that's important. Now stand up. I want to see the final effect."

I stood. In the mirror, an efficient professional person looked back. A person who could blend. Gabriella went to her desk, a white baroque number like Marie Antoinette might have possessed, and fetched some ivory stationery from the top drawer along with a silver-lettered black card. *Director's Circle*, it read.

She tucked the card into my shirt pocket. "Go into the main entrance, the one next to the Rodin. You will pass the event on your right, in the piazza. Do not attempt to enter. Go into the lobby, show them this card, then take the skyway to the Stent Wing. Follow the staircase to the fourth floor. Face the Anish Kapoor—"

"The what?"

"An enormous stainless steel dish in the Contemporary collection, you cannot miss it. The service elevator is down the hall to your right. Take it to the private parking lot. A quick left and you will be in the piazza."

She opened one of the note cards and pressed her lips to the paper, leaving a crimson kiss. She tucked the sweet nothing into a matching envelope, then picked up a fountain pen and wrote Jean Luc on the outside. She licked the seal, closed it, and handed it to me.

"Take this. If anyone stops you, tell them you are making a delivery to Jean Luc Dubois. Tell them you are required to make this delivery personally, that it is from Gabriella. Tell them to call Jean Luc if they are suspicious. He will vouch for you."

I took the card. "What exactly am I delivering?"

She handed me a vase of flowers from her desk, two dozen white roses in an etched crystal decanter. I took the bouquet and held it as she assessed me with a critical eye. I could hide almost my entire upper body behind the voluptuous snow-white explosion.

"There. Very professional." She took me by the shoulders and squeezed. "Remember, head up, stomach in, feet pointed straight ahead."

I did as she said. She smiled brightly.

"There. That will do very nicely."

Chapter Twenty-five

The High Museum of Art, a stark white and gracefully imprac-
tical series of interconnected buildings, proved a challenging
place to infiltrate. Designed like an enormous cylinder plopped
into an even more enormous cube, with narrow white stairways
looping around the periphery and white columns looming like
pale tree trunks, its Stent wing was a place of dizzying confusion.
Especially for someone clomping about in unfamiliar clogs with
two dozen white roses blocking her view.

I came in the lobby as instructed, through the glass cross-
over and up the coiling staircase, winding higher and higher as
I passed the cold-eyed marble statues, the blown-glass Tiffany
bowls. On the fourth floor, two employees in black sweaters
chatted next to the fire extinguisher, their attention locked on a
group of teenagers rollicking dangerously close to a ten-foot-tall
stainless steel dish that fractured and reflected the room back
upon itself in shards of light and color.

The Anish Kapoor. I patted my back pocket for Gabriella's
note. Then I ducked into the service elevator and took it straight
down to the ground floor where it opened—as promised—into
the piazza's back entrance. The service portal. I held my roses
high and stepped into the scurry and bustle.

Getting into the white tent was a snap—all I had to do was
keep up with the streaming tide of waitstaff. Inside, the tent
buzzed with conversation so effervescent it practically bubbled,

and I knew that Chelsea was somewhere in that froth of color and laughter. I also knew that she was protected by a boundary of velvet ropes and discerning eyes. The guests knew it too. They realized they were on display, and they expected to be—like all precious art—defended from the sticky fingers of the riffraff.

I kept a brisk pace, using the flowers as cover. Memories flooded my brain, and I tried hard to ignore them. The spring dance. The winter formal. The inevitable lectures that resulted when I violated some protocol of daintiness and womanhood. The main area smelled like hair spray and perfume, but close to the buffet table, I caught the scent of fresh bread, the salty tang of prosciutto. My stomach growled, and I pressed a hand to it.

Across the room, in the VIP corner, the Amberdecker sisters held court. Evie wore a lady-like suit—navy, with white piping—but as I watched, she discreetly turned her wrist and checked her watch. Eager to get back to work. I put down the flowers, picked up a tray of sparkling wine, and made for Chelsea, who stood as far away from her sister as she could get and still be in the VIP area.

She was impossible to miss, dazzling in a cobalt halter dress, her shoulders glowing with an Aspen tan. Her honey-colored bob rippled with expert highlights, showcasing brilliant blue eyes and softening her assertive jawline. She was an Amberdecker, all right, to the manor—and the manner—born.

I stepped behind her. "Excuse me, Ms. Amberdecker?"

She looked my way, her smile polite. "Yes?"

"We need to talk."

The wariness solidified into annoyance. "Who are you?"

"A friend of the family. And unless you want me to start blabbing the name Lucius Dufrene over the place, you need to head to the ladies' room—by yourself—where we can talk without being disturbed."

She glared, hard, the softness evaporating. "What do you want?"

"I want to do this discreetly."

She put two and two together, made her decision. "I'll be there in five minutes."

"Make it two. And if anybody besides you comes for me, I start talking, and don't think for a second—"

"I heard you!!" she hissed, then turned away.

I'd been dismissed. I waited ten seconds to make sure I wasn't being beset by bodyguards, then I collected my roses, straightened my shoulders, and went into the restroom to wait for her.

I'd been perched on the edge of the marble vanity for barely sixty seconds when Chelsea blew in like a petite hurricane. "Who the hell are you?"

"Tai Randolph."

She made a face. "Evie put you up to this, didn't she? Well, you tell her to go back and dig in the dirt some more, I am not asking Jeremy for any more money! She's on her own with that damn exhibit!"

"Evie? No. This isn't about her at all."

Chelsea put her hands on her hips. "You've got five seconds to explain before I call—"

"Your fiancé, I know the drill. And he'll have some nicely dressed men with hardware on their belts come and escort me out. Then he'll threaten to take every penny I own. He'll ruin me." I sighed. "Been there, done that, got the restraining order. But see, here's the thing. I can't call fancy lawyers. The only real weapon I have is my mouth. And I am not afraid to use it."

"I don't have to talk to you."

"You don't. But you will have to talk to the police. Who will be calling once they learn your little secret, which they will. Lucius Dufrene's life is about to be an open book, and your part in it is bound to come out. The part before he got skeletonized on your family's property, I mean."

Her lip twitched, and the color drained from her face. "I had nothing to do with that."

"Regardless, without an explanation, you're looking like Grade A Prime suspect material. So you can explain to me, and I can explain to them, or you can—"

She put a hand to her mouth, pressing hard, shaking suddenly. "I didn't...I never..."

I snatched a stool from the vanity and shoved it behind her. She collapsed on it, her complexion greenish. I'd suffered enough hangovers to recognize the signs of imminent upchuckery, so I reached behind me and grabbed the wastebasket. She snatched it away from me and heaved her brunch into it.

"Goddammit," she hissed, then shoved her face inside and retched some more. I let her get it out. Finally she stopped heaving and put the wastebasket on the floor. I snatched up a handful of paper towels, wet them, and handed them to her without a word.

She accepted them just as silently, then turned on the stool and faced the vanity mirror. She wiped her mouth, then pulled a travel toothbrush and a mini tube of toothpaste from her purse. I noticed the bracelet—turquoise and silver beads with one large bead pressed tight against the pulse point of her wrist—and realized this was no hangover she was battling.

"That bracelet not working?" I said.

She leaned forward, patting her cheeks with the wet paper. Didn't reply.

I gestured to her wrists. "I used to work on a dive boat, so I recognize a motion sickness bracelet when I see one. The terrycloth bands work the best, but I guess those would clash with your outfit."

She swished a mouthful of water in her mouth, then spat it in the sink. Kept her eyes on her reflection.

"How far along?" I said.

She kept ignoring me. I understood. I also knew that she'd completely misunderstood my threat about her "little secret" and I felt a pang of guilt.

"Look," I said, "I don't care if you got knocked up or not, and neither do the police. None of my, or their, business. Frankly, I can't imagine anyone caring in this day and age, but whatever. Like I said, your business. I do need to know about Lucius, though. So tell me what I need to know, I'll leave, and you'll never see me again."

"We were screwing," she said, pulling a tiny pot of foundation from her purse. "He worked on Richard's crew one summer. I was bored. He was hot. What else do you need to know?"

"Any idea who might have wanted to kill him?"

"No."

"Did you?"

She glared at me. "Why would I kill him?"

"Did he hurt you?"

"What? Hell no!" She returned her attention to the mirror. "You want to find out who killed him, you gotta find somebody who cared. And I didn't." She turned in the seat and looked at me. "Didn't care when we were doing it, didn't care when he left. Found a replacement in two seconds flat."

"Rich, good-looking girls always can."

"Damn straight."

"Your mama and sister and fiancé cool with this?"

She glared again.

"Ah. They don't know."

She blinked at me, and for a second I thought I saw tears. Or maybe a flash of real emotion. And then I understood. She was, after all, throwing up in a trash can, her purse tricked out like a morning sickness field kit. There was a wedding coming up, a hastily assembled one, and there didn't have to be. If there was one thing a rich woman could get in Atlanta, it was a discreet way out of her particular difficulty.

I lowered my voice. "You either really do love him, or you really love his money. I can't tell which."

She ignored me. She had the mascara wand out, her eyes dry now. "I had no reason to kill Lucius. No one in my family did. He didn't matter that way."

"So you and his girlfriend didn't have a fight?"

"Cat? And me?" She made a noise of disgust, pulled out her lipstick. "That chick is batshit. She texted me once, called me a whore. I told her that if she tried to contact me again, I'd have put her away, like straightjacket put away. I was not interested in her redneck drama. If you're looking for somebody who hated Lucius, talk to that dumbass with the skateboard and the stupid tattoo."

"You mean Fishbone?"

Chelsea applied an expert layer of berry-colored lipstick, her eyes on the mirror. "Yeah, him. He and Lucius were always fighting, drugs and money, money and drugs."

"Fighting arguing or fighting fighting?"

"Both."

"About what?"

"Mostly that Lucius had ditched him for a smarter, better partner. Some guy he met online."

"Do you think Fishbone could have killed him over that?"

She shrugged, pursed her lips in the mirror. "Don't know, don't—"

"Don't care, right. Got it."

She popped the cap back on the lipstick and slipped it in her purse. She stood, then stepped around me and headed for the door, dismissing me as easily as she had Lucius and Cat and Fishbone. We were all the same to her—redneck trash. He'd been good for a quick roll or two, but I was merely an inconvenient obstacle.

She paused at the door. "If you breathe a word of this to anyone, you will pay. I will hurt you where you live. I promise you."

And in that second, as the words hit me right between the eyes, Chelsea Amberdecker looked exactly like her mother.

Chapter Twenty-six

A misty fog shrouded Stone Mountain's summit, almost obscuring the Confederate generals carved into its side. During the summer, the park filled up with stroller-pushing mommies in running gear, buff guys taking the stepped trail up to the top. But this day, with a cloudy sky and temps barely above freezing, I had the giant hunk of quartz and granite mostly to myself.

I huddled under a pine at the base of the rock, the perfect vantage point for scoping out the parking lot and the handful of skateboarders gathered in its far corner. The pavement attracted only the hardcore this winter afternoon, but not one of them was Fishbone. I shoved my hands in my pockets and tried to avoid impaling myself on a yucca plant. I wished I'd brought coffee. I wished I had warmer gloves. I wished—

"Have you found what you're looking for?"

I whirled around. Trey stood behind me, his trench coat buttoned tight against the bladed air.

I glared at him. "What are you doing here?"

"Looking for you."

Across the park, one of the teens popped his board at the top of the stairs and rode the handrail down like a surfer taking a wave. The wheels guttered and rumbled, a monotone growl.

I crossed my arms. "So you're stalking me now?"

"This isn't stalking. I'm standing right beside you."

"You're supposed to be working."

"I *was* working, but then I went by your shop at one—"

I smacked my forehead. "Oh shit! I forgot."

"—and you weren't there. Which was not in itself alarming, so I went ahead with the new monitor installation, but then I received a call from Gabriella—"

"Damn it! She ratted me out, didn't she?"

Trey shot me a sharp look. "No. She was calling because the Lost and Found department at the High Museum called her because someone found your cell phone in the restroom, and since hers was the last number you'd dialed—"

"Oh hell!" I patted down my pockets. "My phone's gone!"

Trey pulled it from his pocket. "Gabriella called Jean Luc, who said that he had not seen you. So I told Gabriella I would pick up your phone—which I did—and activate the tracking on your car—which I did—which is why I am standing here right beside you, which is not stalking."

He handed me my phone. Sure enough, the screen showed a GPS map of Stone Mountain, my Camaro a blinking red light. I'd wondered how effective the system was back when Trey had had it installed around Christmastime. Now I knew.

I slipped the phone in my pocket. "Aren't you going to ask what I was doing at the High?"

"Gabriella explained. It was the reason she was concerned enough to go there herself to look for you. A valid concern, I might add."

He had a point. To my astonishment, however, he wasn't annoyed, or angry, or even lecture-y. He was calm and cool, almost mellow.

"You're taking this very non-hypervigilantly," I said.

He cocked his head, thinking. "That is true, yes. It was not true ninety minutes ago, however, but Gabriella gave me something for that." He pulled a tiny bottle from his pocket and squinted at the handwritten label. "Kava, chamomile, avena sativa, and vanilla."

I stared at him. "She drugged you."

"Not drugs. Herbs. Like in tea."

I examined him more closely. No, not drugged, just…

smoothed. Calm, clear-eyed, maybe blinking a teensy bit slower than usual, but as sharp as the wind off the mountain. He returned the pills to his pocket, pulling out a pair of surveillance binoculars instead. He seemed to be settling in for the afternoon.

"Don't you have to get back to work now?" I said.

"Marisa sent me home. Personal leave. She told me to track you down, yell at you, and then get myself together before I set foot in her building again. Her exact words." He moved closer to the scant shelter of the tree and put the binoculars to his eyes. "So that's why I'm here. I would like to know, however, why *you're* here."

I sighed. Time to out with it. So I told him about my visit with Chelsea, and how like Cat, she'd implicated Fishbone as having a conflict with Lucius, probably drug-related. I left out the pregnancy part. I'd given my word, after all.

"And so, since all roads were leading to Fishbone, and thus, to Stone Mountain, I decided to check it out. Not that I've spotted him."

"Would he be six-four with a tattoo of a fish skeleton on the right forearm?"

I held out my hand. "Give me those binoculars."

Trey handed them over. Sure enough, a new guy had joined the action down below. Even in the freezing weather, he wore a tank shirt over loose stovepipe jeans. His black hair fell almost to his waist, a thick ill-maintained tangle held back with a red and navy bandanna, but it was the ink on his right forearm that caught my eye—a tattoo of a leaping fishy skeleton. I watched as he took a flying leap off the steps, grabbing the edge of his board and flipping it under him in a one-eighty, his wheels crushing dead leaves as he crisscrossed the pavement.

I lowered the binoculars. "I wonder how fast he is on that thing."

Trey shook his head. "You have no authority to pursue him."

"I don't want to pursue him, I want to talk to him."

"And how do you plan on doing that?

"I'm going to walk over there and open my mouth."

"That's not the best plan."

"You have a better one?"

He shook his head again, keeping his eyes on Fishbone. The breeze now carried the unmistakable pong of marijuana, although I was more inclined to blame the young couple giggling furtively on the park bench than the guy doing kickflips in the parking lot.

"What exactly are you trying to accomplish here?" Trey said.

"I want to ask him about Lucius."

"Why do you think he'll tell us anything?"

"Not us, boyfriend. Me."

Trey folded his arms. "I don't think—"

"It's non-negotiable. You reek of cop. I know you can't help it, but you do."

"Nonetheless—"

"You can be backup. You're always yammering about backup."

He made a noise of annoyance. "I don't yammer."

I handed him his binoculars and then quickly, before he could protest, I scurried down the wet leaves and gravel to the parking lot. Fishbone had propped his board against the restroom door and was grabbing a swig from a can of Red Bull. He saw me coming, wiped his mouth with the back of his hand.

I pointed at his arm. "Nice tattoo. You get that around here?"

"Nah. Back in Jersey."

He took another pull on the Red Bull. Down the road to our left, I saw a flash of silver and blue easing around the curve—the Stone Mountain police, coming to roust him and his crew.

I cursed under my breath. "Listen—"

But it was too late. Fishbone had already seen the cruiser, and before I could stop him, he snatched up his skateboard and took off at a dead run.

Up the freaking mountain.

I bolted after him, elbows pumping, Trey's voice ringing in my ears. Fishbone had gotten the jump on me, and he was fast—really damn fast—but he had a skateboard he wasn't willing to give up, which slowed him down considerably.

"I only want to talk!" I yelled.

Fishbone fled the rock face and ducked into the line of trees. He ignored me. I heard Trey behind me, yelling my name. I ignored him. I wished I had my sneakers instead of the damn clogs, wished I was wearing jeans instead of pants, wished Fishbone would trip or something, anything to give me a chance to explain.

"I'm not the police!" I yelled.

But it didn't do any good. Fishbone had his sprint on. He jumped a fallen log, dodged a boulder, then pounded off down the side trail into the woods. I followed. My lungs burned, my heart thrashed. All I could hear was the huff-puff of my ragged breathing, and all I could see was the collapsing tunnel of my vision.

And then he was gone. Poof. Suddenly, I was chasing nothing. I listened hard and heard fugitive noises up ahead—underbrush crashing, branches snapping—but I saw no sign of Fishbone. I bent over, dizzy, cursing myself and Fishbone and the inopportune Stone Mountain police.

In a minute or so, I heard more footsteps, coming from behind me, a runner's rhythm. Trey. He slowed to an easy jog and stopped right in front of me, hands on hips. He wasn't even breathing hard.

"I told you that was a bad idea," he said.

I sank to the ground and leaned back on my elbows. "Shut up."

"What did you say to him?"

"Nothing! So don't…crap crap crap!"

I closed my eyes against a wave of dizziness. My breath was still coming hard and fast, making puffs of fog in front of my mouth. I could feel Trey's eyes on me with their laser scrutiny.

"Lie back," he said.

"I'm fine."

"Do it."

Suddenly that seemed like a really good idea. I flopped backwards onto the pine needles, the muscles in my arms and legs quivering. I stared up at the sky, let the cool gray press against my face like a wet washcloth. I could see Trey's black leather lace-ups in my peripheral vision.

"You watched the whole thing?" I said.

"Yes."

"And you didn't think of—oh, I don't know—helping me catch him?"

"No."

Of course he hadn't. I'd gotten that speech before—civilians and detainment rights and blah blah blah—so I didn't argue because I didn't feel like listening to it again.

"So you stood around doing nothing just so you could lecture me about it?"

"No. I did it so that I could find out where he was going, because fleeing up the mountain made no sense." Trey jabbed his chin toward the street. "According to the GPS map, this trail leads to a cut-through which leads out of the park and into town."

I blew out a frustrated breath. "So you let him get away."

"Of course not. I simply re-adjusted my post to the edge of the parking lot where I could monitor the cut-through with the binoculars. From there, I saw him go into a store near the park's perimeter."

"What store?"

Trey pulled up a different map on his phone, this one of the Stone Mountain downtown area, and held it so that I could see. Sure enough, there was a tiny square highlighted just outside the park's boundary. I checked the legend—Grindshop. And then I remembered what Cat said, that Fishbone lived with a brother who owned a store in Stone Mountain.

I struggled to my elbows. "Think hard, boyfriend. Is there any law that says I can't go into that shop and ask whoever I find in it a bunch of questions?"

Trey put his hands on his hips. It was fascinating to watch the tug of war going on in his head—the control freak versus the street cop. In the end, the adrenalin boost from his sprint up the mountain tipped the scales.

"I can't think of one," he said.

Chapter Twenty-seven

Grindshop had once been a single-family dwelling—now it was an oddball black sheep among the tidy mom-and-pop stores on the edge of town. Neon graffiti bubbled along the brick walls, and the front window was a patchwork of sun-faded leaflets, stickers, and peeling yellow tape. The railing along the sidewalk bore the dings and scratches of a thousand slides, and cigarette butts littered the ground.

I pulled open the front door, Trey at my heels. And then he stopped, suddenly, like someone had smashed his brake pedal.

I stopped too. "What's wrong?"

"I can't go in there."

"Why not?"

He turned away from the door and put his back to the bricks. "Olfactory association."

I took a deep breath and caught it then, the cloying odor of marijuana disguised with patchouli incense. And something else, something pungent and chemical. Trey folded his arms and kept his eyes straight ahead, his index finger tap-tap-tapping against his forearm. I put my hand on his shoulder and he flinched, his breathing erratic.

Uh oh. One of those associations.

"How bad?" I said.

"Very bad." He licked his lips, tilted his head back. "Major drug bust, the Sinaloa Cartel. They had a dog fighting ring. And a third story balcony."

"You got dog bit?"

"No."

"Somebody threw you off a balcony?"

He shook his head, then flexed his fingers, deliberately uncurling the fists he'd made. And then I got it.

"Oh crap."

"Indeed." He shook his hands out, took another deep breath. "Go in without me."

"But I need you to tell me if he's lying or not!"

"I can't. You go ahead. I'll stay here. If he tries to leave, I'll…" He closed his eyes. "No, I won't. I'm just going to watch. From right here."

"But—"

"Go."

I went, suppressing a twinge of panic as the door shut behind me. The interior was small and cramped, with stained concrete floors. Shelf after shelf of skateboards lined the walls, along with tee-shirts and bandannas and wheel kits, all of it—every bit of it—covered in skulls. Some scary, some surreal, some flame-eyed, others with eye sockets as empty as the grave. The scent of marijuana permeated the air, layered with…I frowned, took a long sniff. Despite the place's overall grunginess, it smelled like the cleaning aisle at the supermarket, soapy and chemical and fake-lemony.

I heard a noise behind the counter, and an older version of Fishbone—same long black hair, same slouchy clothes, wearing a fedora instead of a bandanna—approached warily. "Yeah?"

"I need to talk to your brother."

"He's not here."

"Yes, he is." I pointed. "He's behind that curtain. I can see his shoes."

The scuffed Nikes under the beaded curtain jerked from view. The soap smell was stronger near the counter, and I had to concentrate to avoid sneezing.

The brother looked me up and down. "Who are you?"

"Not a cop. Not a detective. Just someone who needs information. So we can do this easy—which means you shove your brother up here and I talk to him for a little minute—or we can do this hard—which means my partner and I call the real cops and they come down and let the dogs have a sniff around. And let me tell you, the dogs ain't gonna be fooled by whatever that smell is. They're gonna find whatever you've got hidden in here. So which is it gonna be?"

The man jerked his head toward the curtain. "Marcus! Get your ass out here and talk to the lady."

I heard a sigh, and Fishbone AKA Marcus came from behind the curtain. He held his board against his skinny chest, glaring annoyance from behind a hank of black hair. "What do you want?"

I slapped a photo of Lucius on the table. "You know this guy?"

He looked at his brother, who nodded. The brother was keeping far too close an eye under the counter. I knew what I kept under the counter in my shop, and I was betting Fishbone's brother had the same thing, locked and loaded. I chanced a quick look over my shoulder at the front door, relieved to see Trey pacing in front of the threshold.

Fishbone chewed at his thumbnail and shrugged. "Yeah. So what?"

"So he's dead. Been dead a while. And every time I ask who might have wanted him dead, your name comes up."

"I didn't kill him! I didn't even know he was dead! I thought he left town!" Fishbone shook his head violently, hair flailing with the motion. "He owed me money, why would I kill him?"

I stared at him. If he was pretending ignorance, he deserved an Oscar, because it was a very convincing performance.

"I'm also hearing that you were his connection. Is that true?"

He looked at his brother again. Now the brother looked nervous too. Fishbone shook his head again. "I don't know what—"

"Of course you know, but I don't care. I care that somebody caved in Lucius' skull and shoved him in a coffin where he stewed for almost two years."

"It wasn't me!"

"Glad to hear it. Do you have an idea who it might have been?"

"Lucius hooked up with a new connection, somebody in a chat room online, one of those Tea Party freedom forums. Guy would take just about anything in trade."

"Even bones?"

Fishbone shook his head. "Don't know anything about bones. Lucius mostly traded credit card numbers. And there was stuff he stole from that redneck group he hung out with and that old guy he worked for."

"Dexter at the Confederate shop?"

"Yeah, him. Guns and knives, some ammo. It all went to trade."

"Was Dexter involved with any of this?"

Fishbone laughed. "Him? Nah. He didn't even know he'd been robbed until Lucius skipped town."

"Did he steal anything from you?"

The brothers looked at each other and said nothing. I sighed.

"So he stole your stash, which you of course didn't report to the police. Anything else?"

"Two autographed trick boards and everything in the cash register. Probably traded them online too. I told him not to be messing around those sites, terrorists and mafia and shit." He looked suddenly animated. "You wanna know who killed him, that's who did it. Fucking mafia."

That made three people I'd talked to—Cat and Chelsea and Fishbone—saying the same thing, that Lucius was involved in some shady dealings with an unknown person he traded with online. And while the Goodfellas theory sounded a little far-fetched to me, the fact that I was hearing it again had my ears pricked.

"Did you trade with this connection?"

"Hell no, I'm straight-up face-to-face. Old school all the way." He scratched his thigh. "Look, I didn't kill Lucius and I don't know who did. Can I go now?"

I thought hard. I may not have figured out who Lucius' shadowy web connection was, but I knew one thing—Dexter hadn't been involved. My uncle had been a lot of things, but computer literate was not one of them. He'd have sooner been caught at the ballet than in a chat room.

I pulled one of my business cards out of my back pocket and scribbled Garrity's new work number on it. "Yeah, I'm done. But here's my number in case you think of anything else. And here's the FBI's number if you get in trouble with the mafia." I rapped the counter with my knuckles. "Don't play around with this, dude. There's one body on the ground so far. You don't want to be number two."

Chapter Twenty-eight

When we got back to the shop, Trey insisted I shower and put on clean clothes since I, to use his exact word, "reeked." Which I did, a peculiar blend of sweat, old pot smoke, and the chemical wallop of the shop's air freshener. So I washed my hair twice with his shampoo, then put on freshly washed jeans and one of his ancient Atlanta PD sweatshirts, items I'd liberated during my most recent plunder. When I got back downstairs, he was lying on his back under the counter, wiring the new monitor into the security system video feed.

I scrubbed my hair with a towel. "Do you need some help?"

"No." The sound of rummaging intensified. "Did I leave the screwdriver up there?"

"It's behind your head."

"Oh."

He retrieved the screwdriver and returned his attention to the installation. The effects of whatever Gabriella had given him were wearing off—I could see the first spit and flare of exasperation coming back—but on the whole, he was remarkably calm, especially considering the afternoon he'd had.

"Trey? I know how olfactory triggering works—neural connectivity, hippocampal activation, all that."

He stopped messing with the screwdriver and looked at me. "You took my book."

"Borrowed it. On Eric's recommendation. So I get why you pegged at the skate shop, but why not earlier, in the park? I could smell marijuana there as well, pretty strong, so I know you could smell it too."

"I could, yes." He pushed himself to standing and went to the computer. "I don't know why it happened in one place and not the other."

He double-checked the four-plex video feed, making sure that he had access through his cell phone, through my cell phone, through the laptop. He wouldn't be satisfied until all the deadbolts were deadbolted and the locks locked, until he'd made certain no villains lurked in any nook or cranny.

I sat on the counter next to him. "Does it happen a lot? Olfactory triggers?"

"Somewhat. But usually not so…violent."

I slid an inch closer to him, catching the mingled scent of starched cotton and soap and his evergreen aftershave. Yes, I knew about olfactory triggers. I exhaled softly, ran my foot along his calf…

He didn't look up from the computer. "Tai—"

"I know, I know." I snatched my foot back. "You have a strategy."

"I do."

"Well, you'd best speed it up. I am officially love-starved, boyfriend, and it sucks."

He raised his head and regarded me with fresh curiosity. "Love-starved? Really?"

I froze. There it was. The L-word. And there was Trey—patient, polite, but not backing down one bit.

I felt a blush rising. "I meant to say sex-starved."

"Oh."

"Because I'm not…I mean, it's not like…you know."

The words hung in mid-air, but the universe was swinging like a metronome, back and forth. Tick tock. He crossed his arms, then deliberately uncrossed them. Shifted his weight to neutral stance and then back to natural, as if he couldn't figure out what he wanted to do next.

"Yes," he said. "I know. I think I do anyway. Do I?"

I could feel the blood draining from my head, raging in my chest. He was waiting, I was waiting, each of us waiting for the other to do…what? And I knew that one move from either of us would tip the balance, and we'd both tumble, head over heels, into something vast and maybe endless, like the expanding edge of the universe.

And then my damn phone rang. It buzzed and vibrated and shrilled, insistent and impossible to ignore.

Trey didn't even blink. "That's yours."

"I know."

He glanced at the readout. "It's Richard."

I cursed under my breath. *Now* he decided to call me back.

The phone rang again.

I sighed. "Can we put a bookmark here? At this exact moment? And come back to it later, when the freaking phone isn't ringing off the freaking hook?"

Trey nodded. "Of course."

But he was wrong. It was gone. Whatever he'd been about to do, whatever I'd been about to say, it had crumbled. The moment dissolving. There was no use snatching at it. It was like ashes blowing on the wind.

I cursed again and picked up my phone. "Hey, Richard, thanks for returning my call."

Chapter Twenty-nine

Trey wore the suit and jacket despite my warnings that we would be in-field, and that with reenactors, that meant literally. This particular field lay in a private stretch of woods next to the park, one of the oddly shaped properties with boundaries like a snake trail, sometimes bordering the battlefield, sometimes bumping up against subdivisions or commercial parking lots. Despite the patchwork landscape, once we got past the parking area, the aura of civilization crumbled. The moonlight covered the ground like a wet spiderweb, and the cold seeped into my pores with a bone-chilling potency.

We tromped in silence, following the trail markers. This far off the beaten path, I could almost believe we really had gone back in time, to the place these mountains had been before the railroads and highways had cut it up into lines of travel and trade.

Trey shoved his hands in the pockets of the black trench and turned the collar up. I tried to imagine him on assignment here—lying on the wet ground for hours, one eye pressed to the scope of a sniper rifle—but the image would not take hold. I could only conjure up the Trey walking beside me, skeeved out and uncomfortable and grumpy as hell. But still there, nonetheless.

"Did you bring some more of those little pills?" I said.

"Yes."

"Maybe you should—"

"I already have."

"Oh. So this is as mellow as you're going to get tonight?"

He huddled deeper into his coat. "Yes."

Great, I thought. I'd have to talk to Gabriella about preparing a nuclear-strength concoction, maybe something with an IV.

"Hang tight," I said, "we're almost there, just over the next—damn it!"

My ankle wrenched sideways, and I started to topple. Trey caught me around the shoulders and held me upright.

"Are you okay?"

"Stepped in a hole. I'm good."

I put my weight on my foot gingerly. The tendon complained a little, but held. And in that moment, my back against his chest, his arm around my shoulders, I felt the unsettling but definite shift in his stance—left foot one step behind, spine straightened, shoulders back.

"Trey?"

"Did you hear something?"

"Something like what?"

He didn't answer. He didn't have to.

The soldier materialized from the fog as if he were stepping from the shrouded mists of time. He was grizzled, gray, in the worn butternut of an infantryman. And he held a bayonetted musket pointed right at us.

"Halt!" he yelled. "Who goes there?"

Trey's hand slid between the buttons of his coat, heading for the holster. I grabbed his wrist. "No! No! No! He's in character."

Trey remained on red alert. "He's pointing a rifle at us."

"It's not loaded."

"How do you know?"

"Because he's in character. Which means we have to be too."

"No, we do not. I—"

"Trey, I deal with these people all the time, let me handle this." I cleared my throat and stepped forward, putting on my best aristocratic drawl. "Sir, we are lost in these woods, victims of a Yankee rampage. I am ashamed that those heinous villains left me only these men's clothes to wear, and my husband here only his evening dress."

Trey shot me a look. *What are you doing?* he mouthed.

Trust me, I mouthed back.

I addressed the soldier. "If you could take us to your captain, we would be most grateful."

He gave us a studied look, then lowered the musket. I felt Trey's muscles relax. He was still on alert, and I hoped to whatever deity was listening that there were no other surprises waiting for us in the deep woods. I'd hate to see one of the rebels get Krav Maga all over him. Or worse.

The soldier spat tobacco juice into the shrubbery. "This way. Hands up. And don't be trying no funny business."

Trey did not like having a bayonet at his back. Not one bit. So I broke character for thirty seconds to explain to our "captor" that he was dealing with a bad-tempered, well-armed ex-cop, and that he should probably dial down the menace a teensy hair. He took a good look at Trey's jacket, noted the well-concealed but telltale lines of a shoulder holster. And then he immediately dropped the weapon. He also kept quiet until we got to the clearing.

"Thank you," I said to Trey.

"For what?"

"For being a good sport about this."

"I'm not."

"Well, thank you for not beating that guy with his own musket. Hopefully this won't take long, and then we can be on our way back to the city. I want to ask Richard some questions, that's all, especially about Lucius."

"That might prove to be a sensitive subject, especially considering that Richard was there the night Lucius most likely died, which makes him a suspect."

"Yeah but…I mean, Richard would never kill anybody."

"Are you sure?"

"Sure enough to come tromping out in the woods to talk to him."

Trey didn't argue. He looked miserable, shivering despite multiple layers of wool and cotton. I stepped carefully in the crunchy wet leaves. An owl hooted above us, and Trey flinched.

"Fine. But be quick about it, please."

I smelled the campsite before I saw it. The odors of cooking fires and meat stews and tobacco smoke wafted over, and my whole body panged with hunger and longing. I reached into my pocket for a sucker, but found only a crumpled wrapper. I gritted my teeth and rubbed the nicotine patch.

"I'll be quick. Don't worry."

The sentry led us to the officer's tent, a rectangular unit set up away from the foot soldiers' A-frames, which in war times would have housed men stacked head to foot like cord wood. But the boys tonight had made a small concession to comfort—each tent housed only two men. Still, I didn't envy them the cold soppy ground and steely night air.

The sentinel stood at the tent flap. "Sir! I apprehended two strangers in the woods, sir!"

Richard stuck his head out, and I did a double take. He looked like a daguerreotype come to life. The neatly trimmed beard now bristled over an officer's frock coat, and he carried a pipe instead of the ever-present cigarettes. I suppressed the shiver that we really had stumbled into a rebel regiment, that our lives really were on the line.

And then Richard smiled. "Hey, you two. You're late."

The sentinel looked confused. "Sir?"

Richard composed his expression. "I'd received advance word that two civilians would be arriving, on the run from Sherman and his damned flank attacks. At ease, soldier. These are good people from a good family, and on my honor and in the name of our just cause, it is my duty to protect them."

The sentinel executed a sharp salute. "Yes, sir!"

"As you were, private. Tell the others that we don't want to be disturbed." Richard held open the tent flap. "Welcome to the headquarters of the 41st Infantry, Company B. Make yourselves at home."

Chapter Thirty

Richard sat in a rickety wooden folding chair next to the kerosene lantern, his shadow a flicker on the white canvas walls. "I'm sorry I didn't get your messages until an hour ago. I have a strict "no technology" rule on my site—no cells phones, no computers, no music—so it wasn't until I made a check-in that I saw you'd called." He gestured toward a stack of matching chairs. "Drag up a seat."

I unfolded a chair and eased my butt into it. "Your men must respect you an awful lot to stick to those rules."

"That's true, yes. But I have ways of making sure they follow orders."

Trey closed the tent flap behind himself. He refused to sit, preferring to stand, as always, with a clear line to the exit. Outside I heard the crackle and hiss as damp logs hit the campfire.

Richard clapped his hands to his thighs. "So tell me what you need. We're thirty minutes from lights out."

"I need to ask you some questions."

"About what?"

"I suppose you heard it was Lucius Dufrene's bones that tornado scattered all round."

"I heard. The cops told me. Of course I figured it out when they showed me that coffin." He leveled a look at me under his eyebrows. "One look and I knew something besides dry bones had been in there."

I put that image out of my head. "How well did you know him?"

"Well enough. He was a member of our unit, plus he worked odd jobs for me at the Amberdeckers'—landscaping, construction. He built that flagstone path at the chapel, planted the rosebushes, helped get things in order for the reburial."

"Did he help with the stained-glass windows?"

"Oh no. Evie wouldn't let anybody but the restoration team near them. Lucius only did outside work." Richard picked up an ash-stained percolator, sloshing it a little to test how much coffee it contained. "I suppose you've figured out about the windows by now."

"I have—I saw the real ones at the History Center. But I don't blame you for keeping that secret, not one bit."

"Rose'll find out Saturday. There will be hell to pay then. But it's for the best."

Hell to pay. Evie had used the exact words. I wiggled in my chair, which creaked in protest, so I gave up trying to be comfortable.

"Did Lucius have contact with any other family members?"

"Rose? No. She keeps to herself." Richard's eyes narrowed. "But you don't mean Rose. You mean Chelsea."

"Since you mentioned it."

He shrugged. "I think those two had a little something going on for a while, sure. Not that either of them told me. I'd have put a stop to it."

"But you knew."

"I suspected. I gave him a stern warning about the dangers of such, pointed out that Rose had a mantel full of marksmanship trophies and wasn't slow on the pull. Either he got the hint or Chelsea got bored and that was that. I never had any problems with him." He gestured with the percolator. "Coffee?"

"Sure."

"Got no cream or sugar, of course." Richard filled two tin cups with the dark brew. "Lucius was the one with me the day I found Braxton's remains over by the ravine. He was a good worker. Strong, fast, didn't complain. A little mouthy, but he was learning. That's why I let him be a part of the honor guard."

I accepted the coffee Richard handed me. "The what?"

"The night before the reburial, our unit formed a four-man honor guard to keep watch at the cemetery, each one of us taking a turn watching the chapel. Lucius had the three-to-six shift. But when Dexter showed up to relieve him, he was gone." He tapped the spoon on the edge of the cup. "We didn't think it was a disappearance, though. We thought he'd abandoned his post. And then we thought he'd skipped town. Nobody thought he was…"

Richard's voice trailed off. Outside around the campfire, raucous laughter erupted. No doubt a tin flask of moonshine was being passed hand to hand. A circle of men, connected by booze and bravado, a rough-and-tumble camaraderie very much like the one shared a hundred and fifty years ago.

"Only one person at a time watched the chapel?"

"Right."

"Where were the rest of you?"

"We pitched camp in the clearing next to the greenhouse and sent one guard to the chapel in three-hour shifts. Evie wouldn't let us set up in the cemetery. She was worried about the campfires messing up the graves. When Dexter got to the chapel that morning, Lucius was gone, but the chapel door was still padlocked. Nothing disturbed. So we went ahead and held the dedication ceremony at nine."

"You didn't open the casket and check?"

He shot me an angry look. "Why would we? We'd closed it sacred and solemn the night before, with the minister's blessing, and we had no reason to disturb those remains, so don't try to blame—"

"I'm not trying to blame you. I'm just trying to figure out what happened, and not only for me. For Dexter. He's looking pretty bad right now."

Richard cursed under his breath. "Fine. Go ahead then. Let's get this over with."

I tried to keep my tone non-accusatory. "Who had keys to the chapel's padlock?"

"There was a key in the house, so anybody in the family had access. Rose, Evie, Chelsea. And your uncle had one, of course." Richard frowned, suddenly remembering. "Except that all his keys went missing. He blamed himself for dropping them in the field, but…you think Lucius took them?"

I remembered the afternoon Detective Perez had shown me the key ring with my uncle's initials and the keys that did not fit. I remembered especially the short jagged one, like a padlock key. And I remembered the other thing I'd learned about Lucius from multiple sources—he was a gifted pickpocket.

"I think that's exactly what Lucius did. That would explain how Dexter's key ring ended up on Lucius' body."

"Damn." Richard stirred his coffee with a flat tin spoon. "I hate being wrong. I knew the boy had a wild streak, but I thought all he needed was a firm hand."

"I've also heard he had a mean streak."

"Where'd you hear that?"

"Does it matter?"

His eyes narrowed in annoyance. "Of course it matters. Some people don't understand. You smell that stew? That's squirrel we got ourselves, this morning. We're crack shots, every single one of us, even on these old rifled muskets. But we eat what we kill, and we kill it clean. No point messing up an animal just for target practice." Richard lowered his eyes to his coffee mug. "But Lucius didn't always mind the mess."

I glanced at Trey and saw the muscle in his jaw tighten. He didn't approve of messes.

Richard stared at his coffee. "Lucius was smart. He'd egg the new guys on. Now boys will be boys, but not everybody came through college, you know? Ain't no cause to go making a man feel stupid."

I bit my tongue on that one. I knew some of the kinds of stupid that flourished around these parts. Some of it needed flushing into the open and taking down. But sometimes people like Lucius bit off more than they could chew.

"Any of those boys have reason to shatter his skull and stuff him in a coffin?"

Richard shook his head. "Being an asshole's not a killing offense. Pardon my French."

At that moment, a young man stuck his head inside the tent. He wore oval glasses rimmed in blue steel—period perfect—and pulled his slouch hat down low over his pale forehead. When he saw us, he blushed and ducked his head.

"I'm sorry, Mr. Richard, I didn't know you had company."

Richard waved a hand at him. "Come on in, Kenny. I want you to meet somebody."

The young man came inside the tent, removing his hat as he did. He wore the worn butternut of an infantryman, a wood-handled revolver holstered at his hip. The lamplight revealed a teenager's cheeks, rough with a smattering of acne, and fawn-brown hair cut military-short. Richard introduced me as Dexter's niece, and the young man's eyes flared with recognition.

"Mr. Dexter was a fine man. I'm so sorry for your loss, ma'am."

My throat contracted, but my voice held steady. "Thank you."

Richard poured whiskey in his coffee. "She's got some questions about Lucius. You heard it was his bones we found, didn't you, son?

"Yes, sir. But I didn't know him that good." His head bobbed in my direction. "Sorry, ma'am."

"You don't need to ma'am me. Tai will do."

"Yes, ma'am. I mean, yes, Miss Tai."

I held my coffee between my hands. "You were a part of the honor guard the night before the reburial?"

"Yes, ma'am. Midnight to three."

"Did you see Lucius acting suspiciously?"

"No, ma'am." His eyes flickered with anxiety, but all it took was a nod from Richard, and he continued. "Lucius came to relieve me at three, just like we'd planned. And then I went back to the campfire with Mr. Richard and Mr. Dexter."

I held the coffee to my nose, thinking hard. Lucius had obviously stolen Dexter's keys before that, including the one that would open the padlock to the chapel. He'd come with a plan to empty the coffin. Getting murdered had ground that plan to a halt. But where were Braxton's bones and the burial goods? Somebody had to have them, and it hadn't been Lucius.

"Did you see anybody else out here that night? Anybody you didn't recognize?"

"No, ma'am. Just me and Lucius, Mr. Dexter, and Mr. Richard."

"Do you know of anyone who would have wanted to kill Lucius?"

He shook his head, scuffed at the earth with his toe. "No, ma'am."

"Did he and my uncle get along?"

"Mostly. Lucius liked to push things. He got in trouble the night of the reburial for wearing a NASCAR belt buckle. Mr. Dexter made him take it off, and he didn't argue. He stuck it in his pocket. But he shouldn't have worn it in the first place, and he knew it."

Outside, another round of laughter erupted, and the first rounds of a ribald drinking song began. Richard looked annoyed.

"Kenny? Take some firewood out to the perimeter. And tell everybody I said lights out."

"Yes, sir." Kenny put his hat back on and left, the cold air rushing it after him.

I watched him go, then turned back to Richard. "You seem right fond of him."

"He's good people. His daddy left them three years ago, but his mama does her best, and I try to help out best I can."

I slid a glance at Trey, whose expression never wavered. He could hear a story without forcing his own backstory into it, but I couldn't. Everything felt like the same story to me, playing out over and over again, nobody ever getting it all right, just making fresh kinds of wrong.

Richard kept his eyes on the tent flap. "He's got a scholarship to Georgia Tech for the fall. I may have been wrong about Lucius, but not Kenny."

In the dark distance, a shot and a series of whoops rang out, and Trey's head snapped around. The cold, the soldiers, the dark pressing wilderness were becoming too much for him. He needed to get back to the city, to the amber glow of streetlights, the buzz of electricity.

I stood. "Thanks for seeing me."

"Sure thing." Richard rose slowly, his hand pressed to the small of his back. "When you get back to civilization, go take a look at our website. I have some pictures of your uncle and me up, back in the glory days when we were the young-uns at the front instead of the old guys barking orders at the back."

"Look at you, getting all techified."

He made a rueful face. "Not me. Kenny. The boy's a computer genius. Makes me glad he's such a good kid. Otherwise he'd be off hacking into the White House or something."

I threw Trey a look. He caught it. But he had something else on his mind.

He cocked his head, looked at Richard. "One more question."

"Shoot."

"Did you kill Lucius Dufrene?"

"You're not seriously…" Richard stared at Trey, eyes flickering in the lamplight. "Of course not."

"Do you know who did?"

"No, I don't. But it sure as hell wasn't anybody with me that night, especially not Dexter." He said it flatly, then turned his face to me, his expression hard now. "It's time for lights out. Be careful on your way back to the parking lot. You don't want to get lost out here."

Chapter Thirty-one

I was grateful to see my Camaro parked right where I'd left it, next to Richard's black pickup. We climbed in quickly, and I cranked the engine, revved it a couple of times. "You just had to accuse Richard of killing Lucius, didn't you?"

Trey sounded insulted. "I did not. I simply asked—"

"Yeah, I heard you. And then you accused him of covering for Dexter. And then he threw us out of the tent—"

"We were already leaving."

"—and now he's not going to be volunteering any more information because you pissed him off."

Trey rubbed his gloved hands together in front of the heater. "Those were important points to establish, especially since—"

"Don't say it."

"—your uncle had means, motive, and opportunity, and Richard was with him almost the entire night when Lucius presumably died."

"Dexter didn't kill Lucius. And neither did Richard."

"I was relieved to hear nothing that made me believe otherwise."

He kept his eyes on the dashboard. Now that we were back in a vehicle, his shoulders weren't quite so hunched, even if the furrow on his brow remained.

I cranked the heater up to full blast. "Did you catch the other part? That Kenny's a computer genius?"

"I did."

"Who didn't know Lucius real well."

Trey shook his head. "That part isn't true."

"I suspected not. But I'm glad you verified it." Despite the heater, my breath still made puffs of fog. "What about the rest of what Kenny said?"

"He was telling the truth when he said he relieved Lucius at the chapel at three, and that that was the last he saw of him. But he was lying when he said that Lucius wasn't acting suspiciously."

"Uh huh. And Richard?"

Trey considered. "Mostly telling the truth."

"Technically true but deliberately evasive?"

"Yes, that. Somewhat. But not exactly. He seemed to be…I can't explain. But he wasn't lying."

I checked my phone. No messages. No service either, not surprisingly. I stuck it back in my pocket.

"You know what I think? I think Lucius filched Dexter's keys so he could get into the chapel. I think he took the bones and burial goods and delivered them to someone else—"

"Who?"

"I don't know yet, but everybody I've interviewed so far—Cat, Chelsea, Fishbone—they've all said the same thing, that Lucius had been working with a new partner, somebody he met online. And I bet that partner was up there that night, to take the loot off Lucius' hands. Because Lucius himself never left the chapel. He died in there. And I bet this secret partner is the one who killed him."

"But how would this partner get on the property?"

"There's a million ways—you saw that as we came in. Duck through someone's backyard, park in a commercial lot and sneak in."

"But your uncle was also there, and—"

"Jeez, Trey, whose side are you on?"

"I'm simply trying—"

"I know, I know. I'm sorry." I tilted my head back against the seat. "I'm tired and frustrated and it's like the answer is hovering two inches out of reach."

Trey fastened his seatbelt. "So what do we do now?"

"Now we go home. We'll figure it out in the morning."

Trey looked relieved. He was an urban creature, accustomed to the cycles of rush hour, at home in the steel canyons of Buckhead. Atlanta was by most standards a green city—I'd seen it from the air, coming down into Hartsfield, the dense emerald canopy of Piedmont and Centennial and a hundred smaller parks. But it was a tame green, civilized and domesticated.

Not like the mountain woodlands, with a night sky so deep black it had texture, and stars so bright they seemed cut from crystallized light. The wild wasn't a metaphor out here. It was real, and close. I could feel it pressing against me, and while it wasn't the salt-rimmed wild of the Lowcountry, I knew it nonetheless. Like an old lover in a new bed.

I took the car into a three-point turn and headed back to the park entrance, driving slowly, letting the tires feel their way down the dirt path. Trey was exhausted, in desperate need of the order and discipline of his black-and-white apartment, his safe space, his recovery zone. He kept his eyes on the windshield as if he couldn't wait for Atlanta to appear in the headlights.

I flicked on the high beams, and a long low shape hurtled across the road. I slammed the brakes just in time to avoid a collision. A coyote. It froze at the edge of the road, facing us head-on, yellow eyes gleaming. Trey locked his door, then reached across me and locked mine with a hard slap, like we were confronting a carjacker.

I shot him a look. "Seriously?"

He huddled in his seat, double-checked his seatbelt. "Keep moving. There's probably more of them."

"And not a single one has thumbs."

He ignored me. I honked, and the coyote loped into the underbrush without a backward glance.

Once we got back to the shop, Trey said goodnight at the door. "Call me tomorrow. I'll be presenting the resiliency design paper at two, so call before that."

"I will." I reached up and tucked his scarf tighter around his neck. "Thank you for coming with me tonight. And this afternoon. I had a good time."

And I had, even when I'd been holding the trash can for Chelsea or pursuing Fishbone across the park or tromping after a faux Confederate in the woods. And I hadn't felt a single pang of panic. Not one. And Trey had managed to keep his gun in his holster the entire time.

"It was…interesting," he said.

"Come on, it was more than that." I adjusted his collar, his skin warm beneath the wool. "Your head may want things calm and boring, boyfriend, but your heart is a tricky beast. It has completely different wants." I patted his chest. "And it *does* want."

He didn't drop his eyes. "I know that."

"Because every time I call you with a problem—snake problem, surveillance problem, uncooperative witness problem—you show up. And you stomp around and scowl and lecture me incessantly. But you show up."

"I do not stomp around."

"Come on, Trey. You're a former SWAT team leader, a Red Dog roughhouser. You're not gonna convince me that you're happy sitting behind a desk pushing paper. You come alive out there, in the wild." I moved closer, close enough to feel the heat of him. "With me."

His eyes dipped to my throat, then further down, and it was as if he could see inside the ivory armor of my ribcage, right into my shivering red heart. And the only thing between us was a threshold. I stood on one side of it in the warm low-lit shop, and he stood on the other in the cold, still night.

And all he had to do was reach for me—one finger, one word, one step—and I would drag him upstairs into my brand new bed and not let him out until we were both sated and spent. But he stood unmoving, his expression sheared clean on the surface, a layer of ice on a frozen river with whitewater roaring underneath. His raised his eyes to mine again, and the yearning in them was so fierce I caught my breath.

"Trey?"

His voice was rough. "Yes?"

"It's the wanting that's hard, isn't it? Because it's all tangled up together—who you are, who you were, when to act, when to hold back."

"Yes, but…" He shook his head. "I don't understand why I can't…I'm trying, please believe me. But I have to figure it out before I can change it. Do you understand?"

I thought of the words that still trembled behind my tongue, the words that no act of will could force to the surface, no matter how hard I pushed.

"Yes," I said. "I understand. With all my heart."

Chapter Thirty-two

The dream was a mosaic of sensation untethered from any real memory. No beginning, no context, only Trey, his hands and mouth, and I knew the wild hammering of his heart for what it really was—fear—even as he buried it in the animal burn of desire. And something was pulling me away from him, and I tried to hold on, but he was smoke between my fingers, and then a sound, rhythmic and insistent…

My eyes flew open. I listened harder, heard only pre-dawn shop sounds. I fumbled for my cell phone and checked the time. Barely six a.m. Surely nobody was…

And then I heard it again, this time louder. Knock, knock, knock.

I clambered to the side of the bed and squinted out the bedroom window. There was somebody in the back lot down below, somebody standing at my door. I opened the bedside table and got my .38, thumbing open the cylinder to reveal five rounds. I snapped it shut just as I heard another series of knocks.

I frowned. No-goodniks didn't usually knock. So I put on my robe, and—with silent apologies to Trey, who had been trying to break me of bad concealed carry habits—shoved the revolver into the front pocket and went downstairs to the back door.

"Who is it?" I called.

"Miss Tai?"

I unlocked the door and cracked it an inch. "Kenny! What are you doing here?"

"I need to talk to you."

"At six in the morning?"

"I've got school in an hour, and I couldn't tell you last night, not with Mr. Richard around."

"Why?"

"Because it's about Lucius." He stared at me with his wide eyes. "Please?"

I opened the door all the way. "Get in. And make it fast before I change my mind."

He accepted a mug of coffee, taking one polite sip and then holding it between his shaking white hands.

I sat opposite him. "You weren't entirely truthful last night, were you? You *did* know Lucius pretty well. And he *was* acting suspiciously the night of the reburial."

"Yes, ma'am." He ducked his head. "I didn't want to say anything, but…there's something the police need to know."

"So tell them."

"I can't."

"Why not?"

"I'll get in big trouble. And then I'll lose my scholarship, and if I lose that, I can't go to college." He looked up at me, fiercely agitated. "But I didn't do anything wrong! I didn't mean…"

He bit his lip, breathing hard. I glanced up at my deer head. The red light behind its eyes glimmered, recording every word. Trey was listening, probably with his finger poised to dial 911.

"Hang on a sec," I said.

I turned off my cell phone and went to the deer head. I looked it right in its glassy eyes, breathed a *sotto voce* "sorry" into its mangy ear, then reached behind the left antler and switched off the audio feed. I kept the video—a small placation, so that Trey wouldn't drive his ass over and yell at me, which he would do if he suddenly couldn't see me—but I knew that if he heard something incriminating, he would be required by that merciless left brain of his to turn Kenny in. And I couldn't have that. Not until I'd heard what he had to say.

I turned back to Kenny. "I can't promise to keep the police out of this. But I can try, I can promise you that. And I'm big on keeping my promises."

He looked at the deer head, looked at me.

"Okay," he said.

I made him hot chocolate first. This he actually drank, the cocoa foam staining his baby mustache. He suddenly looked about eight years old.

"Do you know what the Darknet is?" he said.

"One of those role-playing games? Like Dungeons and Dragons?"

This earned me a tiny flicker of a smile. "No, ma'am. It's like the Internet, only without the safeguards. Like the frontier. And it's a dangerous place if you don't know what you're doing."

"But you do."

"Yes, ma'am." He leaned forward, suddenly surer of himself. "You need connections, go-betweens to vouch for you. And if you break the rules, bad things happen."

"Bad like what?"

"Bad like your life gets hacked. They can send Trojan horse viruses into your computer that'll fry everything on there—no more programs, no more documents, just slash-and-burn code. There's sick people on the Darknet. Kiddie porn rings, hit men. But worst of all is the RBC."

"The RBC?"

He dropped his voice. "Russian business community. You don't mess with the RBC, not even accidentally. And they rule the Darknet, ma'am."

"You mean the mafia?"

"Worse than the mafia. The RBC started back in the Gulag prisons, the baddest of the bad. Now they have entire IT teams working the Darknet. They had connections on the Silk Road—"

"The what?"

He made a patient face. "The drug site the FBI busted last year. It was like Amazon, only instead of books and stuff, you could buy crystal meth and crack and pot."

I stared at him. "You've got to be kidding."

"No, ma'am. " He looked down at his hot cocoa. "That's where this all started. Before Silk Road went down, Lucius asked me if I could help them get on it to get some pot. I told them I could, but that I wasn't going to do it on my computer. So I went to this skate shop—"

"Grindshop. In Stone Mountain."

"Yes, ma'am. I downloaded Tor on his computer, showed him—"

"Wait, wait, slow down. What's Tor?"

"It's an onion router. You know, multi-layered. It encrypts data by bouncing it through a random selection of arrays. All those Wikileaks guys? That's what they used. Turned the government's own weapon against it."

He said this with a pleased smirk, and I realized there was more to this young man than nervous blushes and goody-two-shoes smarts. He was a true rebel, one of the quiet unthreatening subversives that could topple entire empires. If the Confederacy had been composed of his ilk, America would have been whistling Dixie instead of the Star-Spangled Banner.

"Okay," I said, "so you gave him this illegal download—"

"The download's not illegal. It's a proxy server, that's all."

"Kenny. In all manners technical, I am officially an old fogey. What's a proxy server?"

His eyes brightened. "It's how Tor maintains user anonymity. With this download, your computer can act as an intermediary for requests from other Tor users. Only nobody knows who got what, or where they got it, or which specific activities are associated with which IP addresses. But that wasn't the problem."

"What was?"

He hesitated. I put down my coffee and scooted knee to knee with him.

"Look at me, Kenny."

He raised his eyes. He was startlingly obedient for such a rebel, but I knew why. He respected his elders—even though

I winced at the term. It was the government he didn't trust, something he'd no doubt learned at Richard's knee.

"Kenny? If you know something, something that could help figure out who killed Lucius, and you don't share that, then you can get in worse trouble than losing a scholarship. I'm talking jail trouble."

He took a deep breath. "Lucius asked me if I knew anyone who bought relics."

I cursed under my breath. I knew it, I'd known it all along.

"There's collectors on the Darknet," Kenny said. "Real rich ones. Anonymous. Lucius said he'd heard about them from other reenactment units, that they bought all kinds of things, even bones. For thousands, Miss Tai. Thousands."

I kept my voice calm. "Did you ever…"

"No, ma'am! I would never desecrate the dead that way, especially not our men in gray. Never!"

"But you think Lucius did."

He nodded. "Mr. Richard is real clear on the rules. If we find anything on the field, we report it to him and he takes care of it. But about a month before Lucius disappeared, he asked me I knew anything about the underground relic trade."

"Did you tell him?"

"No, ma'am. I don't mess with that. But he was asking."

"You think that's where the Amberdecker bones went?"

"Yes, ma'am."

"And you think one of these Darknet bad guys took the bones and killed Lucius instead of paying him?"

"I do now. Back then, I thought he'd just run off. And that's the other reason I'm scared to death to be talking to you. It's not that I don't trust you—Mr. Richard says I can, and so I do—but there's worse things than jail, Miss Tai, things like getting killed and stuffed in a coffin and—"

"Look at me."

He did. He was scared and brave in equal measure, and my heart went out to him.

"I promise that I will do my best to keep you safe and sound and headed to Tech, you hear me?"

"Yes, ma'am."

I realized I'd stopped correcting him forever ago. I was a ma'am now, a grown-up.

"Good. If things get hinky, and the cops do come knocking, you ask for Detective Dan Garrity. But you have to tell me something first—when you said you showed Lucius how to cruise the Darknet, you used the word 'them.' Who else did you show?"

He looked nervous again. "I don't know if I should say."

"You should. Because believe me, if any one of them decides to save their own neck by throwing you under the bus, they will do it in a heartbeat. Especially Fishbone. That dude is looking for a scapegoat, and he's probably going to need one, so out with it, Kenny."

He looked utterly miserable, but he didn't say anything.

"Kenny? Who are you protecting?"

He raised his eyes, and they were as moony as a calf's. "Catherine Ann."

"Who?"

"She's Mr. Richard's daughter. She's a bartender now, and they don't speak to each other anymore, not since she got in trouble with the law, which was all Lucius' fault. She met him here, at this shop, and they dated for a little while, but she broke up with him right before he disappeared. She's not like Lucius, Miss Tai. She's real sweet and nice, and I don't want to get her in any more trouble with Mr. Richard."

I felt the connection coming together. One plus one was always two, and a rose by any other name...

"She doesn't go by Catherine anymore, does she?"

"No, ma'am. She's Cat now. And if Mr. Richard knew about her and Lucius, and about me being the one who helped him get her that pot...Lord have mercy, Miss Tai."

I sat back in my chair. Based on what Cat had told me that night at Hog Wild, I was pretty sure Richard did know, about Lucius anyway. Trey had been right—he had been hiding something that night in the tent. Which meant that Richard was now at the top of the list of people who might have wanted to crack Lucius' skull wide open and stuff him in a coffin.

Lord have mercy indeed.

Chapter Thirty-three

I dumped a stack of Union uniforms into a crate and shoved them into the closet, almost dropping the phone in the process. "I swear, Trey, it's all I can do not to march myself back into those woods—"

"Promise me you won't do that."

I jammed another sucker in my mouth. I'd called Richard's phone, but of course he wasn't answering. He was still in his pretend officers' tent, enforcing his "no technology" rule.

"How could he turn his own daughter out for a goofy teenage stunt like shoplifting! Or trying pot! That bass-akwards, holier-than-thou—"

"Tai."

"I know, I know. Their story, not mine. But now that I know he's Cat's father, I'm not trusting anything he told us last night, not about Lucius, not about the reburial, nothing. You were right—he really was hiding something."

I grabbed another armful of reenactment wear and crammed it into my last empty box. What the hell, I'd just pile the rest of it in the storage room. What the ATF didn't see...

Trey's voice remained calm. "You need to explain what Kenny said after you cut the audio." A pause. "Why *did* you cut the audio?"

"Because it sounded like he was about to confess something, which means you'd have had to call the cops and have them arrest him. And I understand. Laws are necessary sometimes—"

"Sometimes?"

I heard the bristle in his voice. "But sometimes laws need bending. I understand that you can't, and that's okay. Civilization needs people to work the lines. But I work the edges."

He didn't say anything at first. But I could hear him pondering.

"Did you find out anything useful?" he finally said.

I told him what Kenny had shared. He listened. I hoped he was taking notes, because once Trey got information into flow-charts or outlines, he started to see things. Patterns emerged, like a camouflaged lion stepping out of the high grass.

I grabbed a dust rag and can of furniture polish. "Kenny's got a lot riding on staying out of trouble, and he's a good kid."

"How can you be sure?"

"A bad kid wouldn't have come to me." I hesitated. "Why? Do you see something different? Was he lying?"

"I don't know. I can't read people over video."

"So we don't know if he was telling the truth about any of it?"

"No, we don't." He paused. "What are we going to do about this?"

I couldn't resist a tiny smile. "Uh oh, now you're getting curious."

"I'm simply concerned."

I gathered up the photographs still lying on the counter and put them back into their box. "Don't worry. I may have turned the audio off to keep Kenny out of trouble, but I kept the video on so that *I* would stay out too. I didn't think he was a stone cold killer, but it was nice to know that if he'd tried something, you were watching."

"From forty-five minutes away."

"Still. It was a reassuring feeling."

I hesitated before placing my one photo of Cat back in the box. Now that I knew, I could see Richard in her features—the dark hooded eyes, the prominent cheekbones. I tamped down another surge of anger. I knew I shouldn't layer my story over this one, but I couldn't help it. I seethed with it.

"The more I figure out, the more complicated things get. Now Kenny's blaming the mafia too, just like Fishbone. As if the mob would be messing around with old bones."

My doorbell jingled, and I turned around, almost dropping the phone. Rose Amberdecker stood in my shop. She looked out of place, like a lumberjack come to tea. Behind her I saw the outline of her truck, a four-wheel-drive pickup with mud-stained bumpers. From where I stood, I could see the gun rack and the three firearms that filled it—two slim rifles and a shotgun I recognized as the one she'd had in the woods, the twelve-gauge.

Trey saw her too. "Tai?"

"I know."

"Promise you won't turn off the audio-video feed this time."

"You bet I won't," I said, keeping my eyes on Rose. "Guaranteed."

I hung up. Trey didn't have to worry about losing contact. I wanted his eyes and ears all over Rose Amberdecker.

She was dressed as if she'd come directly from the field—blue jeans, flannel-lined work jacket, hair in the ice-gray braid down her back. She stood right in front of the dedication portrait, looking down at it, not at me.

"Can I help you?" I said.

She didn't reply, kept staring at her own image, and her daughters'. She'd donned no mourning then, and I remembered Evie's story, how Braxton Amberdecker's mother had refused to do the same. Mulish blood ran in the veins of Amberdecker women.

"I remember hearing of your uncle's passing," she said. "I only met him once, when this picture was taken, but Richard says he was a fine man."

"He was." I put a lid on the box of photographs. "Still no luck finding the remains?"

She shook her head. "Evie wanted to continue, but I told her it was no use. The land claims us all eventually."

She appraised me with pale blue eyes. I'd been worried my adventure with Chelsea would come back to bite me, and now here was Mama Bear, teeth bared.

"You sell buckshot here?" she said. "Three and three quarters, double aught?"

I tried to keep the relief from showing on my face. So this wasn't about Chelsea.

"I do," I said, "but I'm technically not open right now. I've got an ATF inspection coming up this afternoon, and—"

"Agent Willoughby?"

"No. Thompkins."

"Willoughby and I shoot together sometimes. Doves. Do you hunt?"

I shook my head. I remembered my one dove hunt with my uncle—the patient dogs, the bang of the shotguns, and then afterward, the gut buckets and smell of singed feathers. It was a sport for the keen of eye, and I knew from Richard that Rose had one. But Rose and I weren't talking sport. She was feeling me out for some reason, and I was both curious and wary.

"I don't hunt, but I do carry dove shot. When I'm open. Which I'm not right now."

She ran her finger along the counter, tapped the hardwood. Her nails were cut short, a working woman's manicure. "Is this all there is?"

"What do you mean?"

"Your shop. Is this everything?

I put down my mug. "There's a storage room, a closet or two. And the upstairs is my apartment. But yes, this is it."

She nodded, her eyes roving every corner. She noted the piles of catalogs and identification manuals waiting to be returned to the shelves, my well-thumbed and dog-eared guides through the world of Civil War-era antiques.

"So your business is mainly relics?" she said.

"Most of my reenactment trade is in replicas. My clients do collect, though—guns, swords, buttons, even glass eyes and bone saws. They keep wish lists, so if I run across something they'd be interested in, I try to snag it for them."

"And do you?"

"Do I what?"

"Snag things?"

She said it with a hefty dose of accusation. I kept my voice level.

"Sometimes people bring in things to sell, usually from their grandparents' barn, and if I see something a client is looking for, I purchase it for them."

She fingered the lock on my display case, empty still, waiting for the knives and swords piled on top to be returned to it. "I get them on my land, you know. Diggers, looters. The sheriff told me I'm not allowed to shoot them." She smiled thinly. "But he said he'd understand if I mistook one for a deer."

I remembered her eyes behind the twelve-gauge. She regarded weapons the same way Trey did, with a utilitarian eye, like she would a wrench or a hammer. Some of my clients were gun nuts, but some were like Rose. I wasn't sure which I found more disturbing.

Her eyes hardened. "Thieves, all of them. Hordes of them, sneaking on from the park."

"Can't you prosecute them for trespassing?"

"I'd have to catch them first, but even then, they don't go to jail. They pay the fine and come back the next morning. But the coyotes are bad along the park edge. One day those looters are gonna find more trouble than they can handle." She ran a finger along the lines of a replica cavalry sword, shiny and new. "Your uncle ever do any digging?"

"You mean the illegal kind? Absolutely not."

She kept her eyes on the sword. "Richard said he had a hard time after your aunt died. Lots of bills. Times like that can make a man see things differently."

"Mrs. Amberdecker—"

"There's shops like yours all over. I see the bullets and buttons for sale, claiming to be from the Battle of Kennesaw Mountain. Claiming to be properly obtained." She turned to face me. "You have any things like that here?"

I took a deep breath, held it for a count of three, then let it out. "Dexter believed in proper provenance, and I've continued that commitment."

"Then you won't mind showing me that paperwork."

"Actually, I would." I moved behind the counter. "I'll be glad to answer any questions you have about my procedures here, which are Dexter's procedures, but you can't see my log book and you can't see my sales registers and you can't see my client list."

Her fingers tightened into fists. "Cut the nonsense. Where are they?"

"Where are what?"

"My great-great-grandfather's bones."

So that was that.

I shook my head. "I don't have them."

"Don't lie to me, girl. I know they weren't in the coffin. The detectives told me that *person* was in there, and not a one of Evie's students has found a thing despite looking for four days. Not a one. That's because they're not to be found. Now I don't know if your uncle took them, or somebody else who worked here, but whoever has them came through this shop to sell them, so you'd best tell me, and fast. Where are those bones?"

So this wasn't about Chelsea, who'd obviously kept her mouth shut about my little visit. I took another three-count breath.

"Mrs. Amberdecker, I have an AFT audit today. The Kennesaw Revitalization Commission is threatening to pull my business license unless I buy some sidewalks. Somebody keeps tripping my security system, and even my premises liability-agent boyfriend can't fix the problem because my neighbor's a bitch *and* I have detectives breathing down my neck because I found a skull on *your* property. And you think I have time to fool with even more bones?" I snorted. "I don't even have time for this conversation."

She fixed me with a stare as narrow and relentless as the barrel of a gun. "You're not taking me seriously. But you should. You really should."

She slammed the door on her way out. It made a friendly little tinkle behind her.

I looked up at the deer head. "Did you get that, boyfriend? Because I think I just got threatened by a woman who drives around with three long guns mounted in the back window of her truck."

Chapter Thirty-four

Agent Cranky Pants was a husky man, with the barrel-like midriff of a former athlete and hair the brown of a good-natured spaniel. His eyes, however, remained locked in a perpetual squinch, his nostrils flared as if catching a whiff of something spoiled.

I sat behind my counter, in my purple slacks and jacket, my one piece of business attire. I wanted a sucker, wanted a piece of nicotine gum, wanted a cigarette. I wanted with bright flaring need as the inspector made a methodical examination of my shop.

"There have been complaints," he said.

I kept my expression neutral. "About what?"

"Several things, actually." He pulled out a piece of paper. "The Kennesaw Revitalization Commission reports that because of zoning violations, you may not be issued a business license for next year."

I suppressed the seethe. "You mean Brenda next door, not the KRC. According to the KRC itself, I have six months to make the necessary upgrades or apply for an appeal."

"There are also allegations that you have been making purchases for an individual without waiting for proper NICS verification, because you and this individual are romantically involved."

"Excuse me?"

"You were heard making an agreement with this individual to trade handguns for…" He managed to look both embarrassed and offended. "Sexual favors."

I was incredulous. "You've got to be kidding. That was a joke."

"It is also alleged that you then destroyed the paperwork surrounding the...arrangement."

"No, that didn't happen either. I was—"

And then it hit me. I was in my shop—Trey and me, all alone—when I made that joke. Except for the footsteps Trey had heard, in the alley where we weren't allowed to have cameras. I took a three-count breath. Then another. I waited until the red cleared from my vision before speaking.

"The individual in question—who happens to be my boyfriend, yes—is a fully licensed security agent with both a professional concealed carry card and an HR218 permit from the Atlanta PD. I have documented every transaction he and I have made, every single one of them legal and proper, and accusing otherwise is more of my neighbor's stuntwork so she can have the whole damn block to herself—excuse me, I did not mean to say 'damn'—but I did not, nor will I ever—"

He held up his hand. "I think I understand, Ms. Randolph. That's fine."

"But—"

"I said that's fine. I'm getting the picture. All I need at this point is your A&D book."

I slid the box in front of him. "I wanted to make it more... presentable. But it's been a hellacious morning."

"If the records aren't complete—"

"Oh, they're complete. Just not neat."

He made a checkmark on his sheet as he reached for the box. I suppressed a gulp. My phone vibrated against my thigh, and I took a quick peek. Richard.

I stood. "Could you excuse me for a second?"

Agent Cranky Pants waved a hand at the door and opened the lid. I hurried out, snatching the door shut behind me.

"You are a lying son of a bitch!" I hissed.

"What?"

"Why didn't you tell me you had a daughter?"

A pause. "You talked to Catherine."

"Damn straight I did. She had some very interesting things to say."

"Where is she?"

"You don't know? Haven't you even looked for her?"

A stray whip of wind slapped my hair into my face, and I huddled closer to the window. Behind the glass, Agent Cranky Pants picked up the A&D book and placed it on the counter in front of him. I turned my back. I could not watch.

Richard's voice was a monotone. "Of course I looked. She didn't want to be found."

"I found her in two hours. You could have done it in less if you'd tried."

He muttered a curse. I pulled my thin jacket around me and wrapped my arms tighter. The wind had bite, like the snap of a feral dog. It chewed through my jacket, scraping shivers down my backbone.

"I made the rules clear—no drugs in my home. She came into my house smelling like a damn hippie, didn't even try to deny it, and then got caught stealing."

"So that was it, your way or the highway?"

"She chose—"

"No, you chose. She made a mistake. Now her name's coming up in the investigation into Lucius' death, which means God-knows-what for her. Or you."

"What does that mean?"

"That means considering that he was sleeping with your daughter right before he died, you just hit a triple play, Richard—means, motive, and opportunity—so you'd better—"

"Catherine was what!?!"

His voice was a mixture of terror and anger and grief and total utter astonishment. Which I had discovered was one of the hardest emotions to fake, even over the phone. But I was too mad to care.

"You heard me. Congratulations, Richard, you have now replaced the freaking Russian mafia as Most Likely To Have Murdered Lucius Dufrene!"

"I didn't kill him! I didn't even know about him and Catherine! Tai, you gotta believe me!"

"Save it for the boys in blue. Because I promise you, Richard, if I find one shred of evidence that you had anything to do with Lucius' death, or Braxton's bones, or the missing relics, I will put that evidence on a silver platter and deliver it downtown in person!"

"But—"

"In the meantime, stay the hell out of my shop!"

I smashed the off button with my thumb, hard, and I held it down like I was squashing a bug until the display flickered off. And then I stuffed it in my pocket and marched over to Brenda's, which was locked up tight despite the lights being on. I banged on the door. She stuck her head around the corner and jerked it back.

"I see you!" I yelled. "I know it was you the other night, in the alley! It's been you all along, tripping my system, eavesdropping around corners!" I banged again at the door. "Listen to me, Brenda Lovejoy-Burlington, if you tell one more official person one more lie about me, or about Trey, I will come over here and personally kick your lily white ass!"

"Your car is parked out back again!" she yelled in return.

"Damn straight it is! And it's staying there! Because it's my space! I can put up a fucking lemonade stand if I want to!"

"I'll have you towed!"

"You touch my car, and I will hurt you, you hear me?"

She stomped up to the door, but didn't open it. "I will not be threatened by the likes of you!"

"You just were!"

I kicked the door once for good measure. Then I took another deep breath—which was not working, no matter what Trey said—straightened my jacket, and went back into my shop. Agent Cranky Pants was right where I left him, eagerly making notations in his notebook.

I cleared my throat. "Excuse me?"

He looked up. "Yes?"

"In my first interview with the ATF, I was asked why I wanted a firearms license. And I answered because I believe in the Second Amendment, which is the truth. But the realer truth is that every night, I lay down with my conscience, not the Second Amendment. I take what I do here seriously. That means I abide by the law. You may find some messiness in this shop, and in that book, but you won't find a single legal violation, not one."

He smiled at me, the first smile I'd ever seen on his face. "Anything else?"

"No, that's it."

"Good. Now may I get back to my evaluation?"

I averted my eyes and headed for the storeroom. My chest felt tight, empty. I shut the door behind me, shoved a stack of targets off the table, and sat. I dialed Trey's number. It went straight to voice mail, which I expected. He was delivering his paper on resiliency systems, so I knew he wouldn't answer. But it was good to hear his voice regardless, his patient, professional voice. When the tone sounded, my own voice felt smoother and calmer.

"So I yelled at Richard instead of going into the woods, and then I yelled at Brenda and maybe threatened her with bodily harm if she touched my car. And now the ATF guy is evaluating the A&D book as I speak. I should have listened to you about organizing it, but that's a big 'oh well' now so…cross your fingers, okay?"

The light from was the casement window was thin, but it was enough to illuminate the mishmashed wreckage I'd stuffed out of the ATF's sight. I heard the chair scrape back in the other room. I ended the call, stood, straightened my jacket. Time to face the music.

As I entered the room, the agent looked up. "Ms. Randolph, I have to tell you. I'm impressed by the accuracy and thoroughness of your information. The organization, however—"

I sat in front of him quickly. "I can explain."

"—is most impressive of all. Logical, coherent, efficient. The color-coding was a nice touch, but the cross index was especially helpful."

I stared at him, utterly baffled. I looked where he was pointing and saw…a cross index. And color-coded tabs. My A&D book was virtually unrecognizable—hole-punched, subdivided, a paragon of order and tidiness.

I swallowed hard. "Thank you, sir. I truly—truly—don't know what to say."

Chapter Thirty-five

A single sliver of light shown under Trey's office door at Phoenix Corporate Security, the only sign of activity in the otherwise dark and cloistered hall. He was alone, the last of the industrious field agents to call it a day. I slipped inside without knocking, closing the door behind me.

He looked up from his work. He'd known I was on the way up—there were no surprises at Phoenix, which was safeguarded like a super-villain's lair—but he wore a confused expression nonetheless. "I thought I was meeting you at the shop."

"Changed my mind."

Trey's puzzled frown deepened, but he didn't put down his pen. His office was as dichromatic as his apartment—ink-black desk, paper-white walls, one bookcase lined with rows of crime foreseeability studies and integrated physical security manuals. The stuff of resiliency design.

I leaned back against the door and folded my arms. "You organized my A&D book."

Trey's expression grew wary. "I did."

"Without my permission."

"Correct."

"When?"

"Yesterday. While you were in the shower."

"I told you I wanted to do it myself."

He didn't drop his eyes. "You did, yes."

I examined him closer. The suit wasn't Armani—it was his Dolce & Gabbana. Still Italian, still black, but cut looser in the arms, more relaxed across the back. I tried to read his expression, but he dropped his eyes to his desk. He gathered the papers and stacked them in his in-box. They'd been in a haphazard pile when I'd walked in, a disheveled mosaic of blueprints and pie charts.

I remembered then all the ways he'd stepped out of the black-and-white and into the gray over the past few days—staking out Fishbone, trudging into a dive bar, driving into the mountains. He'd been freaked-out, discombobulated, out of his comfort zone, and he'd still done it, like a seasick man climbing on a boat over and over again, until the pitch and toss of the waves became exhilarating instead of nauseating.

The realization bloomed with fresh surprise. "It's all part of your damn strategy, isn't it? Deliberately doing something I told you not to do?"

He hesitated, then nodded. "You said you wanted me to seduce you. That requires I improve my ability to tolerate uncertainty and lack of consequential control. So…" He moved a mechanical pencil out of its soldier-perfect formation, then moved it back. "I've been practicing."

The earnest resolve in his eyes utterly undid me. Suddenly, I wanted him more than I'd wanted anything in my life. I unbuttoned my jacket and dropped it to the floor, then stepped out of the puddled fabric.

Trey's expression sharpened. "What are you doing?"

"Undressing."

"Here? Now?"

I engaged the lock with a single twist. "Right here, right now."

"But Marisa is—"

"Still with a client in the conference room, yes. I passed her on my way up."

I kicked my heels off, one into each corner, then hit the light switch with my elbow, plunging the room into darkness illuminated only by the streetlight outside. I walked barefoot toward his desk, reaching behind my head and unclipping my curls as

I did. They fell about my shoulders in a mass of tendrils and ringlets. I stopped right in front of his desk, letting my vision adjust to the silvered darkness. He was eyeing me like a mouse might eye a cat.

"But Marisa doesn't matter," I said. "This is all that matters, this dangerous, transgressive, utterly chaotic moment. You've been doing so good, you really have. Wading in, testing the waters. But it's time to get off the shore and into the surf."

The slacks went next. I got a shiver when the air hit my bare thighs, but the rush of blood warmed me fast. I came around the corner of the desk—Trey watching, not saying a word—and then I took hold of his chair with both hands and spun him to face me.

He shook his head. "Right now, the signal-to-noise ratio is…" He kept shaking his head, dazed and bewildered. "And I can't…"

"Yes, you can."

Trey didn't move—not a muscle twitch, not an eyeblink. He kept his hands on the armrests, fingers wrapped tight, practically white-knuckled with effort.

He swallowed, hard. "You said you wanted me to seduce you."

"You did. It worked. Here I am."

"But you said you wanted *me* to make the first move. You said—"

"Oh, you're gonna make a move, all right. I guarantee it."

I unbuttoned the blouse, revealing a lace-enhanced expanse of genuine heaving bosom worthy of the trashiest romance novel cover. Trey exhaled in a sharp burst. He'd bought me the bra I was wearing, a crimson La Perla push-up that had set him back almost five hundred dollars, and was as precisely engineered as the Ferrari to deliver exactly the kind of high-octane response I was seeing right in front of me.

I smiled. "Your move, boyfriend."

He dragged his eyes back to mine. All I could hear was the hum of traffic and the cadence of his breath, quicker on the intake now, shaky on the exhale. And then—slowly, deliberately—he pushed himself to standing, his chest brushing against mine as he rose, starched cotton and hard buttons dragging against my flushed tender skin. And as he stood, I could feel the heat and stir of every inch of him—every single inch—and I knew that he was watching me burn for him, like a lit fuse racing to the inevitable. And he needed too, was trembling with pure uncut need, even if his hands never left his sides.

Slowly he bent his mouth to my ear, his voice a rough whisper. "Does that count?"

I removed his belt with one practiced tug. "Hell, yes."

Chapter Thirty-six

I drove home slowly, the night an opaque bowl over the city. I could see the Atlanta skyline in my rearview mirror against that matte charcoal sky, my windshield wipers scraping blobs of slush off the glass. I listened to the scrape-squeak rhythm of the wipers and shivered despite the furnace-hot air I had aimed at my feet.

I couldn't stop smiling. And remembering. The papers and pencils hitting the floor in a flurried clatter, the slanting bars of the streetlight both veiling and revealing. The sounds of fabric rustling, the hitch and release of breath, the whispery friction of skin against skin…

I cranked the heater down a notch and glanced at my cell phone. Nothing yet. It would come, though. It always did. Usually something polite, a brief cautionary warning about the traffic or an inquiry after my safe arrival. These little after-messages felt sweet and illicit, like the scribbled-under-the-desk notes of elementary school crushes.

Sure enough, my phone rang as I pulled into the space behind the shop. I smiled and tucked it to my ear. "Your timing is exquisite."

"Did you have any trouble?"

"Not a bit. But the weather report was right—there were some flurries."

"There's more expected tomorrow night."

"I plan on being at your place before that happens."

I sat in the car, listening to the tick-tick-tick of the engine cooling, the soft plop-plop of light rain mixed with snow. My heart warmed at the thought of him. And I kept trying to tell him why, kept failing. And he kept trying to act, kept failing. We each had our walls, Trey and I, mortared and cemented. We'd have to take them down the same way we'd built them, brick by brick.

I pulled the keys from the ignition. "I'm sorry if I ruined your seduction strategy."

"I have no complaints."

I laughed. He delivered the words with his usual deadpan blandness, but I could hear an almost-smile lurking in them. I could also hear the rustle of papers, order-making at his end.

"No complaints here either. None whatsoever." I drummed my fingers on the steering wheel. "It really is hard for you, isn't it? Wanting?"

"In itself, no. But it is difficult to process. Sometimes. So I learned to stop. Not stop wanting, of course, but stop acting. Pause. Analyze. Maintain distance." A hesitation. "It can also be complicated by the...you know."

I knew, yes. The hormonal signatures of arousal and anger were very similar, especially to someone with his neuronal wires crossed. Both were potent, irresistible, all-consuming, running in twin currents sometimes, one masquerading as the other.

"I know. But I have an idea that might help."

"What is it?"

"I'm not telling. It's a surprise."

"You know I don't like—"

"You will this one. Trust me." I opened the door, pulling my jacket tight against the rush of cold. "But don't worry, it's not a surprising surprise, it's a—"

The noise came from my left, a sucking rasping gurgle. I stopped walking, stopped talking.

"Tai? Are you there?"

"I thought I heard something."

"Like what?"

"Shhh!"

The night fell silent around me, only the murmur of faraway traffic and slushy rain and my own rapid breathing. I switched the phone to my left hand and went into my purse with my right. The .38 slipped free from the holster, and I pulled it out, hands shaking. I thumbed back the hammer, holding it down in low ready, finger alongside the barrel.

"Tai, get out of there."

"I—"

"Get back in your car and leave, now. I'm calling 911."

I took a step backward, my shoe catching on a piece of cardboard. The gurgling started again, this time accompanied by a moan, and I swung the gun in that direction. And lying there in the mouth of the alley, sprawled on her back, was Brenda.

I pressed the phone to my ear. "Send an ambulance!"

"What's happened?"

"It's Brenda, she's hurt!"

I knelt beside her, gun in one hand, phone in the other. A pool of blood clotted around her head, but I could hear her talking, muttering, sucking in wet breaths. Her cell phone lay beside her, crushed, as if someone had stepped on it. I looked around, convinced I was about to be shot or clobbered or stabbed, but there was only pavement and snow and night. I put the phone down and put my hand against Brenda's ice-cold cheek.

Her eyes flew open. "No!"

"It's okay, Brenda, it's me. Tai. What happened?"

"They…they…"

"Who, Brenda? Who did this?"

Her eyes rolled back in their sockets, and she convulsed. I saw the spreading blood, more than I'd thought at first, a thick wet stain. My brain supplied the details—bullet wound, center mass—and I shook my head to clear it, shoving down the nausea and thickening shock. The gun in my hand felt heavy and useless, but I didn't know what to do with it.

"Brenda?" I moved my hand to her shoulder. "Are they still here?"

She shook her head back and forth. "Gone, gone, gone." And then she choked and arched her back. I could hear Trey on the phone, Brenda moaning, my own breathing, everything so slow, so stark.

I lay the gun on the pavement beside me, pushed 911 on the phone. Then I pulled off my jacket and pressed it against the wound, murmuring the best words I could, telling her to hold on. And I stayed on my knees, shivering in the bitter cold, until I heard voices and sirens, saw the red strobing lights of the ambulance, felt strong hands pulling me back.

And then I slumped against the wall, pulled my knees to my chest, and waited for Trey.

Chapter Thirty-seven

They put me in the backseat of a patrol car, the perp seat. No handcuffs at least. The EMTs were long gone, having hustled Brenda onto a gurney and into an ambulance, an oxygen mask obscuring her features. Only crime scene commotion remained—blue lights, murmured conversations, the chirp and hiccup of police radios.

Trey was deep in an interview with the uniformed officer who'd reached me first. From my viewpoint, it was hard to tell who was interviewing whom. I knew his goal was as clear and specific as a bull's-eye—find and take down the bad guy—and his frustration at being unable to do so was showing. Any second now, the pacing would start, the restless relentless energy that he couldn't dissipate, could only channel. But there was no channel for him now.

I took another swig of coffee. Two hours ago, he'd been a different man—surrender sharpening to demand then softening again to tenderness. Now he was a laser, an arrow unloosed. Once he'd determined that I was indeed alive and unharmed, he'd left me in the custody of one of Kennesaw's finest and unleashed the protocol on the rest of the team.

Detective Perez joined me. She had her own cup of coffee now that she'd cleared what was officially a crime scene. "EMTs trash everything. Good for Ms. Lovejoy-Burlington, but a major pile of suck for me."

I huddled deeper in the borrowed jacket. "Is she going to be okay?"

"I don't know. Not my field." Perez nodded Trey's way. "Your boyfriend is being somewhat…overintense right now."

"Perseveration." I tapped my right temple. "Artifact of his brain rearrangement."

"Ah." Perez stuck her coffee on top of the car and pulled out a piece of yellow paper, covered with Trey's neat angular handwriting. "He is hammering home a good point, though, about the security system. He says the same thing you did, that it malfunctioned. Someone switched off your electricity at the fuse box, then shot out your back camera—"

"From the alley. Where it's dark and there's a blind spot, vulnerabilities even the most inexperienced perp could notice."

"Correct. So no video of our suspect in action. Regardless, there should have been an alarm because…" She read from the paper. "There was a redundant wireless system, with battery backup, that also malfunctioned, and your boyfriend says the only way this could have happened was if it were disabled too. But it's not disabled, he says. Working fine, he says." She looked up from the paper. "Sure seems convenient, doesn't it? Blind spots? Busted cameras? Mysterious malfunctions that kept the police from responding?"

A curl of ice-laced wind nipped at my ankles, and I pulled my legs under me. "No, it's the opposite of convenient, because video footage would prove that things happened exactly the way I say they did."

"Unless it would prove otherwise."

I put my coffee down on the floorboard. "Didn't you get Trey's statement? Where he corroborated my version of events down to the last detail?"

"I did." She flipped backward through her notes, tilting her head as if in deep thought. "I also took down where he said that you and Brenda had been arguing for several weeks now about the back parking space, and that this very afternoon you threatened her with bodily harm if she touched your car."

I rubbed the bridge of my nose with my fingers, but the headache came anyway. "Yes, I said that, and yes, we had been arguing. It's no secret. But even if it were a secret, Trey would have told you. You can ask him anything, and the answer will fall right out of his mouth most of the time. That frontal lobe damage again. But that also means he's telling you the truth about what happened tonight—"

"What you told him happened tonight."

"What he himself heard happening on the phone," I corrected. "The man's brain is a justice machine. There's no room for mercy in it. If I were guilty, he'd hand me over on a silver platter. He'd be upset about it—maybe even devastated—but he'd do it."

Trey now had his hands on his hips. He took two steps to the left, then two to the right. I kept one eye on him as I continued with Perez.

"Look," I said, "I know you have to give me a hard time. That's your job. But you know I didn't do it. The GSR test came back clean—I haven't fired a gun."

She shook her head. "Easy to fool that test. Wash off the residue with soap and water. You have those, I'm sure."

"Except that you've got my gun. So you know that it hasn't been fired recently, and I know that it's not going to match any ballistics test you run."

"You've got an entire shop full of weapons to choose from."

"None of which have been fired tonight. Go ahead. Check. You can look in my scrupulous log book for a list of every firearm in the place."

She didn't say anything, and I wondered if they were already doing that very thing, checking out all the weapons in the shop, sniffing for gunpowder, shining flashlights down into the barrels.

"What was Brenda doing out back at night?"

"My best guess? She was probably writing a nasty note to somebody parked there. She's done it dozens of times, and not just to me."

Perez pointed toward the shattered camera. "She'd come over here at night? By herself? After hearing a gun go off?"

"She's done it before, on Robert E. Lee's birthday. Ask Raymond Junior if you don't believe me." Then I remembered. "Have you checked her cell phone records?"

"For what?"

"To see if she was calling a tow truck. That's what she'd threatened to do. And I saw her phone lying next to her, smashed like somebody stepped on it."

Perez looked interested. She could see it as clearly as I could. Brenda charging over, calling the tow truck. Being surprised by someone who wasn't me, who wasn't one of my friends. Someone murderous.

But Perez wasn't bending. "Maybe you were the one she was calling to have towed?"

"I wasn't. But it doesn't matter. Because you know as well as I do that if I'd been the one to shoot her, I wouldn't have wasted my time trying to save her. I would have let her bleed out on that pavement."

Perez shrugged slightly, kept her face blank.

"Come on, you know I didn't do it. In your gut, where it counts. So stop treating me like a suspect and start treating me like what I am—an eyewitness, your very best hope for catching a very bad person."

She rolled her tongue behind her teeth. "So let's say you didn't shoot her."

"I did not."

"And she didn't shoot herself."

"She did not."

"Then who did?"

"Now that is the question."

Perez slipped the yellow paper back into her jacket and retrieved her coffee. "Because I could do the usual detective thing and start trying to figure out who wanted her dead. Besides you, of course."

I scowled. "I did not—"

"And I will. Due diligence and all that. But I'm thinking whoever shot her didn't come here to shoot her. I'm thinking they came here to shoot you. So now the question becomes, who wants *you* dead?"

I gave a mirthless laugh. "You're gonna need a bigger notebook, Detective."

"I'm getting that feeling." Perez pulled out her tablet computer, and with one swipe, flared it to life. "So here's what I need, Tai—you said I could call you Tai, right? I need you to tell me everything you've done, everybody you've talked to, everything you've found, and everyone you've pissed off, starting with the day you found that skull. Lucius was a lowlife. But Brenda Lovejoy-Burlington is a citizen. I'm going to find out who did this to her, and you are going to help me do it."

Chapter Thirty-eight

At some point, the sun dragged its way into a leaden sky, but in the fluorescent-lit shop, I barely noticed. I'd fielded the usual personal calls—Eric, Rico, and Gabriella—all asking the same questions. Garrity, however, spoke for exactly fifteen seconds, just long enough to tell me that he was on the way. Thirty minutes later, he was coming through my front door.

I stayed on my knees, a half-sorted pile of tee-shirts in my lap, and smiled wearily at him. "That was fast. You must've come in the helicopter."

"Back in the Crown Vic. Sticking with the classics this morning." He plopped a flat green and white box of Krispy Kremes on the counter. "How are you holding up?"

"Well enough."

I stood, wiped the dust from my jeans, and joined him at the counter. The new suits gave him a dangerously official edge, less like the guy I drank beer and shot pool with, more like one of the impersonal authorities coming and going, opening and closing my life.

He surveyed the room. "Where's Trey?"

"Asleep on the floor behind the counter."

He leaned over to peer at Trey, who was curled up on his side, one arm around a pillow. He looked endearingly rumpled, as vulnerable and sweet as a toddler put down for a nap. Except for the nine millimeter two inches from his fingers.

Garrity managed a small smile. "How long did he last?"

"Until two-thirty this morning. Refused to go upstairs, though, as you can see."

Garrity punched the opening on a coffee cup and handed it to me. There was no smell in the world as tonic as coffee, especially not this coffee, which was heavily dosed with pure cream and sweetened with a shot of doughnut glaze. I closed my eyes at the raw pleasure of it, realizing for the first time how numbed and disconnected I was.

"What about you?" he said. "You slept at all?"

"Not yet. I just finished hosing the blood off the pavement out back." I buried my nose in the caffeinated steam. "Any news from the hospital?"

"Brenda's critical but stable—they say she'll pull through. But she hasn't gained consciousness yet."

"So no word on who shot her."

"None." Garrity threw me his cop look, as serious as a gavel coming down. "Except that they were probably aiming for you."

"So you came to lecture me?"

His expression tightened. "I came to check on you. Because, believe it or not...never mind."

I put a hand on his elbow, squeezed gently. "Sorry. Knee-jerk hostility, not directed at you. Thank you for coming. That's what I meant to say."

"Yeah, I know." Garrity scrubbed his face, raked his hands through his hair, got back to business. "Trey said there was some weirdness with the security system, probably a jammer."

"A what?"

"Wireless jammer." He measured off a space the size of a shoebox with his hands. "It's a device about yea big, blocks wireless signals from coming in or going out. They're illegal as hell, but people still use them, and Trey suspected that might be the case here since something disrupted your system last night. Also—and you didn't hear this from me—it prevented Brenda's cell phone call to the tow truck company from going through."

"I was wondering about that."

"Which makes it my department's concern. Major crimes, FCC violations, all that middle of the pie where the APD and the FBI come together."

"Trey called the FBI?"

"He called *me*," Garrity corrected. "Unofficially. He wanted me to know, that's all."

He said it so casually, one might suspect this meant nothing. But I knew better. Coming from Trey, such a phone call was as intimate as a valentine.

I heard a murmur from behind the desk, followed by a sharp inhale, and I froze. This was how it started, a shift in his respiration, words that made no sense. And then would come the tossing of the head, and sometimes the defensive strike, the instinctive blow. I held my breath, but Trey settled back into deeper slumber, and I relaxed.

Garrity did too. "How's he holding up?"

So I told the story—the dive bar and back woods, the skate shop and Stone Mountain. I left out the part where we ravished each other on the desktop, but kept right to the truth with everything else. How Trey was challenging himself, stepping out of his comfort zone. Brick by brick unbuilding the wall.

"He's doing amazingly well. Except for almost beating this guy bloody with his own musket. And some olfactory triggering." I opened the doughnut box and pulled out a chocolate-glazed. "Which reminds me…Trey mentioned a drug bust, the Sinaloa cartel."

Garrity's eyebrows arched in surprise. "He told you about that?"

"He tried. Mostly he clenched and unclenched his fists, but I gather something serious happened."

"Yeah. His one official reprimand. Mine too."

And then he told me that story. One of the last busts they'd worked together before the accident—Garrity as lead detective with Major Crimes, Trey as point man on the SWAT entry team, the two units coming together to arrest a heavily barricaded drug lord.

Garrity reached for a doughnut. "They ran a dog-fighting ring out back, and it was one of the ugliest, sickest things I've ever seen in my life. Trey snapped. Grabbed the main suspect, dragged him upstairs to the third-story balcony, and for three minutes there…" Garrity blew out a breath. "But then he unsnapped. And we each got two weeks' suspension—him for doing it, me for letting it happen—but I don't regret it. I enjoyed every second of watching him dangle that son of a bitch fifty feet off the ground."

I whistled. "Damn."

"Damn indeed." Garrity eyed me suspiciously. "Are you *sure*—"

"I'm sure. He's kept the gun in the holster and his hands to himself."

"That's a good sign. I guess we'll know for sure tomorrow."

"What's to–oh, crap!" I pressed a hand to my forehead. "Tomorrow's the ninth! Shit, Garrity, what do I do?"

Garrity shrugged. "I haven't got a clue. We seem to be dealing with a new Seaver here." And then he smiled, fleeting and crooked. "Let's try not to break this one, okay?"

Chapter Thirty-nine

Trey slept. I got a broom. In between sweeping, I looked up "how to get blood stains out of polyester" on the computer and checked the news for updates on Brenda. I also double-checked the A&D book—grateful for the color-coded and cross-indexed ease of it—but not a single firearm was missing.

My latest perp had come prepared for murder.

I occasionally peered over the counter to make sure Trey was still sleeping. What would I say to him come tomorrow? Hallmark didn't exactly make cards for such occasions. Happy three years since you almost died? Sorry about the brain rearrangement and having to resign your true calling, but congrats on your unique coping strategy?

The ringing of my phone jolted me back to reality, and I snatched it up before it could wake Trey. It was a number I didn't recognize. "Hello?"

"You are such a liar!"

I bristled. "Excuse me, I—"

"You said you wouldn't tell them. You said you'd keep it to yourself."

I sighed. Chelsea Amberdecker. I'd been expecting this comeuppance ever since she'd upchucked in front of me.

"I didn't breathe a word about the pregnancy, I swear. But the police wanted a detailed list of where I'd been and who I'd talked to and—"

"They came to Jeremy's work! Now everybody's looking at me like I had something to do with that dead guy in the woods!"

"That wasn't—"

"Shut up! I can't even go outside without somebody trying to take my picture. Jeremy is furious!"

I didn't say anything. There was nothing to say. I suspected she was the first of many calls I'd get that day. I'd laid the whole mess in Detective Perez's lap—every conversation, every suspicion, every oddball piece of evidence. I figured if Trey could stick a toe in the gray zone, I could buckle up and play in the black-and-white for a while. But I hadn't spilled Chelsea's bun in the oven.

Her voice crackled with fury. "Jeremy says if they show up again, we'll sue. Slander. Defamation. We'll own your tacky little shop, and you, and everything—"

"Do what you gotta do, Chelsea. For what it's worth, I'm sorry. But I kept my word, so if you—"

She hung up on me. I switched the phone to vibrate and stuck it in my back pocket. Trey was still asleep, hadn't budged an inch since he'd stretched himself on the floor, utterly exhausted. Still life with pillow and nine millimeter. I watched him for almost a full minute—his face relaxed, the wrinkle between his eyes softened—then pushed up my sleeves and got back to work.

Two hours later, I had everything sorted and checked off on the inventory sheet. Every gun, knife, button, blade, canteen, and kepi hat. The next order of business was dragging Dexter's eleven boxes of memorabilia back into the storage room. I started by placing my spanking new first aid kit on the top shelf. Then I shoved in the plastic crate filled with old promotional geegaws, pushing it hard with my foot.

It kept going right through the wall.

I stood there for a minute, completely flabbergasted. I pulled the box out and crouched to examine the wall behind the shelving, expecting to find crumbling plaster. Instead, I found a piece of plywood lying flat on the floor inside the wall, and an empty space beyond it. No water-stained crumbly drywall, no inelegant fixes with duct tape. This was a neatly cut hole, disguised by a plywood rectangle that fit into it as precisely as a puzzle piece.

A hiding spot.

I fetched my flashlight and sent a beam skittering into the darkness. It caught a dusty lump in its glare. I lay on my chest and shoved my arm inside as far as it would go, gritting my teeth against the spiderwebs tangling in my eyelashes, the crunch of insect carapaces under my chest. I closed my eyes, sneezed, and stretched my fingers.

They connected with a cold bundle, gritty with dirt. Fabric, heavy-duty nylon. I dragged it toward me into room, then sat up and gave it a good look. The fluorescents revealed a dust-covered backpack, dark blue with black straps.

What in the blazes had Dexter stuck back here? And why? No wonder his inventory never added up. I opened the backpack and peered inside. It contained a dozen or so individual items, wrapped in old cotton fabric, threadbare and stained. I picked up a bundle as big as my fist and unwrapped it.

A silver locket fell into my palm. It was oval, about two inches high, and although its surface was tarnished and grubby, the intricately filigreed decoration revealed its workmanship. I slid my thumbnail between the edges and pried it open carefully. The left side was glassed, filled with mud that covered whatever had been preserved there, but the right held an engraved message:

Sophia Luckie
Not Lost But Gone Before
1802-1862.

I got a jolt of excitement. Thanks to hours spent browsing my Civil War authentication manuals, I was pretty sure I knew what I was holding—mourning jewelry, one of the more peculiar Victorian fads. I also knew that if the piece was authentic, it could be worth thousands.

I retrieved another wad of cloth from the backpack. This one was about the size of a football, wrapped in the same dingy fabric, and I unwrapped it with a reckless fervor of the relic hunter.

And then I saw what it was. And then I put it down very carefully, still half-swaddled.

"Trey?" I called.

No answer. I took a couple of deep breaths to steady myself. Then I put down the backpack—gently, very gently—and stood. I went back into the main room, directly to the sink in the corner, where I plugged in the new electric tea kettle. While it heated, I took down the box of oolong and spooned loose tea into the filter basket, which I then nestled into the glass teapot. When the water was almost boiling, I poured it over the tea, letting the leaves swish and swirl for exactly two minutes. Then I poured a mug three-quarters full of the golden-brown liquid.

I carried this behind the counter and sat cross-legged near Trey's head, moving his gun out of reach. I balanced the mug on my knee with one hand, ran my fingers through his hair with the other.

His eyes fluttered open, blinking me into focus. "Where am I?"

"At the shop. On the floor behind the counter."

"Oh. Right." He dragged himself to sitting, squinting into the gray light. "What time is it?"

"Almost ten." I handed him the tea. "Here. Drink this."

He held the mug between his hands and breathed in the steam. This was his morning ritual, a mug of hot tea between his hands. Three years ago, he'd been brought back from the dead one sense at a time, and his senses brought him back from slumber the same way.

He blew gently on the tea, regarding me over the edge of the mug. "Tai?"

"Yes?"

"Has something happened? You seem…something."

"Finish your tea first." I lay my hand on his knee and squeezed. "And maybe pop a couple of Gabriella's herbal thingies. You're gonna need all the mellowness you can muster for this."

Chapter Forty

He sat cross-legged on the linoleum floor of the storage room, as did I, the backpack between us. He had one elbow to one knee, chin in hand. The other hand held his tea, cooling now.

"Bones," he said.

"Uh huh."

"Human?"

"Looks like it." I pulled the flap of the backpack open. "Nothing else has a skull quite like homo sapiens. See for yourself."

He peered inside without touching the backpack. The skull rested on top of the other objects, still half-wrapped. But it was not an ordinary ivory skull—this skull was stained the deep rust of red clay, mottled with lighter brown blotches. Just like one might expect from bones buried for one hundred and fifty years in the striated clay of the Amberdecker back forty. Just like the ones in the program brochure from the History Center.

"Braxton Amberdecker's bones," I said.

Trey nodded. "A valid theory."

"There's one thing that doesn't make any sense, though." I held out the square of cloth that contained the locket, then opened it for him to see. "This. I didn't know it was evidence until I'd unwrapped it."

Trey peered closer. "What is it?"

"A Victorian mourning pendant."

"A what?"

"A piece of jewelry designed to commemorate a loved one's death. In this case, Sophia Luckie. Sometimes they held photographs, sometimes a lock of hair." I bit my lip. "None of the family talked about burying Braxton with a locket, or about him carrying one into battle. And it wasn't on the list of burial items that Dexter made either. And I have no idea who Sophia Luckie is."

Trey raised his eyes to mine. "I assume from your description that you touched the locket."

"Yes. Before I thought about it. I assumed it was inventory, but then I saw the skull, which I did not finish unwrapping, by the way, once I realized what it was."

To my surprise, he didn't lecture me. "They'll take your prints for exclusion. But you can't touch anything else. There could be fingerprint evidence there, and you could destroy it, especially on a porous surface like bone."

"I know."

"And such evidence could exonerate your uncle."

"Yes. Or—as you have been continuously pointing out—convict him."

"Or that." Trey's voice softened. "Which do you think it will be?"

I shook my head. "Dexter didn't do this. I know he was there the night before Amberdecker burial. But he wasn't a grave robber, or a thief, or a seller of black-market body parts. Lucius was, no doubt, and I am one hundred percent convinced this is his doing. He's the one who installed these shelves, remember? Dexter paid him seventy-five dollars. But Dexter didn't know about this."

Trey considered. Eventually he shook his head. "I don't think so either. But we still have to call the police."

"I know."

"Because someone did take those bones from Lucius and hide them here. And that person is very likely his murderer."

"I know. Just let me sit here a little while longer. At least until my head stops pounding."

Trey put his tea down and examined me. He knew headaches, every genus and species. After a minute, he unfolded himself and slid across the floor to sit behind me, his legs alongside mine, knees bent. Soon I felt his warm fingertips at my temples, firm and gentle.

I leaned back against his chest and closed my eyes. "I know why I think Dexter's innocent, but why do you?"

Trey moved his hands to the back of my neck and dug his thumbs in hard at the base of my skull. The throbbing intensified, then dulled to a diffuse ache. When he returned his fingers to my temples, the effect was narcotic, as if a floodgate of endorphins had opened into my bloodstream.

"Because you believe he's innocent," he said. "I'm learning to trust your intuition about such things."

"But Lucius couldn't have put them here. He died in that chapel. Which means there's somebody else on the loose, someone who was working with Lucius." I opened my eyes. "Everybody I've talked to has mentioned some shadowy dealer-type he met online. The big question is—if our Internet criminal took these bones from Lucius and hid them here, why hasn't said criminal come back for them?"

Trey moved his fingertips to my hairline. "I don't know. Perhaps said criminal tried to do that last night."

"But why wait until last night? Those bones have been here for over a year."

"I don't know. Perhaps whoever put them there was unable to come back and get them until last night."

I didn't let my brain go to the obvious answer, that Dexter had put them there after taking delivery from Lucius, and that he himself had died before he could find a buyer. The reburial had been in the fall, and Dexter had passed away the winter right after, only a few months later.

I shook off the suspicion. Too many questions, not enough answers, and I had work to do, so much freaking work. I uncrossed my legs and pushed myself up. "Okay, I'm ready."

"For what?"

"To go downtown."

"Technically, the authorities should come here."

"I know. But I can't watch any more official uniformed people pawing through my life, I can't—"

"Tai?" Trey's voice was gentle and unswerving. "They'll come anyway."

I knew he was right. I couldn't shake the feeling of violation, however. First the vandalizing, then the shooting, and then cops plowing through my things, through Dexter's things. I stared into the bag and shivered. At least my bones hadn't been dug up and shoved into a crawl space.

"Okay," I said. "I'll call. But I need to do something first."

I pulled my cell phone from my pocket, swiped it to get the camera started. Trey looked at me, then at the phone. He opened his mouth to object, but I held up my hand.

"I will not unwrap another thing in that bag. And I will not lay a finger on anything I've already unwrapped, I promise."

"But—"

"No buts. If I can be all good citizen and call the police, you can look the other way while I take a few innocent photographs of that locket."

Trey looked at the backpack. Then he looked at me. This was not procedure. This was as gray as gray could be. He made his decision quickly, though, nodding once as he gathered himself and stood.

"I'm going to make more tea. In the next room. It should take me exactly fifteen minutes." He fixed me with a steely blue gaze. "No more. No less."

Chapter Forty-one

When I'd told her what I'd found, Detective Perez had been unamused. "Really? Just stuck behind a piece of plywood that you'd never noticed before?"

"Just like that."

"Any other suspicious hiding places I need to know about?"

"No. You're welcome to look, if you want."

She'd wanted. She'd waved a hand, and her tech team had swarmed all over my shop like uniformed bees. The ME had arrived not long after, the same doctor from the tornado-strewn cemetery, only now he sported a tuxedo. He'd been surprisingly jovial, slipping on the blue latex gloves and heading toward the back, humming to himself. Trey had made more tea and watched the proceedings from behind the counter.

The whole time, Perez frowned and grumped and barked terse orders. She wore a beige blazer over her chunky red sweater, but she had glitter in her hair and a woodblock bracelet on one wrist that spelled out "HAPPY BIRTHDAY MOMMY." She was also smoking with resentment. I had the feeling that on this Saturday afternoon, the very last place on Earth she wanted to be was in my gun shop, yet again.

She planted herself right in front of me. "I am having a hard time with this, Ms. Randolph. It's too easy, too convenient."

"Easy? Convenient? My life is ass over teakettle trying to do this good-citizen thing, and you come in here and blah blah blah about easy and convenient? Shoving the damn box back into the dark would have been easy and convenient. But I didn't. So cut me some slack."

"You get slack when you stop finding body parts."

I humphed, but didn't argue. Perez had all the patience of a scalded cat, and I wasn't about to push her into marching me down to the station. Trey watched and listened, stirring his tea, the silver sound of a spoon going round and round. Then he stopped, cocked his head.

"You have a visitor," he said.

I heard tires on gravel, a door opening and closing, footsteps. Perez angled her body to face the door as Trey put down his mug, the better to keep his hands unencumbered.

Evie pushed open the door. Her finely cut charcoal suit was covered in a fine pelt of rain, her shoes and pantyhose spattered with mud. "Where are they?"

Perez stepped in her path. "Dr. Amberdecker—"

"This is my case, it has been from the beginning, ever since we found those bones. Why wasn't I called?"

"We have yet to definitively establish—"

"Don't pretend you don't have them. My mother heard it on the police scanner."

"This is Dr. Phillip's case."

Evie sent a scathing glance toward the back. "Why? Those bones are obviously antiquities—"

"That's the ME's decision—not yours, not mine—and he's gonna make that decision in the lab this time, not in the field."

"The first time—"

"—was an archaeological matter. This is a criminal one. Those remains are evidence in a murder investigation, a murder that occurred on your land, and they're going to the crime lab."

Evie pulled out her phone. "I'm calling the chief of police. We'll see how this shakes out with your boss breathing down your neck and reporters outside."

A voice from the back room interrupted her tirade. "No need to call anybody. Those bones aren't Braxton Amberdecker's."

The entire room turned as one to stare at Dr. Phillips, who stood politely in the doorway, blue gloves still on his hands. Perez was the first to speak.

"What are you talking about?"

"Those bones belong to a female, probably fifteen to seventeen years old based on the unfused growth plates in the arms and legs. So not your remains."

Evie marched up to him. "What about the burial goods?"

He shook his head. "I have the list, but none of those items were with these bones."

"But—"

"If we find anything, it will be returned to you. But I can tell you right now those are not the bones of a twenty-one-year-old white male. Therefore, they are not Braxton Amberdecker's. There's other stuff that will have to wait for lab verification, but that part is definite."

Evie whirled on me. "You know something about this."

I shook my head. I wasn't about to tell her about the locket. Neither was the ME, and neither was Perez. This was an ace in the hole, and they both knew it, and I had no desire to piss them off further.

Evie remained furious. "Your uncle is behind this, I know he is! I wouldn't be surprised to find several of my family's heirlooms on the shelves with price tags stuck to them!" Her face was a mask of helpless anger and thwarted power. She turned to Perez. "I want her records collected, all of them."

"Done," she said dryly. "The ATF had them delivered yesterday. And if I saw anything in them that I could use to shut this shop down, I would. But I didn't."

Trey tapped his spoon on the side of the saucer and retrieved his mug. "And you won't. Everything was in order."

He came around the counter. He kept his tone deferential, and his expression remained as placid as always. Not an ounce of aggression, but not an ounce of submission either. He was toeing a line in the sand, and everyone, including Perez, was suddenly aware of where they stood in relation to it.

As was I. I folded my arms as he moved to stand beside me.

He held his tea in both hands. "Tai has acquiesced with every official request that has come her way, whether on the local, state, or federal level. She has completed her final inspection by the ATF, opened her records, filed the appropriate paperwork, and in short, done everything required of her in terms of rules and procedures and protocol." He looked at the back room, then back at Evie. "The remains belong to the ME's office now. And the shop is closed. So it's best you return to the History Center, Dr. Amberdecker, and attend to your opening. There's nothing for you to do here."

Evie knew she couldn't win this particular battle, but she was far from abandoning the war. She turned on her heel and stomped out the front door, the bells jingling merrily behind her. Perez pulled out her phone and stepped onto the front stoop into the misting rain, her phone in hand. A private call, not on the scanner.

The ME stood next to me. I could smell cigar smoke on him, and his face bore the flush of a man who'd been enjoying a tipple or two before he'd been yanked into service.

I dropped my voice. "Are you sure those bones aren't Braxton Amberdecker's?"

He laughed. "Unless our boy Braxton had child-bearing hips, yes, I'm sure. And by childbearing, I mean postpartum. This is the skeleton of a woman who'd given birth at least once."

"You said she was fifteen?"

"Fifteen to seventeen. Young, yes, but biologically capable of carrying and delivering a child."

"Could she have died in childbirth?"

He looked doubtful. "My money's on the bullet."

"What bullet?"

"Minié ball. Found it tucked in with the spinal column, which had suspicious nicks on the C4 and C5 vertebrae. You can read it all in the final report. I should have that Monday."

"And I can read it?"

"Sure. It's public information."

"What about the locket?"

He shrugged. "None of my business, not what I was called in to investigate. It may not even belong with this body; you'd have to have the in situ archaeological report for that." He leaned forward conspiratorially. "But this girl's not a member of the Amberdecker family, I'll tell you that much. Based on the extent of ramus inversion in the mandible, I'd say she was of African ancestry."

"Wait, wait. She was black?"

The doctor looked at me like I was an idiot. "That's what I said, didn't I?"

When Detective Perez finally cleared my shop for the second time, she left one officer behind. I could see him parked on the other side of the square in his cruiser, watching. I waved. He waved back.

"So not a covert operation," I said.

Trey agreed. "No. You're supposed to know he's there."

"So I won't do anything dastardly."

"True. But I suspect she left him there for your protection as well. She'd prefer to avoid another shooting, I'm sure."

He'd brewed a fresh pot of tea. I caught the smoky scent of Lapsang souchong. Decaffeinated, yes, but packing enough lysine and amino acids to slap even the sleepiest brain to attention. And while he had the bleary, rumpled look one might expect from a man who'd been sleeping on the floor, something else about him crackled. Even with no five-mile run and no real breakfast and no thirty-fifth floor apartment to hole up in, even though he'd been trapped in the sensory overload of my gun shop for eighteen hours, his brain remained on point.

I came behind the counter and poured a half-cup of tea for myself. I'd combed the spiderwebs out of my hair, but I still smelled like the floor of a closet. "So now what?"

"That depends. What is your next goal?"

A good question. I thought I'd exonerated Dexter, but now that I'd dragged skeletons out of his closet—literally—his reputation was back in the hot seat. I'd also managed to either piss off or frighten every source I'd located, ruining any chances for follow-up. And I had an official Cobb County police officer surveilling me.

I spooned sugar into my mug. "The cops are covering the shooting and the robbery and the first skeleton and the second skeleton and the still-missing skeleton. And even though I'm probably on the suspect list—"

"Definitely on the suspect list."

"Whatever. My point is that I've exhausted the shop investigation-wise. And I've exhausted my own suspect list interview-wise. And I've exhausted my goodwill with Perez everything-wise. So I'm not sure where that leaves me goal-wise."

Trey regarded me over his mug. "May I make a suggestion?"

"Sure."

"Have you considered researching the person memorialized by the locket, Sophia Luckie? As the ME pointed out, since there is no in situ record for the bones themselves, you cannot be certain that they're connected to the locket. But you can—"

"Find Sophia Luckie first, and then use her information to find out who the bones might belong to!"

Trey nodded. His expression was cool, but his mouth held a tiny curve of satisfaction. "Yes. That will in no way interfere with the official investigation, but it might give you some contextual insight."

"Okay, so how in the world do I start?"

"I don't know." He pulled his phone from his pocket. "But I know someone who will."

Chapter Forty-two

Two hours—and two hot showers—later, Trey and I pulled up at the central branch of the Atlanta-Fulton Public Library. It had impressive Bauhaus credentials, but to me its stone and concrete facade resembled an Anglo-Saxon castle mated with an Easter Island monolith. Trey dropped me at the front entrance while he parked, leaving me with a scrap of paper as my only guide to the hamster-cage maze of staircases and hallways inside.

Ophelia Price, it read. Fifth floor. Special Collections and Genealogy.

I made my way through the beige and taupe corridors. Here the lighting was dimmed, the glossy hardwood floor as dark as tree roots. Plainly lettered signs announced the specificities—the Rare Book Room, the city directories, the microfilm and vertical files—and I clutched my paper as if it were a compass.

I found my quarry in the stacks, near the glassed-in display of Margaret Mitchell's typewriter. I cleared my throat. "Mrs. Price?"

She turned in my direction. "Yes?"

She was an African American in her late fifties, with close-cropped salt-and-pepper hair and a forest-green shirtdress that had been ironed into wrinkle-free submission. Her voice held the deep timbre of a classically trained singer—or a prison guard—and I reflexively straightened my posture.

"I was told you could help me." I shoved a photograph of the locket her way. "I need to find this person, Sophia Luckie. And all I have is the information you see there."

She accepted the photograph, gave it a brisk inspection. "You can probably find her. It won't be quick, however."

"I know, needle in a haystack."

"No, a needle in a giant stack of other needles."

"But this needle is very specific."

"So is every needle." She checked her watch. "And the library closes early today because of the snow."

"I know, but Trey said—"

"Trey? Trey Seaver?"

I nodded. She looked at me with sharper examination this time. Suddenly, she was reclassifying me, moving me to a completely different shelf in her mental library.

"He said he worked with your daughter, Keesha. With SWAT."

"He did."

She volunteered nothing else. Neither had Trey. Damn, but I wished he'd found a space at the main entrance so that he could have been standing next to me, bearing the brunt of that onyx gaze.

"Come with me," she said finally. "We'll talk in my office."

In a sea of books, her desk was a tiny island of pristine order. I explained the backstory of the locket—what we knew anyway—and she listened.

"Luckie was a common name in Atlanta," she said, "for both whites and blacks. Oakland Cemetery is full of Luckies, going back to pre-Civil War times."

"The ME said the bones are of African descent. If they belong to a descendant of Sophia Luckie, perhaps she is also?"

Ophelia regarded the locket with intense scrutiny, turning the photograph this way and that. There was a soft knock at the door as Trey eased into the room. She stared at him for two seconds, then waved him in, dropping her eyes back to the photograph. He stood behind me, not saying a word.

"And you think," she said, "based on the coloring of the bones, that they were buried somewhere close to here? In red clay soil?"

"Yes, specifically near Kennesaw Mountain. I also think—based on the intense staining—that she was buried at least a hundred years ago. Later than 1860, though, based on the locket."

"So assuming she is of African ancestry, you have your first question—was she a slave or a free person of color? That determines how you begin the search for her ancestors."

"She was carrying a very expensive locket. Wouldn't that tip the scales to the side of free?"

"She could have been a runaway slave, taking what she could from her captors to barter or sell on the Underground Railroad. Did the ME have an opinion? If she'd been a slave, her bones would have shown it. Hard labor always does."

"He didn't say. I suppose we'll have to wait for the official report for that."

She nodded, and her eyes flashed now with an enthusiasm I hadn't seen before. "There were about forty free blacks living in Atlanta during the Civil War, including the Luckie family. Solomon Luckie, a barber, died when a piece of shrapnel hit the lamppost he was standing under during the shelling."

"Is he the person Luckie Street is named after?"

"No, that was some rich white man. And the lamppost was reconstructed and relit in celebration of the premiere of *Gone with the Wind.* Such is Atlanta."

She scrutinized the photograph again, and her face softened. I knew she was imagining a young black woman, a mother, this locket either clutched in her hand or fastened around her neck. It was a fine piece, well-wrought and lovely, easy to sell for a good sum. Why had she been buried with it? Had it been as a measure of respect? Or had there been a darker motive, like the concealing of evidence?

She shared the same look of concentration that Trey did—eyes narrowed, head tilted to one side. "It's an interesting mystery, these bones, but it's best to start with what you know—the information on the locket. Because if you can find Sophia Luckie, you can find her family tree, perhaps even living descendants. And that is where the real work starts." She looked up at Trey, and I saw the first hint of a smile on her patrician features. "Good to see you again, Trey."

He inclined his head. "You too, Mrs. Price."

"Thank you." She nodded crisply. "Now fetch a chair. This is going to take a while."

◇◇◇

Five minutes later, I was digitally overwhelmed. There were websites for finding a particular grave, searchable by name or date or claim to fame. Sites that indexed birth and death certificates, obituaries, veterans' records. Census and voter lists, land deeds and criminal records. Trey hung out at my shoulder. Even he seemed info-avalanched.

I shook my head. "You're weren't kidding about the stack of needles, were you?"

Olivia Price kept typing. "African American genealogy work is difficult. Prior to 1870, slaves weren't listed on the census population schedules, nor were their names typically recorded in birth, marriage, and death records, the usual ways that genealogists track family lines. Tracing a slave's family tree means refocusing the search on the slaveholder instead. There are several ways to do that—ship manifests, property records, wills, emancipation papers."

Trey moved closer to the computer. "But what if she were free?"

"The Freedman's Bureau records will help, but that wasn't founded until 1865. Luckily for you, amateur genealogists have done a lot of the back work. They know where the blanks are. They're looking for ways to fill in those blanks."

She showed us. As it turned out, there were thousands of people whose main goal in life was putting together their family tree. Some did it for their own familial connection. Others did it for religious reasons, like The Church of Jesus Christ of Latter-day Saints. But whatever brought people together to comb through the past, two traits united the successful ones—they were meticulous and patient.

Exactly what I wasn't.

"So if I can find people who already have this particular Sophia Luckie in their family tree, they can help me figure out who our nameless young woman might be?"

"They can. But as I told you, this is not an overnight process, it's…well, well, well."

"What?"

"You're in luck." She pointed to the screen. "I found what might be Sophia Luckie's grave."

I rolled closer to the screen. Sure enough, there was a burial plot listing for one Sophia Luckie in a cemetery in Wilmington, North Carolina—same name, same dates. I couldn't help myself—I reached out a finger and touched the screen, as if the past really were that close.

Trey got right to the heart of the matter. "What can you do with that information?"

Mrs. Price pulled out a pen and notepad. "Now that I have a geographical base—a city and state—I can go to the genealogy sites and find any family trees associated with this Sophia Luckie. Some of those are public access, some not. Regardless, there's usually contact information for whoever maintains the records."

Trey seemed satisfied. "Excellent."

Of course he was pleased—things were proceeding methodically, procedurally, according to plan. I, however, was feeling less and less trusting of any system. I hadn't wanted to give the bones over to crime scene techs. I knew why the forensics team needed to have her in their cold sterile clutches. Why she needed her measurements calibrated, her bones splayed and photographed under too-bright lights. First came justice, then rest. But it still felt like a betrayal.

Ophelia Price tapped my business card. "Is this contact information okay to share?"

"Share away."

"I can't promise anything."

"I know. But thanks for trying. I can't stand the thought of her being alone, you know?"

For a second, I saw a flash of tenderness again, like when she'd glimpsed Trey coming into her office. She hid a lot of heart beneath her brusque exterior, I decided, even if she was skilled at covering it.

She checked her watch and stood. So did I, and Trey, the three of us standing together in her small, windowless office. Outside the first of the snow was coming, but inside, the world was as tidy and contained as a shadow box.

Trey spoke first. "I need to get the car. Very good to see you again, Mrs. Price. Send Kee my regards."

She flashed a smile his way, lovely and abrupt. "You too, Trey. I'll tell her."

He started to leave, turned back. "Five minutes," he said to me, tapping his watch, then disappearing into the stacks. I started to follow, but the librarian interrupted me.

"Miss Randolph?"

I turned back. "Yes?"

She clasped her hands in front of her, precise and efficient, yet there was something vulnerable in the gesture, almost prayerful. "How is he doing, if I may ask?"

"Good. It's challenging sometimes, but he's up to it."

"Of course. I know tomorrow's the ninth, and he doesn't like being disturbed then, but I always think of him. So does Kee." Her face softened. "Special Ops isn't easy for a woman, especially not a woman of color. But Trey was good to her. She doesn't talk about the job much, but she talks about him. She says he was the finest partner she could have asked for."

I smiled. "He still is."

Chapter Forty-three

Trey drove us out of Downtown, taking the Connector up through the heart of the city. The first snow sifted down, as graceful as a ballet, as sweet as marshmallows. Only flurries for the next twenty-four hours, said the forecasters, the soft edge of the advancing high-pressure front.

Trey didn't trust the weather report, however. He kept a baleful eye on the clouds like a particularly grumpy Chicken Little, waiting for the whole sky to fall in pieces. But for now, the city was calm, the traffic extraordinarily light, even for a Sunday afternoon. He could have let the Ferrari slip the traces a bit, if he'd wanted. But he never wanted. Only in matters of life or death did he open the engine full throttle.

"Did you find what you needed?" he said.

"I did. Mrs. Price was very helpful."

He flipped the heater up a notch and didn't reply. He was back to that robotic passivity again—eyes distant, mouth set in a straight line. My brother described it as "flat affect," a psychological term, but I knew it could change in a split second.

"You were partners with her daughter? In SWAT?"

"I was."

"Keesha?"

He nodded again. I'd learned enough about the structure of police departments to know that only one specialized unit in that already specialized unit required partnering with another operator.

"She was a sniper too," I said.

"Kee preferred the term 'sharpshooter.'"

"And you?"

"I had no preference."

He'd been perfect for the job—smart enough to work the algorithms, steady enough to hit the bull's-eye at a thousand yards—but he'd also felt the dangerous lure of being judge, jury, and executioner with a single pull of the trigger. So he'd turned in his resignation. And then the accident happened, and he lost the rest of his life in one wrenching, bloody night.

He adjusted the wipers. "The traffic report says 400 is clear, so we should get home with no problems."

Changing the subject. I let him. It was the day before February ninth. Not a time to be pulling scabs off still-healing emotional wounds.

"Trey?"

"Yes?"

"I don't have any proof, and I won't until we hear from Sophia Luckie's family, but I don't think it's a coincidence that her bones were in Dexter's shop. I think Lucius hid them there. After he found them on Amberdecker property."

Trey kept his eyes on the instrument panel. "Because of the staining."

"Yes. And I know—Georgia's full of red clay—but that particular mottled pattern matches Braxton Amberdecker's bones perfectly. Lucius had access to both Amberdecker land and Dexter's shop."

"Your uncle had access to both as well. But for that matter, Lucius could have found them on park lands. There are striated red clay deposits there as well. It's a circumstantial case."

He had a point. A logical rational point. Which didn't matter one iota. I had a hunch, as if a ghost were whispering in my ear.

"There's something missing in the story," I said. "I don't know what it is, not yet. These bones connect to the Amberdeckers, though, I'm certain of it. And since we're going to be stuck inside a while…wait a second, why are you in the exit lane for 400?"

He looked at me like I was an idiot. "Because we're going to my place. You always stay at my place on Saturday nights."

"Yes, but that was before Brenda got shot, and the bones got found—"

"Which is even more reason to stay at my place."

"Which is even more reason to stay at the shop. To protect it."

He returned his attention to the road. He couldn't articulate his reasoning, but I'd seen it before. I'd get into trouble, he'd go into crusading knight-at-arms mode, then when the situation cooled off, he'd retreat into the vacuum of his black-and-white apartment.

I swiveled in the seat to face him. "My place is as secure as yours. There's a Kennesaw cop out front, a safe room in the back, and a fully functional state-of-the-art security system throughout."

"There hasn't been a shooting at my place."

"But my research is at the shop! I can't—"

"You can get it in the morning. I'll drive you back."

"But—"

"Tai." He adjusted his grip on the steering wheel, jaw tight. "Please."

I sighed. The snow blew in frenzies and twirls. Already patches of white covered the medians, as flimsy as a negligee. The traffic would steamroll right over it; the airport would spasm for a few hours and then snowplow it into dirty humps. Life would go on. But it was the eighth of February. And Trey had said please.

"Fine," I said. "We'll stay at your place—"

"Thank you."

"But we have to go back to the shop first. I need my car, and my research."

"But the snow—"

"—is barely on the ground." I rested my hand on his shoulder, feeling the muscle tighten and then relax. "Besides, this way you can check the security system one more time."

"Tai—"

"Please."

He thought about it, then flipped the turn signal to move out of the exit lane. "Fine. But be quick about it."

Chapter Forty-four

I awoke the next morning to the pounding of footfalls—rhythmic, steady, muted by the mechanical hum of the treadmill. Trey, back to his routine. He ran with the precise cadence of the long distance runner—head up, spine straight, arms loose. He ran without music plugged in his ears or heart monitors strapped to his wrist, ran with only the rhythms of his breath and body as accompaniment.

I rolled over, dragging the ridiculously plump comforter tighter around me. I'd been so exhausted the night before that I'd crawled into bed in my underwear, leaving a trail of discarded clothes behind me. Now I squinted into winter-crisp light, even whiter than the walls or the curtains, and I knew that thirty-five stories below me, the whole of Atlanta lay in snow-swaddled brilliance.

I burrowed back under the goose down and tried to go back to sleep. My phone had other ideas. I almost ignored it, but one peek at the display, and I changed my mind.

I grappled it off the nightstand and pulled it under the covers with me. "Hey there, Garrity."

"Why the hell is there a guy named Fishbone throwing your name around like it was some get-out-of-jail-free card?"

I sat up quickly. "Fishbone? Seriously?"

"Perez pulled him in. He says you told him to ask for me if that happened."

"Yeah. I kinda did."

Garrity muttered a string of detailed expletives, weaving them into a blinding tapestry of vulgarity. Trey stopped the treadmill and stood, hands on hips, breathing hard.

"I am not your one-stop law enforcement shop, Tai Randolph, I can't…" He paused to collect himself again. "Do you know how much sleep I'm going to get tonight? None. This city is going to turn into crazy town about ten minutes past sunset, when the freaking polar vortex swoops in."

"The what?"

"Check the weather. Things have changed. Now I've got this knucklehead yammering—"

"What's he saying?"

"I can't tell you that."

"Then why'd you call me?"

Garrity started explaining as Trey hopped off the treadmill. He walked over beside the bed, wiping his forehead and chest with a towel, and I caught the smell of the herbal liniment that Gabriella made for him, menthol and rosemary. He waved a hand at the phone, one eyebrow raised. I mouthed *Garrity* at him.

Garrity kept talking. "—and I'd really like Trey's take on it, so as soon as you see him, send him in."

"His take on what?"

An exasperated sigh. "The laundry detergent thefts. From four years ago. Are you even listening?"

"Did you say—"

"Trey will remember. Went nowhere then, but I'm seeing something very interesting this morning, and I'd like to run over the old Sinaloa cartel report with him. When he's up to it."

"He's standing right here. Why don't you ask him yourself?"

"He is?"

"He just got off the treadmill."

"You're at his place?"

"Why wouldn't I be?"

"Because it's the ninth. Remember?"

And then I did. The anniversary. The day that Trey made a fortress of his life, surrounded himself with silence and solitude. And yet there he was, breathing hard and a little puzzled. And there I was, half-dressed and sticky-eyed from sleep. Just another Sunday morning.

I shoved the phone in Trey's direction. "Garrity wants to talk to you."

"About what?"

"Your old Sinaloa case."

Trey put the phone to his ear. He listened. Eventually I saw him pause, cock his head in perplexed curiosity, then go to his desk to get paper and pencil, the treadmill abandoned.

I stayed under the sheets. Laundry detergent—the same item Cat had been arrested for shoplifting, the ridiculous "five finger" dare she'd taken at Lucius' request. And then it hit me, like it had hit me in the skate shop even if I hadn't been able to identify it then, that fake lemony smell that had permeated the place.

Laundry detergent.

I heard Trey talking in the living room, the slide of folders, the tapping of keystrokes. I stretched out under the sheets. I had to get up and get dressed eventually, something warm and layered for heading outside into a white morning as sharp as a scimitar.

No rest for the wicked, they said. Not even on a snow day with a polar vortex bearing down.

Ten minutes later, Trey brought my phone back to me. I moved my legs to make room for him. "Laundry detergent theft, huh?"

Trey sat on the edge of the bed. "Hundreds of bottles at a time, premium brands. Coordinated crews timed for shift changes. They hit across the spectrum target-wise. Small family shops, corner grocery stores, big box retailers, some outlets reporting ten to twenty thousand dollars in losses per month. We found a stockpile of it at the Sinaloa bust I was telling you about."

"Just to be clear, we're talking about the stuff you pour in washing machines?"

"Correct. Which is why it made no sense. Until now, apparently."

"Until Fishbone."

Trey shook his head. "Garrity didn't say—"

"He didn't need to. I smelled it myself. The morning we chased Fishbone and his skateboard into the shop."

"You chased Fishbone. I waited outside."

"Right. Which is why you didn't...except that you did." I grabbed his wrist. "Omigod, Trey! That's what triggered you at the skate shop. Not the smell of marijuana alone, like in the park. The smell of marijuana plus laundry detergent! Like the Sinaloa bust!"

Trey's index finger started tap-tapping on his thigh. "That makes sense."

"And another thing—remember Cat the bartender? Richard kicked her out of the house for shoplifting. Guess what Lucius told her to steal?"

Trey narrowed his eyes. "Laundry detergent."

"Bingo, boyfriend. Which means this thing with Fishbone is connecting some major dots in a major way down at the FBI. And you've been invited to play along."

By the time Trey got out of the shower, I was dressed too—jeans, sweatshirt, running shoes. I had my tote bag fully packed, and a travel mug full of coffee. I'd made tea for him, some of the Lapsang souchong from the shop, which I had waiting on the counter.

He met me in the kitchen wearing his best suit—the Armani made-to-measure, the closest thing to a dress uniform he had. I held out my hand, and he dropped his cuff links into my palm. He was a live wire, barely contained where he stood, and I saw the first hint of the anxious wrinkle between his eyes.

I reached for his wrist. "Stop worrying."

"The traffic—"

"Everything's open from 400 to the Connector."

"But the snow—"

"Barely an inch. All the main roads are clear. No ice. I checked."

I slipped the cuff links into place on his right wrist, then his left. He kept both hands extended, checking to make sure everything lined up properly—shirt sleeves a half-inch below the suit cuff, jacket concealing the holster.

"That will change when the rain starts," he said.

"I know, I saw the new predictions. That's why I'm getting my stuff done before the sun sets."

"What stuff?"

I kept my expression neutral. "Shop stuff."

"The shop is secure. I checked two minutes ago."

He pulled his phone from his pocket and with a quick swipe revealed the four-plex video screen, one quadrant for each of the three camera feeds—the front entrance, the back lot, and the deer-eye view of the main room. He turned it around so that I could see.

I moved behind him and reached for the loose ends of his tie. "I see. But I need to put in a final bit of cold proofing before I settle in here for the night."

He relaxed. "Oh. That's a good plan."

I brought the wide end of the tie over the narrow end, then back over to make the knot. Over and through, tuck and neaten. I was finally getting the hang of tying ties—Windsors, double Windsors, half Windsors—and I was finally getting the hang of lying to Trey. It simply required moving where he couldn't see my face. Not that the lie was a huge one. It was a tiny prevarication, more along the line of Technically True But Deliberately Evasive. It would have set off his alarm bells, however, and he had other things to focus on this morning.

I turned him around and examined the final result. As usual, he was an immaculate portrait of male power and potency, at least on the surface. His inside was a stew of insecurity and confusion, but his outside? Dazzling as a diamond.

I smoothed his lapels, the wool satin-soft beneath my fingers. "Trey?"

"Yes?"

"This meeting with Garrity? It's not a test."

He looked puzzled. "I know."

I placed one hand just below his rib cage. "Then why have you stopped breathing into your diaphragm?"

He paused, then put his hand on top of mine. When he inhaled, I felt the movement of air flowing into the tight places, from his lungs into his belly, a breath that went all the way in this time.

I stood on tiptoe and kissed him. "Much better. Now go kick ass."

Chapter Forty-five

Every grocery store I passed on the way to Kennesaw had a packed parking lot. The city gleamed Christmas card pretty, but the sky was a sheet of threatening gray. I checked the time—six hours until sunset, when the sun would dip below the horizon and the sky would unload several metric tons of ice and sleet. I shivered at the thought and vowed to be safely tucked in back at Trey's apartment, where the heating stayed on and the water stayed warm.

I parked in the lot of the Best Buy, avoiding two kids hurling snowballs at each other while their harried father tried to herd them into a mini-van. Inside the store was hardly more civilized, with shoppers snatching generators and batteries, crowding the cash registers. I spotted Kenny at the help desk, looking harried in his blue uniform shirt, and pushed my way toward him.

I broke to the front of the line. "You and I need to talk. Now."

Kenny looked startled. "What? Why?"

"Fishbone's at the police station, spilling his guts. The cops won't tell me what he's saying." I leaned forward. "But I bet you can."

He shook his head. "I don't know anything, Miss Tai, I—"

"I've been thinking about this mystery long and hard, Kenny. It's got holes. I'm betting you can fill them because I'm betting you know something you're not telling. And either you tell me what it is right now, or I take my suspicions to the cops. Your choice." I rapped the counter with my knuckles. "You've got ten minutes to decide. I'll be in the red Camaro out front."

◇◇◇

Seven minutes later, he climbed into the front seat of my car, shaking his head. "I don't know what you think—"

"I think you've been lying to me. Everybody can talk about the damn Russian mafia all they want, but you're the key to all this, aren't you?"

"No, ma'am!"

"Cut the 'ma'am' crap. Lucius started out trading credit card numbers for drugs, then relics, cutting Fishbone out of the deals. He worked alone then, but eventually he got a partner. You."

Kenny shook his head frantically. "It wasn't me!"

"Bullshit. The Amberdecker bones weren't in the coffin, Kenny—Lucius' were—which means somebody else took them off Lucius' hands. The same somebody who hid a completely different set in Uncle Dexter's walls." I held up the photograph of the re-burial. "And there you are, Kenny, front and center."

"But I didn't, I swear!" He shoved his glasses up with one hand, practically hyperventilating. "I don't know anything about those bones!"

"Then who does? "

"I can't—"

"You'd better. Unless you want to explain this to the police."

Kenny let his head fall backward onto the seat and closed his eyes. "I didn't take the bones. But I know who might have."

"Who?"

"He uses the screen name White Wolf. He's one of the traders in the Rabbit Hole."

"The what?"

"It's a Darknet forum. White Wolf buys and sell things you can't buy or sell other places."

"Things like guns and drugs and illegally procured relics?"

Kenny nodded. "When Silk Road went down, Lucius asked me to find him a new connection. Someone flexible, willing to work trades. So I vouched for him to White Wolf."

"Why?"

"Because Lucius paid me to do it. And I needed the money."

Kenny looked miserable to be admitting this. No doubt he fancied himself a true hacker, motived by principles, not profit. But we all had our needy places.

I cranked the engine. "Fasten up, Kenny."

"Why?"

"Because we're going to my place. And then you're taking me down the Rabbit Hole to meet this White Wolf."

"But—"

"No buts. I'm done with buts. I am getting to the bottom of this once and for all."

He reached for the seatbelt. "Yes, ma'am."

Fifteen minutes after we arrived at the shop, he had the Tor download completed and the Darknet up. He logged into an online forum—headed by a stylized Black Ops bunny graphic with a leery evil grin—then typed a username into the search box. What he pulled up looked like an online shopping page, but the classification system made it clear that this Wonderland was even darker than the one Alice stumbled into. Categories like Food and Gardening were listed next to Pharmaceuticals and Firearms.

"Gun runners," I said.

Kenny looked offended. "Not all of them. Some are patriots."

"Patriots avoiding background checks and ATF restrictions, which means criminals."

"Not always. People come here because they can participate in a commerce system outside of government control."

"And yet illegal goods seem to be the main draw."

I clicked on the category for pharmaceuticals—it featured twenty-seven subcategories, including Opioids, Psychedelics, and Cannabis—but nothing for skeletons. Kenny was ahead of me.

"Click Etcetera," he said.

I did. Skulls. Human hair. Mummified hands. Each of them detailed with a precise description. One skull was so small it would have fit in the palm of my hand, and I had to fight the urge to look away from the screen.

"Lucius traded with White Wolf through this site?"

He nodded.

"How does that work?"

"The site uses bitcoin, a cryptocurrency. You click this box and a message goes to the contact with your username, and they send you a message back if they're interested in buying. If so, the buyer sends a bitcoin payment to your account, and the seller ships the merchandise."

I wasn't sure I'd heard him right. "Like through the post office?"

"That's the most dangerous part. The rest of the transaction is untraceable."

"So where did Lucius have his drugs shipped?"

"The skate shop mostly. Until Fishbone got mad and wouldn't let him anymore."

I'd known the answer before the words got out of his mouth. I was half-listening anyway, more fascinated with the screen. It really was a psychedelic version of Amazon. There was even a little online shopping cart. Sellers with names like Elvish226, Jackleg, and...

"There's our buddy White Wolf." I peered closer. "Omigod, he has an approval rating."

"Ninety-six percent. He got dinged for sloppy packaging once. You can see that in the buyer's remarks. Otherwise he's very reliable."

I couldn't quite believe what I was seeing. Back in Savannah, if you wanted illegal pharmaceuticals, you had to find some guy living in his mother's basement or brave the hopped-up crazies over on the Westside. This was sanitized and simple and downright pleasant. Except that it was also the frontier, the Wild West, the Shadow Net. No rules, no tracing, no regulation. And I had one of its denizens a click away from me.

I pointed to an icon of the Confederate Battle Flag. "So is that you? Rebel Yell?"

Kenny nodded. "That shows I'm live right now. Lucius used the name Dirty South."

I pointed to another icon, this one of a slavering snow-colored wolf, fangs bared, a red tongue in a black maw. "And that's White Wolf? Who is also live right now?"

Another nod from Kenny. He was mightily unhappy to be sitting there with me, but he was cooperating. I scooted closer to the screen.

"Send him a message. Tell him you're inquiring about a piece of merchandise."

Kenny typed out my words. They sat there on the page, dangling like a worm on the hook. I had only one real question for this White Wolf—his very name gave me the creeps, conjuring up images of hooded men and burning crosses—but I wasn't sure how to ask it.

And then a reply appeared. From White Wolf. *What piece of merchandise?*

Kenny stared at it. "What do you want me to do now?"

"Scoot over." I moved the keyboard in front of me and typed, *I have information about a recent sale. One with complications attached.*

The cursor blinked, and then White Wolf's reply appeared. *Complications for whom?*

Damn, I thought, he used "whom" correctly. *Complications for both of us,* I typed.

I'm listening.

I typed quickly. *Where are the Amberdecker bones?*

I don't know.

Dirty South delivered them to you.

No, he made the arrangements, but he did not deliver the merchandise. I've heard he ended up in a coffin not his own.

Damn again. So much for the anonymity of the Darknet—White Wolf knew that Lucius and Dirty South were the same person. I had no leverage, no bartering chip. It suddenly occurred to me that I might be tipping this bad guy's hand in a way I hadn't foreseen. Too late, I told myself. The bait had been taken. Time to reel the fish in and pray it wasn't a shark.

I pulled the bourbon out of the drawer and slopped a fair amount into my empty coffee mug. I typed quickly. *The police are asking questions.*

Not of me.

But they will. Eventually.

Is that a threat?

Kenny looked like he wanted to throw up. I swatted him on the knee and kept typing.

No, I typed. *I have no way of threatening you. But if they keep asking questions, they will find your clients, and if your clients are inconvenienced, then you will be too. I want them to stop asking questions, but I need to know something to make that happen.*

The cursor blinked. Finally words started streaming again. *Tell me what you need to know and I will decide.*

I took a minute to drain the last of the bourbon. *Dirty South had a partner. Was it you?*

No.

Was it the old man at Dexter's Guns and More?

How would I know such a thing? The transactions here in the Hole are anonymous.

I hesitated, then typed. *And yet...*

Several seconds passed. *The old man was not involved in the trade. As for the killing, I do not know. I do know that I did not kill Dirty South, nor did I have him killed. Whoever did so cost me a valuable piece of merchandise. Dirty South worked alone. The location of the Amberdecker merchandise died with him.* The cursor blinked. *Unless you have the merchandise he failed to deliver?*

No.

What about the other items he promised? The grouping that came with the locket?"

I thought of the bones lying in a stainless steel bed and got a shiver. So Lucius had been trying to sell them, which meant he was most likely the one who'd stuck them in the wall, just like I'd suspected. Not that White Wolf needed to know this.

25

I know nothing about them, I typed.

That is unfortunate. Should you ever have those items, or similar ones, to offer, please contact me. I am always open to new opportunities. You know how to find me. The cursor blinked. *Just as I know how to find you.*

The cursor stopped blinking, and the wolf icon vanished. White Wolf was no longer live. I looked at Kenny, who was as gray as the sky outside. I pushed my glass of bourbon his way. He took a giant swallow, coughed and hacked.

He wiped his mouth with the back of his sleeve. "Lord have mercy, Miss Tai. What have you done?"

I gave Kenny some hot chocolate and drove him home. The wind was kicking up, fiercer now, dragging the first clouds behind it. That meant the rain was coming. Slow and steady at first, the meteorologists warned, turning to sleet and ice the second night fell. I dropped Kenny off at his apartment complex, waiting until the front door closed behind him before I drove back to the shop.

So Lucius was the sole contact according to White Wolf. Not Dexter. Unfortunately, even White Wolf didn't know who killed Lucius, or where the Amberdecker bones went. But he had known about the other bones, the young woman's bones. And I'd lied to him about them.

Damn, did I want a cigarette.

When I got back to the shop, I opened the faucet to a dribble and duct-taped newspaper a half-inch thick around the exposed spigot in the back lot. Double-checked the security system, because I knew Trey would ask. And then I sat down at the computer, at the now empty screen. He'd ask about this too, how I'd spent my morning. And if I left out chatting online with a black market businessman, the omission would shine in my face like a bare bulb.

My phone rang. Trey. I breathed a silent bit of gratitude that he couldn't read people over the phone.

I put it to my ear. "Hey, I was about to—"

"Stay there. I'm on my way."

"Why?"

"I have sandbags for your car. And chains of some kind. Garrity sent them. Have you finished at the shop?"

"I have, but—"

"Good. I'll see you in seven…No, eight minutes. We'll drive in together. But I have to tell you something first."

"What?"

"I'll tell you when I get there. It's very…something. I'll have to show you."

And then he hung up. I sat back in my chair, watching a clump of dirty snow fall from the roof and splatter on the gravel. Two hours until sundown.

Chapter Forty-six

Trey blazed into the shop eight minutes later on the dot, his coat billowing, snow rushing in behind him. He clutched an armload of file folders to his chest, and I barely had time to stand before he unloaded everything on the counter. I caught one notebook before it toppled to the floor.

"Trey! What in the—"

"Sorry. It's a long story, and I'm a little...something." He shook snow from his hair. "First I have to tell you why I was wrong. Of course I was right too, but that came later."

"What are you talking about?"

He started sorting the folders into piles. "The detergent thefts. The Sinaloa cartel. The distribution networks. We were looking for a traditional organizational structure—discrete branches stemming from a single source. We could never find it. Now I know why."

He was amped, almost hyper. I'd seen him get frustrated—that was when the pacing started—and I'd seen him over-whelmed—that was when the wall came up—but I'd never seen him quite so manic.

"Trey? Are you okay?"

His head snapped up. "What?"

"You're dialed to eleven, boyfriend."

"Oh. Right." He jabbed his chin toward the tea station. "I suspect the Lapsang souchong you purchased was not decaffeinated.

I snatched up the box. The label was a string of indecipherable characters featuring a serene white teacup pillowed on a cloud bank. "But I got it on Buford Highway! From a real old Chinese man! He said—"

"He lied. Or was wrong. I haven't had caffeine in years, not since I joined the sniper team, because I never knew when I'd get a call-out, and zeroing a rifle is extremely difficult with caffeine in your system. Not your system, mine, I mean. Not that I have to zero rifles anymore, but—"

"Trey. You're babbling. Stop it." I put my hand over his heart; it was racing like a hamster on a wheel. "Maybe you should take some of Gabriella's herb thingies to neutralize this."

"I took the last of them. They didn't work." He blew out a sharp breath. "It's rather disconcerting. Nonetheless, it does quicken the mental processing, it certainly does. Which brings us back here, to our detergent theft problem."

He tapped the papers emphatically. His eyes were twin blazes, as sharp and blue as pilot lights. "We were all stuck—Major Crimes, SWAT, all of us—because the investigation would reveal different networks, but they seemed to be self-contained. We'd make the arrests, charge the offenders, send them to prison. But we couldn't link them to the larger network."

I paged through one of the folders as he spoke. It was thick with arrest records, most of them for misdemeanor shoplifting. I saw his name on a few of the reports, read the lines in the dispassionate language all cops wrote reports in—clipped, precise, without an ounce of descriptive lingo.

Trey stood at my shoulder. "When Garrity moved to Major Crimes, one of his first assignments involved tracking the movement of illegal drugs from the 75/85 corridor into the communities. Distribution networks. He discovered one particularly effective unit under the Sinaloa cartel, but he could never figure out how they moved the currency."

I was confused. "How does this involve laundry detergent?"

"I'm getting to that." He handed me another file. "I told you about the multiple arrests we made involving laundry detergent—always one size, always one brand. We found a stock-pile of such at the Sinaloa stash house. I knew it had to be drug-related—maybe an ingredient in the drug-making process, maybe scent-masking—but I never figured it out. Until now." He paused to let the next words sink in. "The detergent was the currency."

"The what?"

Trey spread the materials out for me to see. "Street currency. A single one-hundred-and-fifty-ounce bottle of premium laundry detergent was worth ten dollars in illegal drugs. Customers paid street-level dealers with the detergent. The dealers then traded it back to cooperative local markets, most small grocery stores, where it was then returned to the shelves. It was the ideal street currency—untraceable, easily stolen, easily funneled back into the legitimate market, and not illegal to possess." He pushed the pieces of paper into the center. "See for yourself."

I looked where he was pointing. I saw a jumble of columns, a list of names. "They were laundering money with laundry detergent?"

He thought about that. "Yes."

It all came together in my head. "The skate shop. It was the delivery spot. People brought in detergent, took out drugs."

Trey exhaled in satisfaction. "Exactly. Which is what…the person with the tattoo…"

"Fishbone?"

Trey pointed his pen at me. "Right. Fishbone. That's exactly what Fishbone was explaining to Garrity this morning. In return for reduced charges, of course. And protection."

"Protection?"

"Yes, for him and his brother both. Because even though the skate shop operation is very small, the online criminal network Lucius connected it to is very…" Trey braced himself against the table with both arms. "Very…"

"Huge?"

"Yes. Enormous. More so than we ever suspected, more so than Fishbone and his brother wanted." He nodded toward the countertop. "See for yourself."

I scanned the collection of police reports, press releases, newspaper articles. It was a record of the Atlanta Metro Major Offenders Task Force doing exactly what it was supposed to do—connect local criminals with their larger organizational support system and bring both down in the process. And now there was a fresh series of indictments, the first series of charges against a confederation of former Gulag prisoners with disturbingly familiar nationalities—Ukrainian, Armenian, Latvian, a veritable encyclopedia listing of the former Soviet states, plus a smattering of Polish and Romanian names.

My head went swimmy. "Oh hell. It really is the Russian mafia. Just like Kenny said."

Trey looked like Christmas morning with a pony under the tree. "The specifics are redacted until the search warrant is unsealed, but you can see the pattern regardless. The information has been right there, but we never had the...the ..."

"Key?"

"Correct. But now we do. Now it's a multi-national investigation with the FBI, the Justice Department, felony indictments at the corporate level. Because now we understand its structure."

"Which is?"

He pulled the cap off the pen with his teeth. Instead of a flowchart, he drew a circle. Then he surrounded that with a second circle, and that with a third, like he was drawing a target.

"Each small drug operation, like the skate shop, was a circle. A single line made up of many single points—many single criminals connected on that circle. Follow the line, and only that line, and it goes around and around. You begin where you end. No links to the larger organization. No way to get to the center." He picked up one more folder. "The black market antiquities trade. Another circle. What Garrity discovered from Fishbone is that the key isn't going around the perimeter of the circle. It's finding the point on the circle that takes you to the next circle."

He drew lines across the circles, creating what looking like a spiderweb. And then he put a dot in the very center, at the intersection of all the lines.

I stared. "The spider at the center of the web."

Trey tossed the pen onto the drawing. "Garrity's words exactly."

"But how does Lucius fit in?"

"That's what Garrity and I were trying to figure out this morning. He suspects Lucius' murderer is on one of these circles, the point where the drug trade and the antiquities market intersect. We haven't found that point yet, but when we do…" Trey looked at me, eyes bright. "It will exonerate your uncle entirely, I am sure of it."

And then I saw it. The name. But not just the name, the *translation* of the name. I got a chill.

"Trey? What is this?"

He followed my pointing finger. "Known accessories in a particular Eastern European network. Some are in prison, others out of extradition, others at large."

"What about this one? Belovuk."

Trey nodded. "Serbian given name. It means—"

"White Wolf, I see that." I was shaking now. "He's the link, the point on the black market antiquities circle that connects to the drug circle that connects to the larger organization. He was Lucius' contact, the one who traded him drugs for whatever he could steal. Including bones."

Trey's eyes narrowed. "How do you know this?"

I sighed. "Are you sure you don't have any more of those herbal thingies?"

Chapter Forty-seven

So I explained. Trey refused to sit—he stood as rigid as a marble column, arms folded—and listened as I told him about Kenny's visit, and my web-message conversation with White Wolf, and what I'd learned about Lucius and Dexter and the whole sordid affair. When I was finished, he set his jaw and stared at me.

"This is what you did this morning?"

"It is. Yes."

His voice stayed soft, but his eyes hardened. "What made you decide this was a good idea?"

I felt the first prickle of annoyance. "You should be happy. I put the final puzzle piece in your big damn unsolved case."

"By consorting with a known criminal."

I folded my arms to match his. "I exchanged information, that's all. Cops do it every day."

"You're not a cop."

"Neither are you."

His head snapped back, and I immediately regretted the words. He turned away from me and began gathering up the paperwork from the counter.

I reached out to touch his shoulder. "I'm sorry, I didn't—"

He avoided my hand with a neat sidestep. "No need to apologize. It's the truth. But it doesn't change the fact that you quite possibly jeopardized the entire investigation and endangered your own safety."

"I thought this White Wolf was just some libertarian nut job! I didn't know he was a freaking Russian mobster!"

"If you had suspicions, you should have talked to the authorities."

"You mean the ones who have been trying to blame me for this whole mess? The ones staking out my shop as we speak?"

"Their job is to find the truth."

"Their job is to close the case."

He looked annoyed. "That's the same thing."

"Bullshit."

His expression hardened to match his eyes. "We operate under the rule of law."

"Well, I operate somewhere a little fuzzier with, yes, known criminals. My family tree is crawling with known criminals. Smugglers, moonshiners, thieves—"

"Yes, I know. One of them kidnapped me and then assaulted me and then locked me in the hold of a boat four months ago." He flung a finger at the computer. "This criminal, however, is not related to you and will kill you without hesitation if you get in his way, which is probably what happened to Lucius, which is probably why he's dead. And now you've…you've…"

Words failed him. He gave up trying to explain and stacked the papers, his movements quick but methodical. He stayed silent, but it was the silence of a volcano before it erupts, a silence of ash and smoke and gathering.

"Talk to me, Trey."

"I have nothing to say."

"Oh no, you started this, you're not backing out now." I planted myself right in front of him. "You can go around think-ing in black and white—you can do it literally and you can do it metaphorically and nobody will say boo to you about it because that's your thing now—but I don't have that luxury."

He kept his eyes on the paperwork. "That's not—"

"Yes, it is! You think I like hiding things from you? But I'm damned if I do and damned if I don't, and I will not stand here and be lectured by you, yet again, when the only reason I keep anything from you is because I'm trying to protect you!"

He switched his gaze on me hard and fast, raked his eyes across my mouth. I let him see it, the whole truth, and his expression shifted to astonishment laced with potent, rising fury.

"You believe that," he said incredulously. "You really do."

And my sensible voice was yammering in the back of my head—*shut up shut up shut up!*—but there was another voice—a shriller, louder voice, red-eyed with an equal fury—and that was the voice that started coming out of my mouth.

I popped my hands on my hips. "Screw it. You're not getting protected anymore. You can deal or don't deal or lock yourself in your apartment, I don't care, because I have *had* it with you, Trey Seaver, and the ATF, and the cops, and the fucking Kennesaw whatever-the-fuck commission, and every other goddammed—"

"Stop talking."

"—overbearing, head-up-their-ass *authority* trying to be the boss of me—"

"I said, stop talking!"

"And another thing—"

He moved like a lightning strike, sweeping my computer off the counter with a backhand blow. It crashed into the fresh plaster, where it shattered with a crack of glass and plastic. The screen went black as the drive died, and then there was only Trey's rapid ragged breathing, and the hornet-like whine of pure rage singing in my head.

And then I saw it in his eyes—the SWAT cop stare—and I knew he could do whatever he wanted at that moment, that not a thing could stop him. Not me, not the rules, certainly not the scrambled circuits of his brain. He clenched his hands to fists, and I remembered the coyote, the howl, the wild edge of the night.

I felt the chemical floodgates open—adrenalin and cortisone, fight or flight, tooth and claw—and with a sickening flash, I took an inventory of the weapons around me—the board on the floor, the wrench on the counter, the gun in the drawer—before

I remembered I wasn't dealing with some random bad guy—it was Trey standing in front of me—but my body and brain didn't see any difference. All the training he'd insisted on kicked in, and my feet moved into neutral stance, and my hands opened, and I tried to make my mouth form his name, but my throat had closed.

Trey blinked. And he transformed right in front of me, like melting. He looked down at his hands, then at me. And he saw my fear, saw it clearly. He went pale, and the tremor started. And I wanted to go to him, I really did, but I couldn't make myself move forward.

He exhaled in a burst. "Tai…"

"You need to go."

"I—"

"Now."

He hesitated for only a second, then he averted his eyes and headed for the door. Quickly, without looking back, without taking his things. The stupid bells jangled behind him. And I didn't budge until I heard the roar of the Ferrari, the kick-up of gravel, the screech of tires.

And then I sank to the floor, put my face in my hands, and sobbed.

Chapter Forty-eight

I sat next to the wreckage of my computer. Small shards of plastic here, bits of coiled wire there. I picked up a piece of meshed metal and held it to the light.

Rico's voice was gentle. "Did you try calling?"

"He won't answer his phone."

I could hear music at the other end of the line. Rico was having a Snowpocalypse party at his apartment, gathering a charmed circle of poets and artists, singers and activists, maybe even a movie star or two. Once I would have been there with him. Instead I sat with my knees against my chest on the floor of my shop, ten minutes past sundown, all alone, with a rising storm outside.

I slumped backwards against the counter. "This sucks."

"Of course it does. Y'all are all up in each other's stuff right now. What did you expect?"

"I expected it to get better. But it's not." I thumped the back of my head against the wall. "It hurts."

"Good."

"Rico!"

"I'm serious. People take all this hard fake stuff and put it on the outside, and that keeps all the soft real stuff safe on the inside, and that is the exact definition of armor, baby girl. And you two have taken it off. And that's where it gets real. Skin in the game real."

"This was a little too real."

"What do you mean?"

"I mean I was scared."

"Of what?"

"Trey."

No response. But the music got quieter, which meant he'd gone into the bedroom and shut the door. "Tell me exactly what happened."

I explained as best I could. Sometimes with Trey, the rush of anger flared with a different kind of heat, and in the past, I'd responded with a matching, primal hunger. But there had been none of that red-blooded drumbeat this time. This time I'd felt only fear, cold and pure and irresistible. And now I felt a different kind of fear, the anxious kind, the kind that left my heart sore and my throat raw.

"I swear, Rico, I can't think of him out there by himself, hurting and confused, and me here, stuck in this freaking shop. But I remember that look in his eyes, and I get…Damn it!"

The restless itch started in my legs again. I recognized it from before—the first twinge of a panic attack—and I tried to breathe it down, but that wasn't happening.

"I have to get outside," I said.

"What?"

I scrambled to my feet and shoved open the front door. A blast of cold hit me like a slap in the face. The square outside was sheened with snow, the trees heavy with ice, the streetlights tingeing everything a tawny amber. I sucked in a lungful of the crisp air, wet now, sharp as a razor. There wasn't a single ounce of tobacco in the shop. I'd have smoked anything, even a scuzzy, stale, lint-pocked cigarette from the bottom of my tote bag.

I rubbed my arms. "Jeez, Rico, I gotta get it together."

"You gotta get your ass back in that shop."

"In a minute." I took another breath, relieved when it went all the way in. "It didn't feel like a betrayal when I did it, any of it. I knew Trey wouldn't have liked me talking to Kenny by myself, but I didn't know that was going to lead to the damn

Russian mafia, and he had so much else on his mind this morning, and—"

"That's not why you didn't tell him, and you know it."

I kicked the curb, sending a tiny plume of ice and snow into the air. I didn't argue because he was right. I'd been laying claim like a gold rush prospector—my shop, my parking space, my A&D book, my investigation—all in an effort to control something that couldn't be controlled, something I couldn't fight any longer.

The tears started again, and I cursed softly. "Everything's all mixed up, Rico—Trey and Dexter and the ATF and the cops and that poor girl's bones. I can't help thinking that could be me one day, a dusty skeleton shoved in the back of the closet, no name, no resting place, no people to miss me."

"Careful, baby girl. You're working yourself into a one-woman pity party."

I tilted my head back against the brick and blinked back the tears. "I think he killed her, Rico."

"Who?"

"Braxton Amberdecker. That girl died on Amberdecker land, I know it. What if they made up that story about him disappearing in the Battle of Kennesaw Mountain and then hid him out until he died and then buried him in an unmarked grave in those woods? What if that's why they put his sister in an asylum and destroyed her journals, because she knew the truth?"

"Whoa, whoa, whoa. That's a whole lotta 'what ifs' there."

I wrapped my arms tighter around myself. "I swear, once this city unfreezes itself, I'm going to prove it."

"How?"

"By digging up Braxton Amberdecker."

"You don't know where he is."

"I bet I do, thanks to a tip from a Russian mobster."

"And where is that?"

"I'll tell you if I'm right."

In the square, I saw the headlights on the police car flare bright. Then the blue lights on the dash followed, a kaleidoscopic spin, as the cruiser pulled onto the street.

"So much for that," I said.

"For what?"

"My sentry just abandoned his post."

"No surprise, probably got another call. You think these people can't drive on good days, wait till you see what happens with a little ice on the road." Rico paused to take a swig of something. "Keep your door locked up there in the boonies. You don't want things to get all Donner Party and shit."

I laughed, even if it was half-hearted. Laughter echoed at his end of the call too, his poet friends coming in, wondering where he was. His community. His people. At my end, there was only a silence coming down like the night, and the rising cold.

I went back inside the shop and shut the door, stamping the slush from my feet. And that was when I saw it, the tiny red flicker behind the glass eyes of the stuffed deer. I walked over and stood under it.

Rico's voice was concerned. "Tai? You still there?"

"I'm here. But I have to go."

"All right, but you be careful up there all alone."

"I will," I said, and hung up.

I didn't tell him I wasn't exactly alone anymore.

Chapter Forty-nine

I tilted my head back, looking the deer right in the eye. "I know you're watching me. I can tell, you know, even without the little red light to give you away."

I sat cross-legged on the floor, put my chin in my hand. The shop was quiet, save for the chirps of various surveillance equipment, a noise like well-behaved robot crickets. I could hear the drip drip drip of the faucet, the hum of the electric lights, the muffled roar of the gas heater. The noises blended into the smells—gunpowder and leather and tobacco and strong coffee—and I realized with a pang it was the smell of home.

"It's okay. I watch you too sometimes. Like when I come to bed and you're already asleep. Some days I can't believe you're real and not a figment of my imagination." I fixed my eyes on the red light. "You're probably close to Buckhead by now. At least I hope you are. It's nasty out, and getting nastier."

As if in response, the wind surged, and I heard a branch snap and tumble to the ground with a muffled thud. I held my breath waiting for the electricity to flicker, but the current stayed on. So did the red light.

"You left all your paperwork. I'll put it with mine. And then when the storm's done, we'll dump it all on your dinner table and see how it connects. Because I'm betting it does. I'm betting the skeleton in my closet and the skeleton in the Amberdecker woods and the skeleton we still haven't found are all part of one whopping story, and if anybody can figure it out, it's you and me. We make a great team, boyfriend. Which reminds me."

I leaned over and dragged my tote bag into my lap. I pulled out a piece of paper and held it up.

"This isn't finished yet, but here's the idea I was telling you about, my contribution to your seduction strategy. Besides me learning to be more patient, of course." I unfolded it and turned it to face the camera. "It's a flowchart, see? It starts with a single box here—that's you, taking one step forward. One step. Then based on the response you get from me, you choose the next action. It's all linear except for some…what do you call it? Circular non-divergence? And you're *quite* familiar with this section already, so nothing new there. Except for this sequence…" I pointed to the lower right corner. "It may seem a little odd, but just go with it, trust me."

A spatter of sleet lashed the window, mixing with the snow. Soon it would freeze, and the power lines singing in the whiplash wind would grow heavy with ice. The shadows of the tossing tree branches wove patterns on the wall.

I tucked my knees against my chest. "I suppose you saw my little freak-out when I was talking to Rico. You told me that PTSD triggers are complicated, but mine is pretty specific—it's feeling trapped. Rooms. Circumstances. Expectations. Anything where I'm not in control. And when one hits, it's Savannah all over again, those hours before I finally found you, when I didn't know if you were alive or…not. So last Sunday, when you locked me in the safe room and went off into the darkness, that was a trigger. And now, with the storm, and you out there somewhere, where I can't get to you…"

My voice broke, and I focused on the red blinking light. I recognized the vulnerability behind that ruby glow. Trey had covers for his empty places, perfectly engineered ones that camouflaged the abyss below. He wasn't the only one. And as I sat alone in that cramped messy room, all the memories flooded back—every kiss, every hesitation, every blush, every sideways glance, him in the dark bottom of that boat, lifting his head at the sound of my voice, him in the dark of the bedroom, his mouth against mine—and I got dizzy with the weight of what he meant to me.

"Trey Seaver, I know you'd never hurt me. I know it with my whole heart. I know the kind of damage you're capable of inflicting—and yes, that's scary to see, I'll admit—but you are the best man I know, good and true all the way to your middle. I keep saying, over and over and over, that I'm not going anywhere. And I'm not. I'm right here." I squared my shoulders, took a deep breath. "And I've got something to tell you. It's something I should have told you when I first figured it out, and as soon as I lay eyes on you again—"

My phone started ringing.

I smiled up into the red light. "Took you long enough." And then I put it up to my ear. "Hey, boyfriend."

But the voice on the other end was unfamiliar. "Excuse me?"

Not Trey. I yanked the phone down and checked the display. It was an unknown number, from an unknown area code. I put it back against my ear. "I'm sorry, I thought you were...who is this?"

A hesitation. "I'm calling for Tai Randolph?"

"Speaking."

"This is Professor Geoffrey Walker. I've been told that you may have found the bones of my great-great-grandmother?"

Chapter Fifty

I stammered a little. "Excuse me, could you repeat that?"

"Ophelia Price gave me this number. She said that you've discovered bones that quite possibly belong to my great-great-grandmother, Josephina Luckie."

"Yes, yes, yes." I scrambled over to my tote bag. "I'm sorry, it's been crazy here."

As I pulled my papers from the bag, I sketched out the story for him—the backpack of bones, the mourning jewelry, the forensic details the ME had shared. He listened. I could feel his excitement mounting.

"We never thought we'd find her. She moved to Atlanta in the late 1850s with her aunt—the Sophia Luckie memorialized on the locket—but when her aunt moved back to North Carolina, Josephina stayed in Georgia, moving in with her brother and his family. She was supposed to flee Atlanta with them, but she never returned from gathering provisions, and they had to leave without her, barely ahead of Sherman's troops. There's a memorial in the family plot and an empty grave but..." His voice cracked with emotion. "How did her remains get in your shop?"

"We're still trying to figure that out, but it's looking like a relic hunter who used to work for my uncle hid them in the wall, probably to sell on the black market."

His end went silent. I glanced up at the wall—the red light still flashed—then pulled out the papers Ophelia Price had printed for me.

"Dr. Walker, if you'll send me all the information you have, I'll do the same for you. Tomorrow. In case you don't know, it's blowing up a snowstorm of epic proportions here in Atlanta, and since my computer is suddenly defunct..." I directed a pointed glance at the deer head. "...my cell phone is my only link to the outside world."

"Yes, yes. Of course. Although we don't have much—the few letters she sent, anecdotal recollections from other family members." His voice went emotional again. "All we've had of her has been the story, which some of us assumed was more fiction than fact, and a photograph."

I got a tingle. "You have a photograph?"

"Yes. It's posted on the genealogical website my cousin maintains. Shall I message you the link?"

"Oh yes, please do."

Another pause while he got his voice under control. "I know you're still trying to figure out the story, but...were there other bones with hers?"

I got another tingle. "We don't know—the remains were removed from their original burial place. Why do you ask?"

"She was supposed to be bringing her betrothed with her to the meet point. She never mentioned his name, only that he was a freeman, and that he was bringing provisions from his home for the trip. He had a sister, the letters said, and this sister was providing food and gold and clothes, but they had to sneak it out past an unsympathetic older brother. Josephina planned to marry him once they got north of the Mason-Dixon line, then head west."

"Her fiancé didn't make it out either?"

"Nobody knows. The final shelling started, and the rest of the family decided that they couldn't risk staying any longer. Travel was severely restricted then for all persons of color, free or slave, and they had to move when they had the chance. They had no choice, not with the baby to consider."

"Josephina's baby?"

"Yes. A little girl. Today Josephina seems too young to be a mother, seventeen, but given the context of the time, she was of marriageable age. In her prime, actually."

I thought of the Minié ball, the probably fatal wound on her vertebrae. She'd left her child with her family to meet her soon-to-be husband, but had instead been shot in the back before she could return to them.

"The baby survived?"

"A minor miracle, that. Josephina's brother raised the girl as his own." A pause. "We've always suspected Josephina lied about the child's parentage. She told her brother her betrothed was a freeman, but the baby could have passed for Eastern European. The child chose to identify as black, however, even though it cost her a lifetime of privilege."

"So you suspect Josephina's betrothed was white? Or do you think...I'm sorry, I don't know how to ask this question delicately."

"It's always the question, isn't it? Josephina was a free black woman, but that provided very little protection from the predations of white men. She could have been raped. She could have sold herself for money or food. Or the child really could have been the child of her betrothed, as she claimed. We'll never know."

"And she never said?"

"No. She was a teacher, Ms. Randolph. She worked with churches to provide religious instruction to the enslaved workers on the plantations, secretly sneaking in reading and writing lessons when she could. It was a dangerous endeavor, illegal in antebellum Georgia, and it put her in close contact with white slave owners who would have been very unhappy with her. If she became pregnant through such an encounter, she would have lied about it, most assuredly."

Something was trying to put itself together in my head, but the threads weren't weaving together properly. Something Ophelia Price had said. Or was it something Evie Amberdecker had said? Or was it...

Dr. Walker kept talking. "We're of mixed ancestry, Ms. Randolph. Indigenous people, specifically Cherokee and Muskogee, African American, Northern European to make it interesting. Even a soupçon of East Asian. My ancestral line is rich and diverse, but I identify as black. Would you like photos of me too?"

"Yes, please. Whatever you've got."

"Certainly." He chuckled. "You can easily see the resemblance between Josephina and me, even though she's the more attractive."

I clicked the first link. And I lost my breath.

There was the face of Josephina Luckie, with the locket around her neck, the locket I'd held in my hands. She possessed the long, high-cheekboned features I'd seen on the Ugandan women at the History Center, dark skin, a rounded nose, and piercing eyes. Her dress was that of a Victorian gentlewoman, but her eyes flashed with defiance.

The second link revealed a handsome man with cocoa skin and neat black dreadlocks. He was straight up beautiful, and deceptively young-looking—close examination revealed that the dreads were shot with steel-gray threads and the angled jawline bore the first softness of post-middle age. The caption identified him as Dr. Geoffrey Walker, head of the African American Studies program at a university I recognized from the annual top ten lists. I could see Josephina in his eyes, his nose…

But not his chin, his assertive square chin. A chin I recognized. And the threads started knitting themselves together.

"Dr. Walker? I don't know how to say this, but…Dr. Walker?"

There was no reply.

I looked at my cell phone. Call ended. I pressed redial but the little icon on my screen went round and round.

I banged my fist on the counter. "No! No! No! Not now!"

But it was futile. The inevitable overloading of the cell phone towers, overwhelmed with the call volume of an entire city freaking out. At least I still had electricity, which meant that the deer head was broadcasting over the Wi-Fi, and Trey was listening, dear Lord, I hoped he was listening.

I looked up at the deer head, pointed a finger at it. "Don't go anywhere!"

Outside, the wind howled as pellets of ice pelted the windows with ballistic regularity. I dumped my tote bag on the floor and found the catalog from the History Center. I flipped to the photograph of Braxton Amberdecker—young and handsome, his jaw set firm and strong. I placed the cell phone image of Geoffrey Watson next to him, and saw it clear as day.

The Amberdecker chin.

Josephina *had* lied—her child's father was no freeman, he was Braxton Amberdecker. I remembered Evie's story, of Violet Amberdecker being reprimanded for bringing teachers in for the slave children. Josephina had been such a teacher. And the story came together with such force that I had to sit down again.

I looked up at the deer head. "Violet was the sister in Josephina's story, the one who was secretly giving her and her lover supplies to flee the Siege. That's how Josephina's bones got on Amberdecker land. She went to get provisions. From Violet. Violet knew everything. That's why her family destroyed her journals and locked her away. Because she knew that Braxton was in love with a black woman, that he was deserting the Confederacy and his wife—even his unborn baby—to be with her and his other child, to get them out of Atlanta, and she tried to help them do it. And she knew that somebody on the plantation killed them both, shot them with Minié balls and buried their bodies in the woods."

I studied Josephina's face as the storm blasted the windows. She'd been a force of nature too, born free, which was a loaded and inaccurate word for describing being black in a white-dominated world, but she'd wielded that edged freedom like a sword. And she'd paid with her life.

I looked up at the deer head. The red light behind the glass eyes was no longer flashing. Trey had signed off. I felt a pang in my heart. And then the realization hit me—there was another reason that light could be off.

I pulled out my phone, then cursed. First the cell phone towers, now the Wi-Fi. And then, without even a flicker of warning, I heard a soft click and the room went totally, utterly, and completely dark.

Chapter Fifty-one

I spent the next sixty seconds cursing the darkness. I cursed the general meltdown of technology too, then cursed some more just to hear myself curse, a human voice against the storm outside. And then I gathered my wits and opened the supply box Trey had brought. It was a survivalist's delight—candles and matches, batteries and protein bars, solar rechargers and handcrank flashlights.

The romantic in me chose the candles first. I lit a few and lined them up on the counter, then spread a blanket on the floor in front of the deer head even though Trey couldn't hear or see me anymore. The system's battery backup powered its essential components, like the emergency alarms and the interior monitors. So the cameras still recorded, and the monitors still worked inside the shop, but without the Wi-Fi, there was no way Trey could tap the feed. And even if the towers came back up and a 911 call went out, neither police nor ambulance could respond, not until the roads cleared. I was essentially on my own.

So I poured another cup of coffee before it went cold and sat on the blanket, wrapping a second one around my shoulders. I turned off my useless cell phone to conserve the battery. And then I hunkered down to wait out the storm.

"They were secret lovers," I said to the deer head. "They took advantage of Braxton's Missing-in-Action status after the Battle of Kennesaw Mountain to flee the city, but they went back to the Amberdecker plantation to get provisions from Violet. That's where they were murdered. By Nate Amberdecker. His own brother."

There was no one to hear my words, but they sounded true enough in the dark cold. Josephina's story mentioned an older brother, unsympathetic, that she and Braxton had to sneak the provisions past. They'd not succeeded. Nate had discovered the two lovers making off with the money and food that Violet had supplied, so he killed both of them and buried them in the woods. Only he didn't get away with the crime undiscovered— Violet knew.

"They've all known," I said, and my voice echoed back to me. "Starting with Violet, who got shut up in an asylum and drugged to death so she'd stop talking about her dream, about her brother dying in the woods. But it wasn't a dream, not at all, and the cover-up has continued with every single Amberdecker since. They've known Braxton was an adulterer and a deserter, and that Nate murdered him and Josephina. And they've known those bones were out there somewhere, the ones that would tell the truth, so they never developed the land, never allowed excavation. And that's why they want those bones back so badly, so they can shove them in the ground again, so nobody will figure it out. And one of them was willing to kill me to make that happen."

I looked up at the deer head. Still no red light.

"Damn it, Trey, where are you?" I said, louder now. "I need you to hear this, right now! I'm cracking the whole damn case, and I'm stuck here until—"

The popping crunch of tires on gravel broke through my tirade, and I saw headlights swing across the back wall. Not the Ferrari. No, this was a deeper rumble, unfamiliar on this deserted night, a night when there should be no traffic. I stood, and was surprised to find that my hand automatically went to my gun-less hip. And I heard Trey's voice as clear in my head as if he'd been standing there—*what do you do now?*—and I knew the answer to that.

I hurried behind the counter and got my carry bag from the safe. I pulled the .38 from the holster, opened the cylinder to check it. Fully loaded.

I looked out the front window. The square outside was dark and empty, every business shuttered and locked tight, except for the massive black truck parked askew at my door. The engine sputtered to a stop, the driver's door opened, and a familiar figure stepped out, boots crunching in the ice and snow.

Richard.

I double-checked the locks, including the industrial-grade deadbolt. Then I put my back to the wall and both hands on the .38.

He banged at the door. "I know you're in there, Tai!"

"Go away!"

"Let me in and I'll explain everything!"

"I figured it out myself! Now get off my property!"

He banged some more. The headlights from his truck pierced the darkness of the shop. It was a four-wheel drive, capable of running roughshod over ice and snow, hell and high water. He didn't need my shelter, and he wasn't getting it.

"I'm the one who found that girl's bones, Tai, right next to Braxton's! I know who she is and I know who put her there and I know why Rose doesn't want anybody to know!"

"So do I!"

"Then you know why she's coming to kill you!"

I felt a new chill, one that had nothing to do with the storm. I tightened my grip on the gun. It was cold. I liked it cold. The cold made it was clear where the gun ended and I began.

"Tai!"

"I'm listening."

He blew on his hands and stamped his feet. "I found two sets of bones in the woods that morning. Right away I knew one had to be Braxton—I saw the bayonet—but when I told everybody about it, Rose had a fit. She told me to march back out there and destroy them, both sets, but I told her it was too late, that Evie had already called the archaeologist's office. Rose told me to pretend I'd only found one set and to destroy the others. But I couldn't, I just couldn't, so I got Lucius to help me bury them back near the park line."

"That was a big mistake, considering he promptly dug them right back up again and hid them in the walls here."

"I know that now."

"Did you know he took Braxton's remains too?"

Richard shook his head vehemently. "I thought they were in the casket, I swear I did. I didn't realize Lucius was dead either, not until the morning of the tornado. And then you found the girl's bones, and Rose found out about them, and she knew I'd lied…look, just let me in, okay?"

I sighed, then unlocked the door and opened it a sliver. Richard stood on the welcome mat, shoulders hunched, face raw from the cold.

"I don't have Braxton's bones," I said.

"I know," he replied. "I do."

He unslung a drawstring bag from his shoulder and held it in my direction. I stood there, staring, sleet frosting the heavy canvas, but I didn't put down the gun.

"You found them near the chapel, didn't you?"

He nodded. "I dug 'em up under the flagstone path. Lucius had a cache there, probably built it when he lay the path during the restoration."

"Does Rose know you have them?"

"She will when she sees that path dug up. And then she'll come for me. But she's going to come for you first. She came for you once already, only she got your neighbor instead, and when she sees that hole in the ground, she'll come for you again. And I can't let that happen, Tai. I'm sorry for the rest, by God I am, but I'm here now, and I'm going to keep you safe until I get Rose Amberdecker to justice." Richard took a step forward. "Now let me in."

I raised the revolver. "Oh no, you don't, you're—"

I heard the crack of the rifle and the whine of a bullet at the same time, and I threw myself on the floor. Richard bellowed and went to his knees, the bag still in hand. He lunged for the doorway, and I dragged him inside as another bullet shattered the front window, leaving only the burglar bars for protection. The emergency alarm tripped, filling the room with flashing red lights and shrieking sirens. I slammed the door, locked it. Through the slanting snow, I saw a figure coming across the square—Rose, two long guns in hand—and I crawled behind the counter, Richard right behind.

He sagged to the floor, one hand pressed against the red stain blossoming on his shoulder. "Aw, shit. I'm shot."

I knelt in front of him. He cursed and clenched his teeth as I pulled his jacket back. It was a clean exit wound, a through-and-through in the left shoulder, but it bled like a stuck pig. He'd been shot from behind. I hadn't seen Rose across the square, but that was no surprise. The bulldozers provided excellent cover. Richard had been lucky that the storm had dropped visibility to virtually nil. Otherwise, she'd have picked him off first shot.

I heard boots kicking at the front door, a rifle butt banging in broken glass. I fumbled in the drawer under the cash register until I found the spare speedloader. I was moving from memory, from training, and if Trey had been there, I would have kissed him on the mouth for making me stuff that stupid thing full of bullets over and over again, because it was by rote now, even though my hands were shaking and my vision was collapsing, and I was sick, and cold, and tunnel-visioned.

Rose emptied some rounds into the lock—which held, by the love of all that was holy—but she was using the shotgun now, not the rifle. Any second she'd come at the lock with a buck slug, and the door would fall open like a freaking red carpet.

"Rose Amberdecker!" I yelled. "I got enough ammo to put a hundred holes in you. So you stay the hell out of here, you hear me?"

She fired through the broken window again, but said nothing. I knelt next to Richard. "Can you crawl?"

"I think so."

"Good. Stay low and follow me."

"Where are you going?"

"The storage room."

"But she'll—"

"Not my storage room, she won't."

There was a shotgun blast at the door, and that was enough for me. I scrambled for the back using the counter as cover, Richard right behind, the bag of bones still clutched in his hand.

Chapter Fifty-two

Rose kicked the door in just as we cleared the threshold of the storage room. I slammed the door behind Richard, listened as the deadbolts engaged with robotic precision, then moved to the far corner, my back against the wall. I kept the .38 out, and I kept it pointed right at him.

Richard took a step in my direction, but I shook my head. "You stay right there, or I'll put a fresh bullet in you."

Rose kicked at the door, but it wasn't budging. Three more kicks—rapid, violent, wrenching—and then a final thud as she flung her whole body against the door. She shot at the handle, but it held. Another blast and the shrieking alarm ceased. And then I heard Rose's voice on the other side of the wood.

"I got no quarrel with you, girl. You open this door, and you can walk out safe and sound. Richard too. It's the bones I want."

I ignored her—no way I was falling for that line. I switched the gun to one hand, pulled up the shop's security monitor with the other. One click, and I got a panoramic 360 of the front room, brilliant in the blaze of Richard's headlights, then a quick switch shot to the outside cameras, which were a blizzard of black and white.

Richard pressed his hand against his shoulder. "This is all my fault. I should have seen this coming sooner."

"Yeah, you should have. But this isn't about you, it's about a whole line of dark-skinned descendants who don't even know they're Amberdeckers."

He was pale, and in shock, but I saw no surprise on his face.

Anger bloomed in my chest. "You knew all of this too, didn't you?"

He stared at the far wall. "Rose told me that part when I found the bones the first time. She needed me to understand why that second set of bones could never see the light of day. She said it was necessary to protect the family, that if I really cared about her and Evie and Chelsea, I'd do what she asked. And God help me, I almost did it, but I couldn't go through with it. I told Rose I had, though, and she believed me. Until you found the bones in the wall."

"How did you figure out where Braxton's bones were?"

"Once I decided Lucius hadn't had help that night, I decided he had to have hidden them somewhere near the chapel. And then I remembered the pry bar you found out in the field."

I remembered it too. Hefty, solid, deadly. "You mean the murder weapon."

Richard winced. "Yeah. And I wondered why anyone would have needed it. The coffin wasn't locked, and Lucius had Dexter's keys to the chapel."

"He needed it for the flagstones. To pry them up so that he could hide the bones underneath."

Richard nodded. "So a couple of hours ago, I drove up through the park and went in the back way, so that Rose wouldn't see me. Found the stone he'd hidden them under first try." He grimaced and pulled his arm tighter to his chest. "I started putting everything together the night you came to the encampment. I decided Rose must have come for the bones the night of the reburial, to destroy them like she thought I'd destroyed the girl's, and then when she found Lucius there, and an empty coffin, and that pry bar…"

So that was what Trey had seen in Richard's face the night we met him in the woods—the painful growing realization that the woman he'd served for thirty years was a killer.

"I knew Rose was a hard woman, but I never figured she

would…" He tilted his head back against the wall, closed his eyes. "I thought I knew her, but I didn't. And I'm done with her."

I heard regret in his voice, but also the bitterness and anger that come from deep betrayal. And then I understood.

"You're in love with her, aren't you? That's why you've never said anything about any of it."

"It doesn't matter. We're not getting out of here alive. She's a crack shot. And she's got nothing to lose."

He didn't look at me, but I could see he was disgusted with himself. Not as disgusted as I was, but pretty disgusted nonetheless. In the hall, Rose rattled the door again, and his attention jerked that way.

"Don't worry," I said. "That door is UL-rated Level Four, which means Rose isn't getting in without a tank. So settle in. We're going to be here for a while."

But Richard wasn't going to make it a while, as Rose probably knew. He was still bleeding and getting paler. I pulled Trey's brand new first aid kit from the shelf and kicked it over with my foot.

He reached for the box, looking sad and hurt and angry all at once. "You don't have to stand over there. I'm not gonna hurt you."

"All the same."

"Tai—"

"I let you in my safe room. That's as far as I'm going. Now get some gauze and bandages and tie that up before you die."

He got to work clumsily. In the silence I could hear Rose in the shop, opening drawers, rifling through boxes, overturning shelves, looking for anything she could use to get into the room. Richard opened the gauze with his teeth, winced in pain as he fumbled with the wrapping.

I cursed, tucked the gun into the small of my back. "Give me that."

He did. I pressed the bandage against the seeping hole, then wound the gauze to hold it in place. It was still bleeding profusely, and his skin had gone ashen.

"I figured out that Nate killed Braxton and Josephina," I said. "Violet knew the whole story too."

"They've all known the story, Tai. Every generation of them."

"Evie and Chelsea?"

He shook his head. "No. Rose gave the secret to me instead. And it was going to die with me."

I felt the anger rise again. "Braxton took a bullet between the eyes. The girl was shot in the back, the ME says. Running for her life. You were good with letting their stories die with you too?"

He shuddered, but not from horror or guilt. He was going down fast. The wound probably wasn't fatal, not of itself, but the loss of blood and rising shock would get him soon. And then I'd have an unconscious person to deal with, and I had enough on my hands. I went back to the door, pressed my ear against it. The shots came fast—pow pow pow—and I jumped back, my heart banging in my chest.

But the door held. Of course it did.

I took my .38 in hand again. At least we had ammo, enough to last till Doomsday. *We*, I thought bitterly. As if Richard were on my side. He was on the side of whoever wasn't trying to kill him. Rose had time on her side—up to a point—so she could afford to be patient and thorough. But she could never be as thorough as Trey. The door would hold. I had faith.

"And Brenda?" I said. "You did figure out that Rose was the one who shot her, right?"

"I had no proof."

"But you knew."

He refused to even look at me. "I didn't want to admit it, but yeah. I knew."

My temper sizzled. "So you know that was supposed to have been me that night, bleeding out on the pavement. How far were you willing to go for her, Richard? What was next, pulling the trigger yourself?"

"Doesn't matter. She's going to kill us both now."

"Not in this room, she won't."

Richard coughed, grimaced in pain. I tried to gauge how much blood he'd lost and couldn't, not beneath the heavy coat. I felt the first nibble of fear—maybe he was right, maybe there was no way out.

I pulled my phone out and checked it one more time, but there was still no service. I cursed. "Freaking blizzard."

Richard screwed up his eyes at me. "That's not why your phone's not working."

"What do you mean?"

He glared. "How do you think I figured out she was the one who shot Brenda? She stole my jammer, Tai, the one I use in field to keep the boys from using their cell phones. It's how she kept the security system from going off when she broke in, how she planned on keeping you from calling the police."

I crossed the room quickly and knelt in front of him. "Are you telling me the towers aren't flooded, that the only thing keeping me from calling 911 is your jammer?"

"Yeah. Probably."

"Where is it?"

"In her truck, most likely."

"How do you stop it?"

"Push the power button."

I stood up. Suddenly I had a Plan B. Not that the cops could get to us with the snow screaming down, the roads slick with black ice and blocked with accidents. But if Rose somehow managed to breech the safe room, at least there was a chance…

One the screen, Rose leveled the shotgun and shot at the door again, this time in pure thwarted anger. I watched her pace the front room, running down her options. As long as the police couldn't arrive, it was a standoff, but she was running out of ideas. That was a bad thing. People without ideas were two steps from desperation, and if she got desperate, she'd get reckless.

"It's okay if you run," Richard said, his voice hoarse. "Your Uncle Dexter—"

"—wouldn't have left you for that crazy woman to murder, and neither am I. Regardless of what went on before, you tried to do right at the end. So—"

And then I heard it. A rustling at the window. A quick look at the screen told me it wasn't Rose, who was still banging around in the front room. I swung the gun toward the window, but I saw nothing except the snow and ice beating against the panes. But then I heard it again. Not a rustling. Three light taps. And then I heard the voice, barely above a whisper.

"Tai! It's me."

I lowered the gun as disbelief washed over me. "Trey?"

Chapter Fifty-three

"Of course it's me. Don't shoot."

My heart skipped a beat as I stuffed the pistol into the back of my jeans and scrambled on top of the display table. Trey waited, ice crystals in his hair, his coat billowing in the sleeting wind. He was holding onto the windowsill with bare white fingers, his teeth chattering as I cranked open the glass.

I stood on tiptoe. "How in the hell did you get here?"

"I'm standing on the dumpster. I told you this window was easily—"

"Not the window, here, at the shop!"

"Oh. That. I never left."

I slipped my hands through the opening and held his cold face between them. "Jesus, Trey, where have you been?"

"I parked on the other side of the square so you wouldn't see me. Or hear. But I could see and hear you. Until the electricity went out, and the towers went down—"

"The towers aren't down. It's a jammer. In Rose's truck."

His eyes flared. "I knew it! I told you—"

"You did. You told me a lot of things. And I'll be very happy to keep listening if you can get us out of here."

"I will." He hesitated. "I'm sorry I frightened you. Earlier. And broke your computer. And—"

I pressed fingers over his cold mouth. "Not now."

"And I wanted to come back in, especially after the things you said, but I couldn't. And then I saw Richard, and then I could, but before I could, I heard the rifle shot, saw you both move inside. And then I saw Rose come from behind a bulldozer, but I couldn't get a clear shot, because I couldn't get a clear background, not with you somewhere in the shop, and...I am so sorry."

"Me too. But that's for later." I wiped his ice-crusted hair from his forehead. "Right now I need you to get us out of here."

"That's my main goal." He looked beyond me to the security monitor. "Why is she doing this? What does she want?"

"She wants Braxton's bones, and she's willing to kill me and Richard to get them."

"But you don't have—"

"Actually, I do."

"You what?"

"I'll explain later. Can we make a run for it?"

He shook his head. "From where she's standing, she can cover both the front and back doors."

"We can't stay here much longer." I jerked my head toward Richard. "He's been hit."

"How bad?"

"Bad enough."

Trey peered beyond me to where Richard slumped in the corner. The rain slanted in mercilessly, and the wind howled behind him. Trey's eyes didn't reveal an ounce of mercy either.

I shook my head. "We can't leave him here. He's in this mess because he tried to protect me. She'll kill him out of pure spite, and he doesn't deserve that."

Trey blinked, and I saw his priorities rearranging themselves. Richard, no longer a bad guy, was now reclassified as hostage in need of rescue. A different flowchart, different protocol. I was dying to pepper him with questions, but knew I had to let him think. He had experience with barricaded shooter scenarios. I had zip.

He did a quick calculation. "How are you for ammo?"

"I've got every bit of it in here. Plus every long gun in the shop, still in the gun safe."

"What can Rose access?"

"Nothing except the reenactment supplies. Clothes, camp-ware...oh shit."

"What?

I looked down at the video screen. Sure enough, Rose had found the kerosene. She looked demonic in the flashing emergency light—her white hair wild, her face dirty, shotgun held in one hand while she dragged the plastic jugs out with the other. She had no way out, and she knew it. The airport was shut down, every interstate a parking lot of spun-out wrecks; even her massive four-wheel drive truck wouldn't get her out of the city. But it would get her back to her property. And she could burn the shop down before she left, pick us all off like rabbits when we tried to run. And then the fire would turn everything to ash, and the papers would call it an unfortunate accident. A candle falling over, a dropped cigarette. Of course this was how Tai Randolph would go, they'd say, that girl never could manage anything.

I gritted my teeth. "I am not letting that bitch burn down my life. I swear to God, Trey, I—"

"I know. Let me think."

Trey readjusted his position. He was soaking wet, shivering harder. He didn't have long before hypothermia set in.

"Stay here," he said. "Don't open that door unless she sets a fire and you have no other option. If I can find the jammer and disarm it, I'll do that first, so keep your phone on. Call 911 as soon as you can."

"Wait, what are you going to do?"

"I'm going to neutralize the threat."

"What does that mean?"

His voice was soft and terrifying. "You know what that means."

I grabbed his hands. "No, no, no! You can't do that. You're not a cop anymore, they'll send you to prison this time. You have to—"

"I have to do what's necessary."

I grabbed his collar and held tight. "You find the jammer, call 911, and then run, you hear me?"

"The police won't be able to get here in time."

"Damn it, Trey, don't—"

He pulled free of my fingers, to the edge of the dumpster where I could not reach him. He had that look of trying to make words happen, trying hard. But then he gave up trying, and I watched as his expression shifted, becoming stiller, flatter, reserved and relentless. I watched him become an assassin, right in front of me, as cold and merciless as the night.

I felt tears spring to my eyes. "No. Please no."

But a swirl of snow wrapped him like a shroud, and when it cleared, he was gone.

Chapter Fifty-four

I pressed my face to the window, but all I got in return was an icy slap of wind. Trey was out there in the night, part of the howl and storm, and I was stuck in the safe room—again. I felt the surge—itchy, restless, like nausea if nausea were bright purple and two thousand volts and toxic as mercury.

I clenched my teeth. "No no no! Not now!"

But I could feel the panic spreading. It would take me down if I stayed in that room. I climbed down to where Richard slumped in the corner. He'd gone quiet, which meant shock was setting in. And although he deserved every ounce of pain wracking his body, he didn't deserve to die.

I kicked his foot. "Get up, we have to go."

He moaned and slumped sideways. I bent down and grabbed his chin. His eyes fluttered open, but his pupils were dilated, his gaze blank.

"Damn it, Richard, Trey is about to take on a woman with a fucking twelve-gauge all by himself, and I am not going to sit in this room while he does it."

But Richard wasn't going anywhere. Behind me, the video screen revealed Rose. She'd already emptied one container of kerosene and was opening a gallon of lamp oil, twisting the cap with one hand, holding it with the other. The shotgun stood beside her, propped against the counter. She had no reason to think she might need it. No way to know she was in a sniper's crosshairs.

I'll do what's necessary, he'd said.

I cursed, shoved an extra speedloader in my pocket. The door would lock behind me automatically, protecting Richard. If I could get it open quietly, I could use the hallway as concealment. It would let me get the drop on her—no way she could get the shotgun up in time—and I had a wall to duck behind if she did.

I took a deep breath, feeling the panic melt and a new feeling rise, a quickening heady sensation. So this was what it was like for Trey, sliding into the plan, the protocol, the flow. Everything made sense, so clear and clean…

I pulled out my .38, warm now from my body. One more ammo check—locked and loaded. One more check of the video screen to make sure Rose was still occupied. Then I eased the door open and slipped into the hallway.

The smell of kerosene hit me first. The emergency light above the door still pulsed bloody red, and the headlights from Richard's truck threw a curtain of blinding light through the front windows. It illuminated Rose, standing at the counter now, the shotgun a foot away. My training unfolded like a map—solid stance, slight lean, both hands on the weapon—and I took a deep breath and stepped around the corner.

I aimed right at her heart. "Freeze, Rose!"

She dropped the lamp oil and lunged for the shotgun. She was quicker than I'd expected and managed to grab it, but I pinged a shot into the counter, and she froze, clutching it right above the stock.

I put the sights back on her. "Drop it. Now."

She was breathing hard, her sides heaving. Not fear—fury—as defiant as she'd been the first time I'd spotted her.

She glared at me. "What are you gonna do, girl, stand there all night? Nobody's coming. You're all alone."

I kept the gun aimed at her chest. "That's where you're wrong."

And from somewhere out of the blinding wall of brightness, Trey stepped into the shop, his silhouette a blur against the brilliance, his shoes crunching broken glass. He looked murderously surreal in the flashing red light, his weapon drawn, his voice cool and firm.

"Get back in the room, Tai."

I kept my stance. "No, *you* get in the room. If anybody's getting shot tonight, I'm doing the shooting."

"No, you're not. Get in the room. I'll deal with this."

This, he'd said. Not *her*. Rose switched her attention his way. She didn't drop the shotgun. I could see her running the possibilities—how quickly she could grab the trigger, which target to take down first, could she get us both with one pull—and I knew she'd tumbled down to her last option, that she was in the desperation zone. Her eyes switched from me to Trey and back to me. Calculating.

I shook my head. "Don't you even think about it. You might get one of us, but not both. And the one of us you don't get will put you down, Rose Amberdecker, like a dog, but not before you scream and beg and bleed and die for a very long time. Because as you pointed out, we are all alone out here."

Trey stayed silent. No orders, no demands. I squinted at him again the light. He had his finger on the trigger, primed for imminent threat. All Rose had to do was make a suspicious twitch, and he'd drop her. One shot, one kill. And as I saw him standing there in the bright merciless glare, the cold dead darkness behind, I realized that he wanted her to try it. He was giving her the space to take that move because he wanted to shoot her, wanted it very badly.

And I knew it wasn't restraint that held him back. He was simply waiting for the trigger. And she was going to give it to him, any second now. And I wanted desperately to go to him, put a hand on him, bring him back from the edge, but I wasn't about to cross his muzzle range, wasn't about to stand so close that Rose could whip the shotgun up and take us down together.

I forced myself to sound calm. "Trey?"

He didn't answer, didn't lower the gun.

"I'm gonna get her weapon now. You cover me, okay?"

No response.

"Hey? Boyfriend? Answer me."

Trey blinked. A shudder rippled through him, and he let out the half-breath he'd been holding. He slipped his finger alongside the barrel, nodded.

"Copy that. I mean, yes. You're covered. Get her weapon."

I didn't hesitate. I tucked my .38 back into the small of my back and snatched the shotgun out of her hands. She didn't protest, probably because Trey still reeked of loose-cannon dangerous. But she glared hot hate at me as I proceeded to unload her weapon.

"I've got lawyers," she said. "Mean smart ones."

"You're gonna need them. Because I am shouting this story from the rooftops, to anybody who will listen." I pumped the magazine, dumping the cartridges on the floor, one by one. "Braxton and Josephina. Their baby. That whole other line of Amberdeckers you've pretended didn't exist for a hundred years. I talked to one of them this very afternoon. Their story is gonna be front page news."

"You've got no proof."

"I've got plenty, especially once I get Braxton's bones and all his DNA into evidence."

Her eyes blazed. "Those belong to me."

"No, they don't. And they never have." I took a step back, out of her range. "It wasn't enough that Braxton's bones went in the ground. You had to go get them out of his damn coffin, probably gonna burn them to ashes, but Lucius beat you to them. So you killed him with the first thing you could grab, the pry bar. Only the bones weren't in the coffin."

Her chest heaved, but she didn't speak. I put the unloaded gun on the floor and kicked it to the corner, put my .38 right back on her.

"You thought the same thing everybody did—that Lucius had had a partner that night, someone who took the bones off his hands. So you shoved his body in the empty casket and searched his apartment the next day. But you didn't find anything, and when the bones didn't turn up, you kept quiet. Until the tornado." I raised the gun a smidgen so that she was staring straight down the barrel. "And me. You didn't see me coming either. But the best part is, the bones were right under your nose the whole time."

She remained silent. Trey too. Up close, I could see the wreckage of his clothing. He had to be on the verge of collapse. Rose looked on the verge of collapse too, and I probably wasn't far behind. And then it hit me with a wallop—we were still alone in the darkened snowbound shop, me and Trey and a vengeful murderess, with Richard bleeding out in the back room.

"Trey?"

"Yes?"

I stepped closer to him. "So…what now?"

"Now we wait."

"For what?"

He cocked his head, listening. "For that."

And then I heard it too—the low drumming whine, coming closer, the only noise in a city frozen solid.

A helicopter.

It appeared as suddenly as a UFO, and even from a hundred feet below, I could feel the whoosh and swirl of the wind coming through the broken shop window, the savage chop-chop-chop as it swooped and hovered. It landed in the middle of the square, kicking up tornadoes of silted ice and powdery snow, shredding the steely air, gracefully, powerfully.

A Black Hawk. With FBI emblazoned on its side.

The hatch opened and Garrity jumped out, his dark gray coat flapping in the wind. He made a slashing motion across his throat, and the engine whined to a halt. He jogged toward us, but I didn't drop the gun, not even when he came busting through my ruined door, gold shield flashing in the fierce-white light, S&W in hand.

He looked from me to Trey to Rose, then back to Trey. "What the hell?"

I gripped my own gun tighter. "About freaking time."

Chapter Fifty-five

The next ten minutes were a blur—darkness and noise and grunts and orders. Even when Garrity slapped the handcuffs on Rose and dragged her out the door, I didn't put my gun down. One of Garrity's men had to peel my fingers off the grip. Patiently. Carefully.

They stabilized Richard and loaded him on a stretcher. He grabbed my hand as he passed, his lips moving but no words coming. I lowered my ear to his mouth.

"Catherine," he wheezed.

"I'll do my best," I said.

The men hurried him inside the copter, and Garrity shot the pilot a thumbs up. The silence vanished, drowned out by the crystalline whine of the engine, gathering for the upmount.

Garrity raised his voice to a shout. "We'll get to Grady, and I'll be back here in—" He put a hand to his earpiece, cursed. "Never mind. Massive pile-up on 285. Go back inside and stay there."

Trey stared in astonishment. "What?"

"I'm serious. This is triage. I got room in the copter for two extra people—that's Rose and Richard."

"But procedurally—"

"You want procedure, fine. I'm deputizing you." He jerked a thumb at me. "Her too."

I shoved my hands in my pockets. "Cool."

But Trey was having none of this. "You can't do that. Only the sheriff—"

"Lalalala, my friend. I don't wanna hear it. Go into Tai's apartment and stay put until I get somebody here. Collect the evidence. Get warm. We'll deal with this later, once hell stops freezing over."

He held a hand to his ear in the universal gesture of "call me" and loped to the helicopter. The door closed, and the copter rose into the air. Trey watched it rise, then followed it with his eyes all the way over the horizon. It left only descending quiet in its wake, and yet he continued to watch its vanishing point, squinting against the wind.

I stood next to him. "You called Garrity."

"I did. As soon as I found the jammer and dismantled it."

"It was in Rose's truck?"

He nodded. "I called 911 too, but I knew they couldn't get a unit here in time. But Garrity..." He cocked his head, his eyes still riveted on the empty sky. "Garrity has his own tac team and access to a Sikorsky Black Hawk."

I took his hand, squeezed it. "You miss it, don't you? Being a cop?"

"I do." He looked at me, and the fierce desire in his face was almost too much to bear. "But missing is as complicated as wanting now."

I moved closer to him, huddled under his wet coat. I remembered his finger on the trigger, the violent trembling anger fueling him. He'd been a timebomb. And he'd cut the right wire, defused and emptied himself before ignition. And now he was my boyfriend again.

I chose my words carefully. "That thing that happened back there, with Rose? That was close."

"It was. I'm sorry."

"No need to apologize. But we do have to deal with it. All of it."

"All of what?"

I looked into his face, took both his hands in mine. "I know you've worked hard to create a life that makes you feel safe and protected and in control. The job, the apartment, the rules. God knows you've needed what calm you could scrape together. But you need this too. You need to be in the action again. You've got a fire heart, boyfriend, and I don't even know what that means, but I know it's true."

He looked down at me, so serious, so vibrant, so practically pulsing with vitality I was surprised the snow didn't melt around him in a wet submissive circle.

"I know something else too," I said. "This is the first February ninth you've spent out of your apartment in three years."

He looked surprised. "It is, isn't it?"

"It is." I managed a smile. "So what are we going to do? Because keeping things locked down is not working for you."

"It's not working for you either. No matter what I do or say, you still…you know."

"I know. I have a fire heart too."

He nodded. "Then we need to deal with that as well."

We. The two of us. My heart thumped harder, and I grew light-headed, my whole body strumming with the post-adrenalin crash. I started walking toward the shop, pulling Trey after me. He followed, our footsteps making squeaking sounds in the snow. And his hand was cold, but it was in mine, and he was holding it so tightly my fingers ached, but it was a good ache. I savored it, reveled in it, let it rush up my arm to meet the ache in my heart, which was also good.

He kept his eyes on the gun shop. "Tai?"

"Yes?"

"Promise me you won't ever let me hurt you. That you'll do whatever it takes to keep that from happening."

"Trey—"

He stopped walking, but didn't let go of my hand. "Promise."

I turned to face him, and he met my eyes straight on. The night behind us was as silent as the grave, the ground before us shadowy and treacherous.

"I promise," I said.

Back in the shop, we climbed the stairs through the freezing, kerosene-riddled shop to my apartment and shut the door on the whole mess. We dried off with the pristine white towels I'd pilfered from his place, then changed in the dark, the bathroom shades pulled against nothing but flurries and flat darkness. I listened to the small human sounds—the slide of fabric against skin, the rustle of hangers—as we undressed and dressed, trading wet freezing clothes for sweatshirts and pajama bottoms and thick dry socks. I could hear his teeth chattering as he folded the fabric—evidence now—and put each item into a separate plastic bag.

He finished his task and motioned toward the bed. "Sit."

"I'm fine, I—"

"Please."

I sat. Trey watched to make sure I was staying put, then went into the closet and got one of his washcloths. He ran water until it was warm, then filled the sink and dipped the washcloth. He moved to stand in front of me and lifted my chin with one hand, dabbing lightly at my face.

I closed my eyes. "I have something to tell you."

"I know."

He concentrated on my forehead. Even when the tears started—slow, like first thaw—he didn't stop. With every gentle stroke, he removed another layer of blood and sweat and grime.

I opened my eyes. "You know what I'm going to say, don't you?"

"I think so, yes."

He went back to the sink and dipped the cloth in the water again and wrung it out. I watched him, so precise and efficient and tender. I lost him in the watery blur of the tears, which I could not blink away. But I knew he was there. I got lightheaded, and I knew I had to do it quick, without looking down, like flinging myself off the high dive.

I licked my lips. "Okay. Here goes. God help us both, Trey Seaver, but…I love you."

He didn't move, didn't blink. He simply nodded as he folded the washcloth into a tidy square. I had no idea why his brain seized up at such times—an EEG of the moment would no doubt have captured the frantic swirls and dissonant flashes and neuronal firing. But he was trying, despite the hiccups, despite the grit in those gears.

"Trey?"

He held up a finger. "Ten more seconds, please."

Exactly ten seconds passed. Then he turned to face me. And then he took one deliberate step toward me. Then another. And then he was striding across the room right to me, no hesitation, none whatsoever, running his fingers into my hair and tipping my face back to kiss me, totally without asking, and I stopped thinking about anything but that singular moment, his mouth on mine—sure, untethered, devastating. I let him pull me upright into his arms, where he held me too tightly, and I didn't mind, not one iota. I opened my eyes, feeling the thump-thump-thump of his heart against mine.

I smiled up at him. "Wow. That was a whole lotta steps."

He sat on the edge of the bed and pulled me down next to him, brushing my hair from my face so that he could look me right in the eye. "Of course I love you. You know that."

And he kissed me again, and I surrendered utterly, took down the armor, opened all the way. And I expected to feel terror, but it was only relief, a sweet wrecking ball surge of it, and exhaustion, a delicious tiredness.

I tilted my head back to look him in the eye. "This isn't how it normally ends, you know. No EMTs, no CSI teams. No interrogations, no fingerprints, no being dragged downtown."

"We have to do that in the morning."

"I know, but that's the morning. It'll be better in the morning."

Outside, clouds lay over the city like tired ghosts, ready to sleep, even as the rain continued its relentless work. According to hope and faith and meteorology, the dawn would be gracious, and in a few hours, the sun would send shards of clean morning light straight down from a clear blue sky. Already I could hear ice crashing to the ground, falling from power lines and pine boughs, the swan song of the frozen world.

He shook his head. "It's going to get worse before it gets better."

"I know. But then it will get better."

I leaned against him. The midnight hush would vanish, yes, but for the moment, it was as comforting as the folds of a weathered quilt. Trey put his arm around me without my having to tell him to do so, and we watched the white expanse through my bedroom window. And it was so familiar, almost pre-ordained, to be where we were, together, the world outside.

"Do I need to get a blanket?" I said.

"No. I'm not cold anymore."

He wasn't, not at all. I lay my head on his shoulder. "Trey?"

"Hmmm?"

"Admit it. I had you at 'I know you're watching me.'"

He made a soft noise in the back of this throat, almost like a laugh. "You had me the entire time."

Epilogue

One Month Later

I resolved to sip the second glass of wine more slowly. The first already buzzed in my head, loosening my balance. My new red heels perfectly matched my new skirt and jacket, but they had me feeling off-kilter, and the wine wasn't helping. Receptions weren't my kind of party, especially not this one, which was chock full of photographers and news crews mingling with forensic anthropologists and a slew of fascinated gossip junkies.

Trey stood at my side. "I'm surprised Evie allowed reporters."

"She said she wanted to tell the whole truth of the Amberdecker story, and heaven help her, that's what she's doing. To every news outlet in Atlanta."

Across the exhibit hall, Evie shared the spotlight with her newfound cousin, Dr. Geoffrey Walker. The two made an attractive pair, even if Evie's composed smile seemed tight. I sympathized. Her mother was in jail, charged with both first-degree and attempted murder. Her sister was conspicuously absent as well, as she was still lounging in the Seychelles on a conveniently extended honeymoon. Even Evie's colleagues in the archaeologist's office kept a wide berth. She was mildly disgraced, tainted and tarnished, and now she stood in the middle of the crowd utterly alone except for the blood kin stranger at her elbow.

But her exhibit had gone on, closing and then re-opening as the debated, threatened, and utterly revamped show that it was.

Now another portrait hung in the hall—Josephina Luckie's. Her remains were leaving Atlanta, however, going home with Dr. Walker to be interred in the North Carolina cemetery where her empty grave waited. Eventually, Braxton's bones would accompany her, and the war-crossed lovers would rest eternally side by side, less intimately than when they'd lain tangled in the Kennesaw clay, but perhaps more peacefully. It must have killed Evie to let them go, those marvelously storied, red-marbled bones. But let them go she had.

I stared up at Josephina's image, her dark skin and bold gaze in stark contrast to the heartbreaking softness of Braxton's features. Could true love really have flourished in such hard ground? Or had theirs been a tale of mutual desperation and inevitable reckoning?

The crimson bones kept their secrets, kept them tight.

The present-day story was still telling itself. Richard had his own reckoning on the horizon, charges ranging from improper disposal of a body to evidence tampering. Detective Perez had thrown the book, and she'd had an impressively hefty book to throw. But he'd had a visitor at his bail hearing, a sunglassed and unapproachable Cat. She'd left without speaking, but she'd shown up. Which—as I knew very well—was an enormous deal.

Garrity and his new FBI buddies had taken a scythe to Atlanta's street drug business. I'd seen him at the press conference afterward, so tickled he could barely hide the grin. He'd sent a shout-out Trey's way, for the work he'd done back with the Sinaloa cartel and for lending his current expertise to the case. Trey had taken the praise smoothly, but I'd seen the corner of his mouth twitch in a suppressed smile. They were coming after the big dogs next, Garrity told me afterward, the White Wolfs of the world. He said it with an expression very like a wolf's himself.

And then there was me. With a brand new Federal Firearms License framed on the wall. And ballistic-proof Plexiglass windows in the safe room.

I took another sip of wine. "Uh oh. I'm getting looks."

"Of course you are. You're in the news. Again."

"Yes, but not one reporter has used the word 'reckless.'"

"Yet."

He managed to draw the word into two syllables, with a pronounced emphasis on the final consonant. I heard the buzzing of my phone, but I didn't look down.

Trey raised an eyebrow. "Aren't you going to get that?"

"It's just Kenny again."

"I thought he finished your computer last week."

"Yes, but he keeps thinking of new-fangled awesomeness to install, and since I told him money was no object…"

Trey didn't complain. His AmEx Titanium was doing penance for him. I was doing my own penance, most of which involved swearing off the Darknet and always looking him in the face when I spoke.

"Thanks, by the way, for getting your professor friend to put in a good word. Kenny's going to keep his scholarship."

"You're welcome. I was glad to help."

Trey had pulled an old contact out of the woodwork, a Georgia Tech computer science professor he'd once worked with on asymmetrical sniper prediction models. Good words were powerful currency, but they carried their own price. Markers and favors, tokens and boons. They all returned home eventually, empty-handed and needy as prodigals.

I put the wineglass to my lips, dismayed to see that it was empty. Across the room, I saw Geoffrey Walker step closer to Evie, put a hand on her shoulder. Her face softened, and she sent a genuine smile his way. She would be fine, Dr. Evie Amberdecker. She was tough enough for the truth, even a landslide of it.

"I think I'm ready to go," I said.

Trey didn't argue. He'd been ready to go for a while. He'd come because I'd asked him, but he was keen to get us back to his apartment. I knew why. My new outfit covered equally new La Perla undergarments in a matching flame red, and we still had unexplored sections on the flowchart.

"I'll get the car," he said, already headed for the exit.

I waited for him out front, pulling my coat around me, winter nipping at my knees. Milder now, with wet spring on its breath. I couldn't see the Ferrari, but I heard it growling from around the corner.

"Excuse me, miss?"

I turned. "Yes?"

A woman stood there—black fitted coat, black bobbed hair, porcelain skin, red-lipped smile. She handed me a notecard, heavy ivory stock, with my first name written on the envelope in a swirling cursive.

"You dropped this," she said.

"No, I didn't."

She smiled wider. "I'm sure you did."

And then she walked away, heels clicking on the sidewalk. She walked so quickly she was out of sight before I could open the envelope. I pulled out the card just as the Ferrari swung to a stop in front of me.

There was only one line inside the card, written in the same flowing script as my name on the front—*And I will give you all the kingdoms of the world and their glory*—but there was a photograph, taken at the summit of Kennesaw Mountain, black bare branches reaching into a winter-blue sky. In the image, a woman stood next to an iron cannon, gazing out over the landscape, Atlanta a distant shimmer of steel on the horizon. She had her back to the camera, but I recognized her riotous hair. I put my hand to the same hair, tidied now, no longer tossing in the high mountain wind.

Trey came around to open the car door for me, stopping short when he saw my expression. "Tai? What's wrong? What's happened?"

I looked up at him. "I don't know, boyfriend. But something has. And I suspect I'm going to find out what it is, real soon."

Author's Note

Tai and Trey's Atlanta is a place of bustle and leisure, nature and steel, tradition and edge, just like the real Atlanta. These two Atlantas co-exist easily in my imagination, like kissing cousins, but any native to the area will recognize some differences between my fictional version and the actual one (the most obvious being that in Trey and Tai's Atlanta, nobody spends nearly enough time waiting in traffic).

Tai's gun shop resides in my imagination; the city of Kennesaw is real, however. You'll find it slightly northwest of Atlanta, and it really does have a city ordinance requiring every head of household to maintain a firearm and ammunition. It also has a store specializing in Confederate memorabilia—Wildman's Civil War Surplus (although any resemblance between Tai's shop and this one is purely coincidental).

Trey's Buckhead neighborhood also exists, even if there isn't a bar called Hog Wild there. Most of the other places I describe—Stone Mountain (both the hunk of granite and the city beside it), the FBI field office, the High Museum of Art, the Atlanta History Center, and the Atlanta Fulton Public Library—are also real, as is Kennesaw Mountain Battlefield National Park. And while you won't find any Amberdecker plantations along the park's borders, the rest of what Tai says about the Civil War history and the complicated geography of the area is true.

If you're interested in learning more about the research that went into this book, you can check out my ever-changing

Pinterest boards: *The Civil War*— devoted to the War Between the States, especially Georgia's part in it; *Criminal Behavior*, which explores villains and scams and nefarious wrongdoings, including the ones that show up in *Deeper Than the Grave*; *Trey and Tai's Accessories*, a collection of my protagonists' clothing, automobiles, and weaponry; and *Trey and Tai's Atlanta*, which includes an interactive map of the metro Atlanta landmarks that have cameo appearances in the series. This fourth book also has its own board: *Deeper Than the Grave Research*. You can find these and my other writerly and readerly boards at *www.pinterest.com/tinawh*.

To receive a free catalog of Poisoned Pen Press titles, please contact us in one of the following ways:

Phone: 1-800-421-3976
Facsimile: 1-480-949-1707
Email: info@poisonedpenpress.com
Website: www.poisonedpenpress.com

Poisoned Pen Press
6962 E. First Ave. Ste 103
Scottsdale, AZ 85251